MW01713776

YOU HAD ME AT WAFFLES

The Story of Emily and Adam

To: Sheila
Enjoy the ride!
♡ Tracy

You Had Me at Waffles

Copyright © 2025 by Tracy T. Wright
All rights reserved.

No part of this publication may be reproduced, distributed, or transmitted in any form or by any means, including photocopying, recording, or other electronic or mechanical methods, without the prior written permission of the publisher, except in the case of brief quotations used in reviews or critical articles.

This is a work of fiction. Names, characters, businesses, places, events, and incidents are either the product of the author's imagination or used in a fictitious manner. Any resemblance to actual persons, living or dead, or actual events is purely coincidental.

Published by Tarenley Media
For rights and permissions, contact: tracywrightbooks@gmail.com

Follow the author at https://tracywrightbooks.substack.com or on TikTok, Instagram, or Facebook @tracywrightbooks.

ISBN 978-1-0694776-2-0

DEDICATION

For my friends—the ones who make life brighter, funnier, and yummier. Thank you for reminding me that love stories come in many forms, and some of the best ones begin with maple syrup and a group chat.

Chapter One

The mimosa bar had collapsed fifteen minutes before guests arrived.

Emily Levine crouched beneath a folding table at the Niagara Falls Welcome Pavilion, silently cursing both plastic folding tables and her life choices. Her hair was frizzing, her button-down stuck to her back, and she was pretty sure she was out of options to save the event. Fantastic.

"Everything okay down there?" came a chipper voice from above.

With effort, Emily took two deep breaths and pulled herself together. She stuck her head out. "Perfect! Just rethinking my career choices. How's your day?"

The intern blinked. "We're out of name tags."

Of course they were.

Emily stood, brushing herself off, adjusting the laminated "Event Director" badge clipped to her shirt. She forced a smile. "Right. No problem. Just hand people sharpies and tell them to be creative. It's a tourism brunch, not the G7."

The intern scurried off.

Emily exhaled, took a beat, and surveyed the room. The small room in the Niagara Exhibition Center had been transformed—sort of. There were various booths for their tourism partners set up around the room, freshly-baked local pastries, fairy lights, and posters and tiny table cards that read 'Sip, Savor, Stay: Discover Niagara.'

It was cute. Somewhat ambitious. Slightly disorganized. Very her.

Despite herself, she felt a small flicker of pride. Not just for pulling the event together with a bit duct tape and blind optimism—but for being here at all. After a few bad years of romantic chaos and, as a result, professional stagnation, this was supposed to be the year she refocused.

No more impulsive relationships, no more getting distracted by the first charming smile that remembered her coffee order.

She was done with all that. Emily had officially rerouted her priorities. No boys. No drama. Just her career, her goals, and maybe—if the universe cooperated—something amazing she could be proud of. Something real.

She checked her phone. 10:27 a.m.

Guests would be arriving in three minutes. Her best friend, Sophie hadn't arrived yet, nor texted. She was probably still in Toronto, being disgustingly domestic with her pilot boyfriend, Daniel. They'd moved in together last month. Now they cooked. They slow danced in the kitchen. They had matching throw pillows.

Emily, by contrast, lived alone, had three waffle makers, two wine-stained blouses, and a job that required her to smile through endless debates about which Niagara wine paired best with brunch.

She shoved her phone away and slapped on her best smile just as the doors opened and the brunch crowd began to pour in.

Emily clapped her hands and raised her voice over the rising hum of voices. "Welcome, everyone! Please grab a name tag—or a Sharpie—and help yourself to some refreshments. The mimosa station is undergoing an unexpected makeover, but we've got juice and free carbohydrates."

A ripple of polite laughter moved through the crowd. She offered a few strategic hellos, waved to a city councillor she only recognized from Zoom meetings, and managed to steer an eager influencer away from filming the half-collapsed mimosa table.

As she traversed the room, she stopped to shake hands, answer questions, and take photos. "Hi, yes, thank you for coming! Yes, we have gluten-free donuts. And yes, the mayor might stop by. No, I don't know if he's vegan."

She fielded three questions about parking, two about bathrooms, and one about whether Niagara was planning a pancake festival. By the time she made it halfway across the room, her cheeks already ached from smiling too wide and her coffee had vanished somewhere between greeting the fire marshal and pretending she didn't notice that some of the fairy lights she had purchased from the dollar store were already beginning to flicker.

But the crowd was warm. Curious. Exploring the booths. Chatting with the tourism partners. Taking photos. This might actually work.

Having a working mimosa bar would have been the crowning touch, but there was no time for that now.

And then, among the crowd, in walked Adam Kostas. Aviator sunglasses, perfectly timed smirk, and a leather jacket that had no business looking that good at 10:35 a.m.

He nodded in greeting when he saw her. "Emily."

"Hey, Adam." Emily blinked. "What the hell are you doing here?"

He grinned. "Nice to see you too."

"Did you come with Sophie?" Emily tried to look around him, but his impressive shoulders blocked most of her view.

"No," he said, removing his sunglasses with unnecessary flair. "She sent me instead. Said you could use an extra hand." He looked around. "Or maybe a plus one."

Emily sighed. "This is a tourism event, not a dating app."

Adam's eyes sparkled. "Can't it be both?" He leaned back against the door frame, glancing around the room with a grin. "Sophie couldn't make it. Last minute work thing," he said, tone shifting slightly, his eyes softening just a little. "She said to apologize. And that she'll make it up to you soon."

Emily nodded, taking a deep breath. She knew Sophie's work could sometimes be unpredictable. At least she'd sent help.

Adam was Daniel's co-pilot and friend. They'd first met over dinner a few months ago. He was a little too charismatic with his easy smile and that whole "I'm-too-cool" vibe that made him impossible to ignore. A little too charming for Emily's liking.

But he wasn't just Daniel's friend—over the past few weeks, he'd been showing up more and more at group events. Dinners. Trivia nights. The infamous IKEA furniture assembly marathon last Sunday. And every time, he somehow managed to slide in beside Emily like a heat-seeking missile. Like it was the most natural thing in the world.

Worse, he remembered things. Her favorite takeout order. The way she liked her tea. That she'd once said red wine made her sleepy, but not white wine. It was... unnerving. And a little disarming.

Emily wasn't sure if it was intentional or if he was just naturally like that with everyone—but it made ignoring him nearly impossible.

"Well," Emily said, dragging her thoughts back to the present, "since you're here, you might as well help. I'm running out of name tags, and the mimosas have... collapsed."

Adam looked over the mimosa bar, where the plastic folding table had caved in on one side, transforming the whole setup into a chaotic slip-and-slide of toppled plastic orange juice bottles and fruit garnish. Luckily, the glass bottles of champagne had survived, sitting innocently behind the disaster zone in ice buckets.

He turned back to Emily and raised an eyebrow. "That looks pretty bad. You need someone to rescue you from this thing? I'm your guy."

He shrugged off his jacket with an "I've got this" vibe.

"I didn't know we were rescuing anything," she muttered, her hands on her hips. "Remember, this is a tourism brunch, not a hostage situation."

"Oh, trust me," Adam said, moving into the room like he owned it. "I've been to worse events. I'm not saying I'm a mimosa expert, but when it comes to saving brunch... well, let's just say I'm *well* qualified."

Emily glared at him but couldn't help the faint tug of a smile. He was completely insufferable, but he was also exactly what she hadn't known she'd needed right now—someone to balance out the stress and, somehow, make everything feel a little less overwhelming.

"Fine," she said, taking a step back. "You can fix the mimosa station."

"Aye aye, Captain." Adam saluted her with mock seriousness. "Consider it done."

As he moved toward the collapsed mimosa bar, Emily felt a

strange sense of calm settle over her. No matter how much she pretended to dislike Adam's over-the-top confidence, it was somehow contagious.

She forced herself to look away, focusing instead on the other guests now trickling in. She straightened brochures on the nearby table, adjusted a poster, and greeted a few newcomers with a smile, handing out sharpies and name tags.

But she couldn't help sneaking glances over at Adam. He was completely in his element. He had fixed the wobbly table, adjusted the tablecloth, and was now expertly recalibrating the mimosa station. No panicking, no flustered fiddling. Just smooth, effortless execution. He had the mimosa glasses perfectly stacked, the juice bottles lined up with precision, and the champagne flowing within ten minutes, and with the same ease and confidence he seemed to bring to every situation. Then he was passing out mimosas, charming the guests who gathered around, his natural charisma shining through.

Emily's frown deepened. She was grateful he was taking it seriously, but she couldn't believe how well he was pulling this off. She had a hard time ignoring the fact that Adam was... actually good.

"Well, I have to admit," she muttered to herself, "he's not terrible at it."

She caught him flashing a grin in her direction, as if he'd somehow read her thoughts.

And just like that, she realized she might need to rethink her opinion of Adam. She had always thought of him as unreliable—the laid-back co-pilot who didn't take things too seriously. But here he was, doing a great job helping her out. Maybe there was more to him than she'd given credit for.

No, she reminded herself sharply. *No boys.*

She had *a plan.* She wasn't about to throw away six months of post-breakup clarity just because someone showed up with a crooked smile and mimosa-related competence. Focus, Levine. Career first. Charming pilots? *Dead last.*

By noon, the event was in full swing. Emily circulated like a pro, handing out pamphlets, posing for photos, answering questions with rehearsed ease. People were enjoying themselves. The room was full. The donuts were disappearing. The mayor was not, in fact, vegan.

The last guests trickled out around 1:30, leaving the once-buzzing room scattered with crumpled napkins, half-eaten mini quiches and, to Emily, the faint smell of success.

She surveyed the room, watching as her team tidied around her, and the partners packed up their booths. The mimosa station had survived. The guests had taken selfies. No one had tripped over the bunting. She'd received compliments on the food. It hadn't been flawless—but it had been enough.

Emily turned to find Adam shrugging into his leather jacket. He was watching her, the kind of look on his face that made her pulse tick a little faster.

"You're smirking," she said.

"I'm observing," he replied. "You pulled it off."

"We pulled it off," she corrected reluctantly.

Adam gave a mock bow. "My work here is done." He paused. "But I'm proud of you. This was impressive."

"Even the mimosa incident?"

"Especially the mimosa incident."

She crossed her arms. "Well, thanks for helping. I owe you one."

He winked. "I'll add it to your tab."

Emily rolled her eyes. "There's a tab?"

"Only for you."

He was *so* flirty. Effortlessly so. The kind of guy who winked like it was punctuation. Did he talk to everyone like that? Did every woman get their own "tab"? Their own cheeky smile and personalized charm?

She shook her head, annoyed at herself for even wondering. Of course he was like that with everyone. Guys like Adam didn't *choose* someone—they just floated through rooms, collecting attention like it was oxygen.

It didn't mean anything.

Emily noticed one of the partners waving to get her attention. She threw a crumpled napkin at Adam. "Thanks again," she said. "Now get out before I draft you into next year's committee."

He laughed and sauntered out with a wave.

And just like that, he was gone, the door swinging shut behind him.

Chapter Two

Adam Kostas was not the kind of man who usually worried about whether he was texting too soon. He'd faced mechanical failures mid-air, a malfunctioning espresso machine on a red-eye to Munich, and Daniel's two-hour PowerPoint presentation on "*Cruising Altitude, Cruising Attitude*."

He was a cool-under-pressure kind of guy. The guy who didn't overthink things.

Until Emily Levine.

He stared at his phone, thumbs hovering over the keyboard. The Niagara Tourism Board brunch she'd organized had ended hours ago, but her face—wide-eyed and open, framed by chaotic waves of brown hair—was still annoyingly vivid in his mind.

The mimosa disaster. The way her brow furrowed when she was concentrating. The fact that she'd let him help, even though she clearly hated needing help. And the way she'd looked at him—just for a second—like she was confused by him.

He smirked.

Then frowned.

Then smirked again.

He'd always been able to read people, especially women. But Emily? She was a locked terminal with a delayed departure and no pilot announcement in sight. And for some idiotic reason, that made him want to circle the runway.

It was a dangerous thought.

Adam had long since made peace with his fate: confirmed bachelor, lifelong flirt, occasional relationship escape artist. He'd seen what love did to people—his friends, his family, his coworkers. Tying yourself to someone just seemed like an elaborate gamble. Too many expectations. Too many sacrifices. Too many risks.

He liked his freedom. He liked flying solo—literally and figuratively.

Occasionally, he would feel drawn to a woman. And then the chase would begin. It was fun, sometimes casual, occasionally intense, always flirty, but it would always inevitably end. Like he knew it would. He'd lose interest. They'd want more. He'd panic and end things. Rinse and repeat.

He wasn't built for commitment. Hell, he didn't even believe in it.

He was tempted. God, was he tempted. To send a clever text, to drop a casual compliment, to see if she'd take the bait and banter back. The start of the chase was always the best part—those first charged exchanges, the slow unraveling of curiosity. And Emily had curiosity in spades. She was sharp-tongued and soft-hearted in a way that made him want to learn all her contradictions. But something in him warned him to hold back.

The biggest problem was that Emily was now part of the "crew". They'd just figured out a rhythm. The dynamic. Their new little circle that somehow made the evenings and weekends bearable again. And if he screwed it up by flirting too hard, or worse—if she actually fell for him—he knew he'd lose all of it.

Fortunately, when they'd first met over dinner at a little

Italian place with Sophie and Daniel, she hadn't immediately fallen for his usual charm. Maybe she was immune.

But then came the group trivia nights, the weekend brunches, and the furniture assembly marathons. And he'd loved every second of it.

Well. Not *loved.*

Liked aggressively.

Still. Texting her directly felt... loaded. Too intimate. Too obvious. Too early for a one-on-one text. He made a decision: *Group chat it is.*

He opened the "Flight Club" group chat—named, predictably, by Daniel, who insisted it was ironic.

Adam hovered over the keyboard, then typed:

Adam: *Serious question. How many waffle makers does one woman need before we stage a full-scale intervention?*

He tossed his phone onto the counter like he didn't care. Walked to the fridge. Opened it. Closed it again without taking anything.

The phone buzzed. He jumped for it.

Sophie: *Three is reasonable. One per mood.*

Daniel: *No comment.*

Emily: *You're all rude. It's called being prepared. You never know when you're going to have a brunch emergency.*

Adam grinned. That was Emily, alright. Battle-ready and insult-deflecting with the grace of a barrister.

He glanced at his reflection in the dark window above the sink. His hair was still damp from a shower, the curls already rebelling in three different directions. He ran a hand through them but gave up halfway. It didn't matter.

He picked up the phone again, typing before his brain could stop him.

Adam: *I just think if someone coincidentally owns three waffle makers, they're morally obligated to start a brunch club. I don't make the rules.*

Emily: *You literally just made that rule.*

Sophie: *I support this. Brunch Club has a nice ring to it.*

Adam: *I'll bring maple syrup. The good stuff...none of that fake corn syrup nonsense. Canadian grade-A amber. Like my soul.*

Daniel: *Second that. Please don't let the non-Canadians bring the maple syrup.*

Another pause. This time longer.

Adam could picture her reading it, biting the inside of her cheek, probably debating whether or not to respond at all. Emily didn't do casual well—not when it came to herself. She was a little disorganized, but also the type who overthought thank-you notes and mentally reviewed conversations she'd had three days earlier. She'd never admit it, but she cared. Deeply.

That was probably what scared him.

He waited.

Emily: *Okay, maple snobs. You bring the syrup. Sophie and I will handle the waffles.*

Sophie: *I'm ordering matching mugs. Nobody stop me.*

Adam's grin stretched lazily across his face. There it was—a crack in the armor. She didn't hate the idea. He sat down on one of the stools at his kitchen island, thumbs moving across his screen.

Adam: *So... brunch club, Saturdays? Sundays? We rotating hosts? I need to know what level of maple syrup I'm expected to bring. Like, can I go full sommelier? Or are we keeping it entry-level?*

Emily: *You're insufferable.*

Adam: *But useful.*

Emily: *Fine, but only in very limited brunch-related contexts.*

Adam barked a laugh. There was a strange flutter in his chest again. He ignored it.

Adam: *How about next weekend? I'll bring a new syrup to taste-test. You can judge it harshly while pretending you don't care.*

Emily: *Fine. Yes. If you don't mind trekking down to Niagara, I'll be the first host since I've got the equipment. Bring your passports. Don't be late.*

He exhaled, slower this time.

The conversation wound down after that—Sophie suggesting playlists, Daniel groaning in protest—but Adam stayed with his phone in his hand a moment longer.

He thought again about texting Emily directly. Just something quick. Something stupid.

Congrats on the event!

That brunch would've crashed without you.

You're fun when you're panicking.

But he didn't send anything. Not yet.

Because no matter how much his instincts were telling him to start a private chat with Emily, Adam knew when something had the potential to spiral. And this couldn't be just a crush or a fling, or a throwaway distraction. It could never become romantic. It would ruin the friendship group.

So they would stay friends. Just friends. Connected. Comfortable. Yes. But not too close. Not too connected. Not *too* comfortable. Not too much of anything.

So no, he wasn't going to text her tonight. He was going to stay in the group chat. Keep it safe. Keep it light.

Because if he let himself want her—really want her—there was no world in which he didn't ruin everything. And he kind of liked *this* world.

So he tucked his phone away, leaned back against the kitchen counter, and told himself he was just looking forward to brunch. Every other weekend. With the group. Where he could see her. Casually. From a neutral, emotionally safe distance.

That was all.

Chapter Three

Emily Levine was not okay. Again.

She wasn't in full meltdown mode. Nothing had exploded, no vendors were currently yelling at her, and no one had called her place of work to report a "brunch-adjacent disaster." So in that very specific and generous sense, she was fine.

But in the *I-just-accidentally-volunteered-to-host-brunch* and *Adam-Kostas-is-bringing-maple-syrup* sense?

Yeah. Not okay.

She sat on the floor of her Niagara County apartment, surrounded by three waffle makers, two chipped mixing bowls, and a rising sense of dread. Her phone buzzed beside her—another message in the Flight Club group chat.

Sophie: *Found mugs that say "Let's Waffle About It." Ordering four.*

Emily groaned. Her thumbs moved quickly across the screen.

Emily: *I hate how much I love that.*

She tossed the phone aside and immediately lost it behind a throw blanket she hadn't bought on purpose. It had been one of those impulse clearance-bin purchases. Some would call it ugly, but to her, it was soft and the perfect size for her lap. And by now, it was probably emotionally important.

Emily sighed. She had never hosted a brunch before.

Wait, scratch that—she'd hosted *exactly one* brunch, and the mimosa bar had collapsed minutes before it started. So technically, she was zero for one.

And now she'd volunteered to do it again. On purpose. With witnesses. With people she liked. People she saw regularly. People she'd have to keep seeing if everything went terribly wrong.

Her phone buzzed from behind the blanket. Another message from the group chat.

Probably Adam again.

She didn't move.

Instead, she let her head fall back against the cabinet and stared at the ceiling like the answers might be up there. They weren't.

The Brunch Club had started as a joke—maple syrup snobbery, waffle-related smack talk, a little group flirtation. But now it was a real thing. And she was hosting the first official one.

It should've felt fun. Light. Easy.

It didn't.

Because Adam Kostas—Mr. Maple Syrup Sommelier, Mr. Always-Has-A-Quip—wasn't just in the group anymore. He was *the* group. Or, at least, the part of it she couldn't stop thinking about.

His cocky grin. His curly hair—messy, unruly, yet somehow endearing. The way he somehow made pouring orange juice without spilling it look easy. How could someone always look so… confident? And charming. And a little dangerous.

And that was the problem.

Emily didn't do casual crushes. She wasn't a *dabble* kind of girl. When she fell, she fell hard. Headfirst. No helmet. No exit strategy.

And Adam? Adam was the kind of guy who turned flirty texts into an art form. Who smiled like he already knew your next move. Who'd probably kissed half of Pearson Airport just for the air miles.

And if she fell for him—and it got weird and it didn't work—it would ruin the new friendship structure they had built out of trivia nights, shared meals, weekends and sarcasm. She couldn't risk that. Not for a maybe.

A knock at the door made her jump. She blinked, startled, then scrambled upright, kicking aside a roll of parchment paper and a half-empty can of whipped cream.

She opened the door to find Daniel Carter standing there with a six-pack of sparkling water.

"I come in peace," he announced.

Emily crossed her arms. "Are you my emotional support, Carter?"

"Do you need any? If yes, you might consider calling Sophie."

Emily smiled and beckoned him inside. Daniel kissed her on the cheek as he stepped past her.

"Sorry to just drop in like this. I was in Hamilton for a meeting," he explained. His tone softened. "Thought I should check in. See if you needed help or anything else for brunch tomorrow."

She shut the door and gestured vaguely to the chaos in her kitchen. "Well, it may not look like it, but I think I've almost got it."

Daniel took in the scene—three waffle makers, an array of mismatched plates, and what looked like the aftermath of a batter-themed tornado. A trail of flour dusted the floor like a crime scene. A bottle of vanilla had rolled under the fridge and got stuck there. A rogue spatula was balanced precariously on top of a toaster. One waffle maker was still open, mid-bake, with batter hardened into a tragic brown-beige sculpture. Piles of cooked waffles of varying shades of beige sat in disarray on plates across the counter. Something smelled faintly... burnt.

"Wow," he said. "It's like Pinterest and a food truck got divorced in here."

"I'm very proud," Emily muttered. She stepped around him and began to clear a small corner of the kitchen counter. "Did you know baking soda and baking powder are two completely different things?"

He set the sparkling water on the counter and leaned against it, arms crossed. "Yes, because I'm an adult."

Emily ignored this. "Anyway, I think I've got the waffle batter down. It took a few tries." She tore a small piece of waffle off one of the plates. "Here, try this. This is…" she consulted a torn notepad. "Number thirteen."

Daniel popped it into his mouth and chewed. "Nice crisp on the outside," he said, nodding thoughtfully. "Soft on the inside. Light cinnamon flavor. Not too sweet." He swallowed. "I think we have a winner."

Emily beamed. "Okay, thirteen it is." She picked up a batter-covered pencil and circled something twice on her notepad. "Thank you."

"So," he said casually. "Adam almost came with me."

Emily froze. "Almost?" she asked, too quickly.

Daniel nodded. "He was at the meeting, too. Got weird about it. Said he had errands. Which I think means 'panicked and didn't want to overstep.'"

She picked up a spoon and stirred something aggressively. “He wouldn’t have been overstepping.”

“No?” Daniel raised an eyebrow.

“No,” she repeated, quieter this time. She shrugged. “I mean, we’re friends.”

“Uh-huh.”

She glanced up. “Don’t look at me like that.”

“I didn’t say anything.”

“You didn’t have to.”

Daniel gave her a look that could only be described as *older brother adjacent*. It was almost worse than judgment. It was understanding.

“I think he’s trying to be careful,” Daniel said. He pursed his lips thoughtfully. “Which is funny, because Adam doesn’t usually do careful.”

“Well, maybe brunch is his exception,” Emily said. “Maybe this is sacred waffle space.” She paused, then added, “The holiest of carbs.”

Daniel chuckled. “Or maybe you’re the exception.”

Emily swallowed.

“I’m not trying to push anything,” he added quickly. “Just... I’ve known him a long time. He’s not good at this stuff. Feelings. Staying. But he’s also never been in a group text this long without bailing, so. Progress?”

Emily exhaled. “I just... I like how things are. All of us. Together. As friends.”

Daniel nodded slowly. “I get that.” He watched her for a second, then took in the disarray of mixing bowls and abandoned batter. “Need help getting ready? I’m excellent at taste-testing and pretending I know what *mise en place* means.”

Emily arched a brow. “You offering to whisk something?”

“I’m offering to stand here with sparkling water and give supportive commentary while you whisk something,” he clarified.

She cracked a smile. “Tempting.”

He nudged a cutting board aside and grabbed an apple from her fruit bowl. “Seriously though, you good for tomorrow? Plates? Seating? Backup waffle irons in case of electrical fire?”

“I’ve got three waffle irons. I just tested them and they all work fine.” She sighed. “It’s a personality trait at this point.”

“Could be worse,” Daniel said, crunching into the apple. “You could have no waffle makers and an overinflated sense of brunch confidence. I’ve seen it. It’s dark.”

Emily laughed. She surveyed her kitchen, hands on hips. “Thanks, but I think I’ll be fine by tomorrow.”

He bowed. “Just making sure the brunch queen doesn’t crumble under pressure. You need anything, you call. I’ve got emergency bacon and a solid French toast recipe I stole from a passenger in Montréal.”

She gave him a look. “How do you have emergency bacon?”

He shrugged. “I’m Canadian.” As if that explained everything.

She opened her mouth to argue, but he was already backing toward the door.

“Call Sophie for emotional regulation,” he instructed. “I expect more waffles tomorrow.”

And then he was gone.

Emily stood alone in the middle of her kitchen, still holding the spoon. And strangely, she felt better. Not totally calm, but Daniel’s visit had done something. Grounded her, maybe. Calibrated the panic. It helped to know someone else saw the chaos and didn’t flinch. That someone wasn’t asking her to *fix* anything, just… show up. Do the thing. Try.

She breathed a little deeper. The kitchen still looked like a culinary crime scene, but it didn't feel quite as impossible now.

She went to retrieve her phone from the sofa. Another message.

Adam: *Don't forget. I'm bringing the syrup. Don't mess up the waffles.*

She laughed despite herself. Then sighed.

"Just waffles," she told herself firmly. But she as started to clean the kitchen, at the back of her mind, she worried if her head was making promises her heart couldn't keep.

Chapter Four

By the time the doorbell rang, Emily had already burned one batch of waffles, dropped an entire jar of cinnamon into the sink, and reminded her toaster: "We do not panic in this house."

The toaster was unmoved.

She wiped her hands on a kitchen towel—one that was supposed to be "charming rustic linen" but now looked more like a traumatized dishrag that had seen too much—and tried to pretend she was fine.

She had exactly twelve minutes of calm left in her before she imploded. But she opened the door anyway.

"Welcome to Brunch Club," she said, voice too loud, eyes too wide.

Daniel raised an eyebrow. "Do I need to call someone?"

Sophie stepped in behind him, holding a Tupperware container. "She's probably fine. This is her pre-hostess adrenaline spiral. We've all been there before."

Daniel hung their jackets on the hook. "Have we though?"

Emily pointed a wooden spoon at him. "This is a *very real* spiral. Respect it."

"Duly noted," Daniel said, raising his hands, palms forward.

Sophie moved into the kitchen and placed the container on the counter. Then she handed Emily a gift bag. "You said not to bring anything, so obviously we brought something."

Inside were the mugs Sophie had texted about: white ceramic, hand-lettered in black and red script—*Let's Waffle About It.*

Emily was speechless. Something about the mugs—their shape, their size, the writing—it was perfect. Also, she loved mugs with witty sayings. "We each get to keep one?" she asked hopefully.

"Of course. For Brunch Club members only. You're welcome," Sophie said smugly.

Daniel was busy re-organizing the coffee station while Sophie and Emily unwrapped and washed the mugs when the knock came.

Emily didn't have to check who it was. Her pulse had already answered.

She opened the door to Adam, who was somehow wearing a Henley shirt and jeans like he'd been styled by a brunch deity. He held a brown paper bag in one hand and a large bottle of golden maple syrup in the other.

"Morning," he said, grinning. "I brought offerings."

Her throat might've closed for a second.

"Coffee's in the kitchen," she managed. "Waffle war zone straight ahead."

He stepped inside, removed his sunglasses, and looked around. "Wow. Three waffle makers. You weren't kidding."

"Did you think I was exaggerating?"

"Honestly? Yes."

"Then you clearly don't know how seriously I take batter-based decisions."

He smiled, slower this time. "I'm learning."

Emily turned away before her face showed too much.

The brunch buzzed along in a kind of controlled chaos. Sophie set the table, Daniel took over coffee duty, and Adam slipped into her kitchen like he belonged there.

He moved like he knew exactly where to be without taking up too much space. He manned the waffle station like a pro, flipping each one with a flourish and muttering ratings under his breath.

"Seven-point-eight," he said, sliding one onto a plate. "Slightly uneven edges. Needs redemption."

Emily, who was busy cutting strawberries into slices, looked over his shoulder. "Excuse you, that waffle is a structural masterpiece."

"That waffle is a delicious disappointment," he replied. "The good news is, with three waffle makers on the go at the same time, brunch will be ready in five minutes." He glanced at her. "Honestly? Three waffle makers and we're still getting uneven edges? Do better, Levine."

Emily opened her mouth to argue—but paused instead, watching him rotate one waffle, one out onto a plate, and pour batter into the third with casual, almost aggravating precision. It was… kind of impressive.

She swatted his arm. He caught her hand.

Just for a second. Not long enough to be a moment, but long enough to notice it *could've* been one. Then he grinned and released her.

The apartment filled with the warm smell of waffles, cinnamon, and fresh coffee. With everything plated and steaming, the four of them finally sat down at the table—mugs in hand, syrup and powdered sugar on standby, and the kind of comfortable energy that comes from people who aren't quite family, but aren't strangers anymore either.

Adam took a bite of his waffle, chewed slowly, then held up a hand.

"Eight-point-five," he announced. "Good texture. Strong crisp. Slightly excessive on the cinnamon, but I respect the ambition."

Emily narrowed her eyes. "That waffle is a solid nine-point-two. Minimum."

Daniel stabbed his own. "Seven. Needs peanut butter."

"You can't rate waffles based on toppings," Sophie protested. "That's like judging a novel by the cover font."

"That is *exactly* how I judge novels," Daniel replied. "Also, your waffles are faking confidence."

Emily blinked. "I'm sorry, are my waffles... insecure?"

Sophie leaned forward, grinning. "They're bold. But uncertain. Like they're trying to impress someone at brunch and overdid it on the nutmeg."

Adam nodded solemnly. "Brunch waffles with something to prove."

Emily laughed, shaking her head as she refilled coffees. "You people are monsters."

Sophie smiled at her, then gestured around. "This is really nice though. I missed this."

"Did you not have waffles in New York?" Adam asked, mock horror in his voice.

"We had waffles," Sophie said. "But not like this." She picked up the maple syrup and poured a liberal amount on her half-eaten waffle.

Daniel shook his head in mock horror. "Waffles without real maple syrup is a disgrace."

She shrugged easily in agreement. "There are a lot of things I miss about New York, but Toronto definitely has its benefits."

Emily tilted her head. "Do you like it? Living together in Toronto?"

Sophie paused, then nodded. "Yeah. It's weird. Good-weird. We take turns making dinner. Daniel folds laundry with scary precision. I accidentally bought four throw pillows in one IKEA trip."

"You didn't *accidentally*—," Daniel said.

"I *emotionally* did," Sophie corrected.

Emily smiled, but something tugged in her chest. She used to imagine that kind of domestic chaos with Sophie. They had both lived in New York together at one point, dropping in unannounced, spending time together whenever they could, and always saying they should definitely move in together. But with the timing of job changes, relationship situations, and lease expiry dates, they had never managed it.

"Is your mom okay with you being up here full time?" she asked gently.

"Oh, yeah," Sophie said, waving a hand. "She's great, actually. She's been dating this accountant named Barry who brews his own kombucha. I think she likes having the house to herself now. Every time I call, she's 'heading to salsa night' or 'hiking with Barry's dogs.'"

Emily blinked. "Wow."

"Right?" Sophie said. "She doesn't need me around as much. And I think I needed a little space too. She was always great, just... a lot. You get it."

Emily did get it. The way people you love can take up space without meaning to. The way growing up sometimes meant choosing a different kind of closeness. Her own parents were still in New York, too.

She glanced across the table at Adam, who was busy writing

fake waffle scores in jam on his plate.

He caught her looking. Grinned.

She looked away, heart stuttering.

Focus, she reminded herself. No boys. No distractions. She hadn't left New York, moved away from her family, and rebuilt her whole damn life just to get derailed by a cute pilot with excellent hair who was suspiciously good at everything. She came here to build something. To prove she could do more than survive—she could thrive. That meant career goals, big ideas, clean slates. Not someone who might derail her life plans, then probably forget to text her back in two weeks.

Time passed in a blur of friendly banter, childhood stories, and the syrup bottle being passed back and forth. An hour later, they were still laughing when Sophie finally folded her napkin on the table and stood up.

"Alright, peeps. We've got to hit the road—Daniel's flying out tonight and I still need to help him pack."

Daniel stood as well, expression neutral, sipping the last of his coffee. "She means she needs me to find her other sock and tell her she's doing great at life."

"Same thing," Sophie said, kissing his cheek. Then she hugged Emily tight. "This was amazing. Seriously. You crushed it."

Emily smiled. "Thanks. Next time I'm charging admission."

Daniel hugged her, too. "In that case, next time we're hosting."

They said bye to Adam, and then they were gone.

The silence felt like a held breath.

Emily exhaled, leaning against the edge of the counter. "Well. That was brunch."

Adam spun the now-half-empty syrup bottle in his hand.

"You survived."

"Barely."

"You did great."

She glanced at him, surprised by the sincerity in his voice. "Thanks."

They stood in the kitchen surrounded by the aftermath—plates stacked, mugs half-full, a table full of crumbs and leftover waffle toppings. The waffle makers hummed their cooling-off sound, like tired machines after a long shift.

"I should probably start cleaning up," she said.

"I'll help," he offered, already grabbing plates.

They moved around each other easily.

At one point, they reached for the same mug, and their fingers brushed.

Emily froze.

So did he.

Then he gently tugged the mug from her. "I've got it," he said. "And for the record? You didn't just host. You set a standard for the next one."

Emily looked up. "And you? Do you always… help clean up after brunches?"

He smirked. "Only when the host owns three waffle makers and has a syrup tolerance I respect."

She laughed, and it loosened something in the air between them. After tidying the table, they moved to handle the dishes together—Adam rinsing each item and handing it to Emily to place in the dishwasher.

"I think this was a good idea," she said finally. "Brunch Club."

He looked at her for a long moment. "Yeah. Me too."

She turned back to the dishes, heart thudding in her chest.

They worked in silence for a few minutes.

Finally, Adam set the last plate in the drying rack and dried his hands. He looked at her like he was considering something, then gave a brief shake of his head.

"See you next weekend?" he asked, voice low. He went to the door to put on his shoes.

"Yeah," she said, almost a whisper. "See you next weekend."

He gave her one of his brilliant smiles, a brief hug, and then he was gone.

The door clicked shut.

Emily leaned on the counter again. Then she whispered to no one at all: "Just friends."

Chapter Five

Adam was tired.

The post-flight slump had hit hard—too many hours in the sky, not enough hours of sleep, and exactly half a granola bar left in his flight bag that looked like it had survived a natural disaster.

Niagara County was supposed to be a pit stop. A refuel-and-go. But his brain had mutinied and his body had followed, dragging him into a corner café with the words *Locally Roasted Coffee, All Day Breakfast,* and *Free Wi-Fi* painted on the window like siren songs.

He'd just placed his order—a large Americano and a banana muffin—when the door swung open behind him, jingling cheerfully.

And there she was.

Emily Levine, in heels and a sleek black cardigan, carrying an iPad and a reusable coffee sleeve like some kind of caffeinated goddess of regional tourism.

Adam blinked.

Emily blinked.

"Oh," she said.

"Oh yes," he replied, already grinning.

She took two steps inside and looked him over. She smiled. "What are you doing here?"

"Wow. Not even a hello?" He gave her a slow once-over. "Nice outfit, by the way. Are you running for mayor of Brunch Town?"

"I have a meeting," she said, ignoring the comment. "And you still haven't answered my question."

"I landed an hour ago," he said. "Needed caffeine. Saw this place. Fate."

She snorted. "You don't believe in fate."

"True. But I believe in maple syrup—" he paused dramatically "—which I noticed they don't have stocked behind the counter. Honestly, it's an issue of public interest." He shook his head in mock horror. "A place that serves breakfast without real maple syrup this close to the Canadian border is a disgrace. What are we even doing as a society?"

Emily raised an eyebrow. "Are you lobbying for a syrup mandate now?"

"Honestly? Yes. If elected, I promise to restore maple dignity to every breakfast place."

Her lips twitched. "Can't believe I'm saying this," she muttered, walking up to the barista, "but I actually agree with him." She ordered a flat white.

Adam leaned casually on the counter. "I'd like to file a complaint, actually. No grade-A Canadian maple syrup? That corn syrup imposter just doesn't cut it." He shook his head. "Good thing I always bring my own."

The barista—a young woman with a purple buzzcut and a name tag that said *Bree (she/her)*—looked mildly alarmed.

Emily gave him a sharp look. "You bring your own syrup to cafés?"

"Not usually." He reached into his bag and pulled out a small travel-size glass bottle. "But I like to be prepared."

Bree stared at him. "Is that... real maple syrup?"

"It's *the* real maple syrup," Adam said solemnly. "Tapped from a sugar bush north of Ottawa by an old man named Benoît who speaks only in riddles and syrup viscosity measurements."

Emily rolled her eyes. "You are not serious."

"I'm always serious about syrup."

Bree handed over his Americano with the careful hands of someone serving an unpredictable customer. "Please don't put that in our coffee."

"No promises," Adam said, tucking it back in his bag. "But thank you for your concern."

Emily accepted her drink and moved to a small two-top by the window. Adam followed.

"Please remember you're currently on the American side of Niagara Falls," Emily murmured.

"Noted." He took a bite of his muffin.

"Are you actually stalking me?" she asked, sipping carefully.

He looked affronted, chewed, then swallowed. He gestured at her. "I could ask you the same thing."

"I work three blocks away."

"The airport is three blocks away, Emily."

She snorted. "You're exhausting."

"And yet," he said, pulling out the chair across from her, "here we are."

Emily eyed him over the rim of her cup. "You look tired."

He smirked. "You look aggressively professional."

She shrugged. "I have to pitch a campaign to my boss in twenty minutes."

"Oh yeah? What kind?"

She hesitated.

He tilted his head. “C’mon. Give me a teaser. I’m working on less than four hours of sleep over the past twenty-four hours, and just sat through three hours of turbulence. I deserve something.”

“It’s just...” She set her drink down. “I want to run a regional series. I’m calling it ‘*Rediscover Niagara.*’ I want to showcase places locals take for granted. Underrated spots. Weekend gems. That kind of thing.”

Adam blinked. “That’s actually... really good.”

Emily raised an eyebrow. “What, you thought I wore black for fun?”

“I thought you wore it to intimidate the breakfast competition.”

She rolled her eyes.

“Are you using Sophie for it?” he asked.

She nodded enthusiastically. “Yes, I’d like to. It would be a collaboration. If I get the greenlight, I want her to be the featured creator.”

Sophie Lin wasn’t just a travel blogger—she was a full-fledged content creator with a dedicated audience, known for her mix of breezy charm and honest reviews. She’d built her brand from the ground up while still in New York, turning weekend getaways into viral itineraries and somehow making Wi-Fi-free cabins look aspirational instead of inconvenient. Now that she was in Toronto, Emily had a feeling Sophie was ready for something new—something closer to home.

“Smart,” he said, sipping his coffee. “She’ll get it picked up fast.”

“If I get the green light—”

“*When* you get the green light,” Adam interrupted.

Emily flashed him a brief smile. “*When* I get the green

light," she corrected. "I was going to ask her this weekend." She paused, considering. She tapped the side of her cup, then made a decision. She turned her iPad toward him. "Okay, fine. You want a teaser? Here's the rough pitch deck."

Adam leaned in, eyes scanning the first few slides. He nodded. "Bright colors, strong visuals, bold fonts, and a catchy title. Bit heavy on the alliteration, though."

She blinked, then snorted. "It's a working draft. Don't start."

"Too late," he muttered, flipping to the next slide. "'Hidden Gems of the Escarpment'—okay, I like this. But if you're planning to take influencers to that sketchy overlook, you better include a waiver."

"It's not *that* sketchy," she argued. "It's scenic."

"It's scenic in a 'here lies someone who chased the algorithm too far and fell over the edge' kind of way," he shot back.

Emily sighed. "Fine. Noted. We'll flag it for safety. Happy?"

"Delighted," he said, then paused on a slide showcasing a lineup of featured businesses. "You've got a good mix here. Artisanal. Quirky. But… why only one business from the south end?"

She blinked. "Because the foot traffic's stronger near the heritage corridor."

"Sure. But if you're pitching this as local and inclusive, you're going to get called out for that imbalance. People talk. Especially small business owners who feel left out."

Emily stared at him, eyebrows raised.

Adam paused, coffee cup halfway to his lips. "What?"

"Don't tell me you're good at marketing, too."

He shrugged. "I'm curious. I pay attention." He paused.

"I've seen brand campaigns go sideways for less."

"Okay," she admitted. "That's a good point."

Adam leaned back in his seat, satisfied.

Emily narrowed her eyes. "Why are you so helpful?"

He gave her an innocent look. "What, you think I'm just another pretty face? That's sexist."

"No," she said slowly. "I just wasn't expecting actual constructive feedback before noon."

"I have layers," he said, sipping his coffee.

She snorted. "You have caffeine and ego."

"Layers," he repeated, looking satisfied.

Emily shook her head, but there was a hint of a smile tugging at her mouth. She turned the iPad back toward herself, fingers dancing across the screen. "I'll revise the lineup."

Adam raised an eyebrow. "So, you admit I was right?"

"I admit you weren't entirely wrong."

He tapped the table. "I'll take it."

They both sat back in their chairs for a moment, letting the tension ease into something quieter. She sipped her coffee. He finished his muffin.

Then Emily glanced at the time and groaned. "I'm late." She gathered her things, but lingered a beat longer than necessary. "Thanks."

Adam nodded. "Any time."

Another notification pinged from Emily's iPad. She sighed and stood, adjusting her cardigan. "Alright, alright, I'm coming," she muttered to no one in particular.

He followed her out the door. "Hey, Em?"

"Yes?"

"Good luck with your pitch." He put his sunglasses back on. They slid into place smoothly. He didn't even needed to adjust them. "I'm sure you'll hit it out of the ballpark."

"Baseball references. Really?" But she smiled. "Thank you. I'll need all the luck I can get."

"And once you get approved—"

She opened her mouth to protest, but he held up a hand to stop her.

"Once you get approved," he continued firmly. "Let me know if there's anything I can do to help."

Her expression softened. "Thank you for the vote of confidence. And the offer." Suddenly, she grinned. "I just might take you up on it."

"No sweat."

She turned to leave, but then paused and turned back. "Do you actually carry syrup in your bag?"

He held it up like a trophy. "A souvenir for an American colleague," he explained.

She shook her head. Then, with a final smile and a wave, she left.

Adam watched her go, the lingering echo of her heels tapping against the pavement.

He stayed there a moment longer, the half-full coffee cup warm in his hand.

What the hell was he doing? He wasn't the volunteer type. And yet he'd just offered to spend his precious time probably handing out brochures and talking about historic stone bridges like it was his life's purpose.

For Emily.

He ran a hand through his hair and sighed.

This wasn't the plan. There *was* no plan. But maybe that was the problem.

Because somehow, without meaning to, without permission

or warning, he kept finding himself in her orbit.

And worse—he didn't want to leave it.

Who even *was* he?

He looked down the street where she'd disappeared, then back at the café. The door jingled behind him as someone else walked out, laughter spilling out into the street.

Maybe bumping into her today had been an accident. Some might even call it fate.

But this? It felt dangerously like intention.

He tucked the syrup bottle back in his bag and walked in the other direction—grinning the whole way, even if he didn't know why.

Chapter Six

Emily had managed to survive a full executive pitch meeting without swearing, panicking, or forgetting her lines—a personal best.

Instead, she'd shown slides, made jokes that mostly landed, and only said the word *immersive* twice, which in tourism pitch terms showed enormous restraint. For once, she didn't feel like a walking imposter badge in heels. She'd owned it. Or at least... rented the moment temporarily.

More importantly, the pitch had landed. Actually landed. As in: nods of approval, actual eye contact, and her boss saying the words *"This could be something."*

Emily rode the high all the way back to her desk—a small corner cubicle at the Niagara Regional Tourism Board, nestled between a poster of the Falls and a ficus someone kept forgetting to water.

She was the youngest department lead on the floor, and proud of it. She'd left New York for this job—left behind the noise and the competition and a shared apartment she'd never really felt at home in.

It wasn't the most glamorous job she'd ever had, and it definitely didn't pay like it. Half the time, she joked she was basically a well-dressed volunteer with a tourism badge. But it mattered. It felt like something she could build.

She'd spent most of her career planning corporate events in New York—rented ballrooms, speaker panels, corporate gift bags no one wanted—but marketing had always tugged at her more. The storytelling side. The chance to make something resonate. This role was a blend of both: logistics and narrative. A test drive for the next version of her career.

And this pitch? This was her first real win. Not survival. Not *"good effort."* A win.

She dropped into her chair, spun once, then pulled up her laptop and exhaled slowly. The familiar hum of office life buzzed around her: someone microwaving leftovers, two coworkers arguing gently about font sizes, the muted ding of elevator doors.

The plan was solid.

Rediscover Niagara: A content series showcasing the hidden gems—the kinds of places locals always said they'd get around to but never did. The bakery with sour cherry scones only available on Thursdays. The converted canoe shack that now sold fresh donuts. The historic ferry dock-turned-latte haven. The elderly couple who sold handmade postcards in the back of their greenhouse.

Emily wanted people to see Niagara through a different lens. Not just a destination. A place to come back to.

She just needed the right voice to bring it to life.

Enter Sophie Lin. Travel influencer. Queen of travel blogging. And—most importantly—the only person Emily trusted not to turn this into some over-polished, hollow-sounding reel that said everything and nothing.

She opened her messenger app, clicked Sophie's name and typed:

Emily: *Okay. Serious work question. Can I call you?*

Sophie's reply came a few seconds later.

Sophie: *Can't speak now, but am I being recruited into a tourism heist? Because yes.*

Emily: *Better. I want to feature you in a campaign. Multi-part video series. Rediscover Niagara. Small businesses, local stories, off-the-beaten-path gems. You'd be the on-camera lead.*

Sophie: *Okay wait. This actually sounds awesome. Tell me everything.*

Emily: *We'd film over two weekends. You'd visit selected spots, try things, talk to owners, make it personal. Nothing scripted—just your usual charm and some high-res B-roll.*

Sophie: *I love this. Like genuinely love it.*

Emily: *Really?*

Sophie: *YES. Let me check with my agent, but I'm 99% in. This is exactly the kind of work I want right now. Local, meaningful, bite-sized storytelling? Count me in.*

Emily: *I knew you'd get it.*

Sophie: *So can I boss you around on set?*

Emily: *Never.*

Sophie: *Fine. But if this is taking up our weekends and postponing Brunch Club gatherings, then I insist there be brunch food. That's non-negotiable.*

Emily: *Obviously.*

Sophie: *Okay, I'm in. Send me the brief. I'll block dates. This is exciting, Em. I'm so proud of you.*

Emily stared at her screen a beat longer than necessary, then let herself grin. She felt a weird, fizzy wave of something almost like pride rising in her chest. Sophie had believed in her even when she didn't fully believe in herself. Having that trust reflected back at her now? It was grounding.

She opened a clean document, titled it *Rediscover Niagara: Sophie Lin Pitch Deck*, and got to work.

An hour later, she was halfway through a bullet point on filming permits when her phone rang. The name across her screen read: Adam Kostas.

She blinked. She let it ring once. Twice. Then picked up. "You're calling me. Like with your voice. Is everything okay? Did Brunch Club dissolve?"

Adam's voice came through, warm and easy. "Hi to you too. No, Brunch Club is holding strong, although I hear there may be some disruptions soon." He paused. "I just wanted to be one of the first to congratulate you on your campaign pitch. I heard you got it, and managed to rope Sophie in, too."

"Wow, news travels fast." Emily leaned back in her chair, twirling a pen. "She volunteered. I merely offered brunch-adjacent food and creative freedom."

"Well played," he said. There was a pause. "Listen, I'm thinking I should come along."

"To the shoots?"

"For logistics."

She laughed. "You're not logistics."

"I can be logistics."

"You're maple syrup and distraction. That's not a production role."

"I can carry bags. Run errands. Taste test local pastries. Charm cranky business owners. Flirt our way out of parking tickets."

"We're not going to get parking tickets."

"You lack imagination."

Emily smiled despite herself. "You seriously want in?"

"Actually… yeah," he said. "I was supposed to be up north this month. Family thing. But my cousin's in Europe longer than expected and the usual trip's on hold. So I've got some free time. Also, the tennis club had a flooding issue, so I'm banned from cardio for at least a week."

She blinked. "That's a lot of unrelated information."

"I just mean," he said, tone a little quieter now, "I've got time. And I'd rather spend it doing something that feels good. With people I like."

The shift caught her off guard. For a second, he wasn't the guy who made jokes and dodged serious moments with easy banter. He was just… Adam. A little less effortless charm. A little more real.

"You're still going to make it chaotic, aren't you?"

"Only in the most helpful way."

She hesitated. Not because he wasn't capable—he was, in that annoyingly natural way that made you wonder if he practiced at home in front of the mirror. But this campaign mattered. It wasn't brunch. It wasn't bickering in group chats. It was her career.

And yet... he'd always shown up. To fix mimosas at her work event. To brunch. He'd even helped clean up and had done a good job of it.

Maybe she did need someone to help her lighten the weight of it. Someone who didn't make it all feel so heavy. Someone who could just... be there.

She'd never worked this closely with someone who made her pulse speed up just by saying her name. Was that risky? Probably. But then again, risk was part of the pitch.

"Okay," she said finally. "But only if you promise not to make a scene when I tell you what time call starts."

He paused. "How early?"

"Like... sunrise early."

He tsked. "Disrespectful," he said. "But fine. I'll be there."

She blinked. "That's it?"

"I already put it in my calendar."

"You use a calendar?"

"I have layers, Emily."

She smiled. "So you've said." She turned toward the window, watching tourists amble past. People with cameras and ball caps and wide smiles, chasing wonder in the everyday.

She wanted to give them more places to look.

"Thank you," she said softly.

"For what?"

"For showing up."

There was a pause on the line.

Then, in perfect Adam fashion: "So... do I get a crew t-shirt or what?"

She laughed. "Goodbye, Kostas."

He was still laughing when she hung up.

And she was still smiling when she pulled up her document again and started typing.

This was a campaign. This was work. This was real now. She took a deep breath, fingers flying over the keyboard, a zing of excitement shooting through her.

Because she knew, if she didn't panic, it might even be *really* good.

Chapter Seven

Adam Kostas did not consider himself a romantic. He considered himself a realist with excellent hair, above-average instincts, and a healthy respect for emotional detachment. He liked things breezy. Light. Simple. Low on drama.

And yet, here he was—sitting cross-legged on a brown industrial carpet in a small conference room on a Saturday afternoon, elbow-deep in filming permits, trying to wrangle them into some sort of order.

The room was aggressively beige. One window. Fluorescent lighting. A small round table with three mismatched chairs and a whiteboard in the corner that read 'Q2 Goals!!' in purple marker.

His leather jacket was slung over the back of one chair—he'd ditched it earlier when the room got warm. Now he was left in just a soft, grey Henley shirt that clung more than he intended and jeans that still had airport lounge wrinkles in them. His curls were a little messier than usual.

He hadn't even meant to be here today. But when Emily said she needed help prepping materials for the *Rediscover Niagara* campaign, he showed up. No hesitation. No calendar conflict.

Just... showed up.

She'd left twenty minutes ago, mumbling something about a meeting with the city permit liaison and how "If I don't come back, assume I've been swallowed by red tape."

So Adam stayed behind. Organized folders. Sorted piles. Pretended he was useful while wondering why the hell he had agreed to drive over an hour from home to work for free on a weekend.

But, he didn't mind. Not really.

He liked being useful. Quietly. When no one was watching. Especially now, with the campaign officially starting. With Emily letting him in—not just to her apartment for waffles, but into this thing that actually mattered to her. He wasn't just showing up anymore.

He was... involved. Emotionally. Somehow. As a friend, a good friend.

He reached for another file folder, popped the clip, and started sorting loose papers into piles: permits, release forms, location descriptions, printouts of maps with highlighter all over them.

And then, between two pages of contact sheets for a cider house and a kayak rental stand—he found the letter.

It was folded neatly. Not labeled. Not on letterhead. Cream-colored paper. Soft ink. No logo. No signature.

If he'd known it was personal, he never would have read it. But when he opened it to check the contents, and his eyes fell on the first sentence, he couldn't *not* read it.

You make everything feel lighter. Like I could stop performing and just be.

I wasn't looking for this. But maybe I needed it.

I don't know what this is, or what it could be. But I know I feel better when you're around.

I think about you when you're gone.

I look at you, and it feels like possibility.

Even if I never say this out loud—I hope you know. I hope you feel it, too.

Adam stared at the paper like it might catch fire in his hands.

The sounds of the office disappeared. The ticking of the wall clock, the quiet hum of the HVAC system, even the slight buzz of fluorescent light overhead—the world dimmed around him, like someone had turned down the background noise of the entire room. The only sound was the fluttering of his own heartbeat.

It wasn't signed. No name. No date. But it was Emily's handwriting. He was sure of it. Her neat, flowing script across the page. Just... words. Raw. Honest. Hopeful in a way that made his chest tighten.

He read it again. And then again.

Emily.

And then he felt his world… shift.

He thought about the way Emily deflected compliments. The way she sometimes smiled with one corner of her mouth when she was uncertain. The way she looked at him when she thought he wasn't paying attention—like maybe, for a second, she saw something he didn't.

This letter sounded like that version of her.

Hopeful. Honest. Quietly terrified.

Adam rubbed the back of his neck, unsure whether he wanted to pace the room or lie down on the floor.

He wasn't supposed to feel this way.

This was supposed to be light. Banter, brunch-related jokes, maybe a few meaningless flirty texts, and zero consequences. Just friends.

But then she'd let him into her kitchen. Into her *plans.* Into her trust.

And now he was holding a damn love letter.

He read it again, more slowly this time. Letting the words sink deeper. Letting them echo through the parts of him that had spent years laughing everything off before it could mean anything.

She had written this for him. She had to have. *Right?*

He knew he should ask. Clarify. Confirm.

But he couldn't. Because the words felt *true*. Because they made sense in the context of her nervous laugh and the way she never texted first but always replied. The way she had let him into this campaign, even though he knew she didn't let people in easily. Not when it counted.

But this letter… it sounded like it had been written from a place that counted.

He sat down hard in the nearest chair, the paper still in his hand. He ran a hand through his hair.

For a guy who swore he wasn't built for feelings, he sure had a lot of them all of a sudden. Hope. Confusion. Panic. Possibility.

Maybe she felt it too. Maybe this was her way of saying it—without saying it. A soft opening. An emotional breadcrumb.

But had she left it behind intentionally for him to find? He shook his head. That didn't make sense. It had been well hidden between forms inside a folder he would have no reason to open.

He started to fold it again, hands careful, like he was tucking away a secret that might crumble if he breathed too hard.

He knew what he had to do. It was obvious. He had to put it back. She hadn't been ready to share the letter with him. Not yet.

So, he would put the letter back. He would wait. He would bide his time. When she was ready, she would give him the letter.

He reached for the folder it came from.

The conference room door opened.

Adam crammed the letter into his back pocket, heard it crumple and held back a wince. Tried to look busy. Tried not to look guilty.

One of the tourism staffers—a tall, lanky young man carrying a messenger bag and a lanyard that read 'LIAM'—peeked in. "Oh, hey, sorry. Didn't know anyone was still in here."

Adam blinked. "Yeah. Just—organizing."

Liam nodded. "Cool. Uh, the permit form from the marina people is missing a signature. Emily said it might be in that stack?"

"Right," Adam said, forcing a smile. He started to look through one of the folders on the table labeled PERMITS.

Liam moved to stand beside the table. "Do you... want me to help?"

"No," Adam said quickly. Too quickly. "I got it. You're good." He expected Liam to leave, but he didn't move.

Liam cleared his throat. "Emily asked me, to ask you, if you would mind bringing the form to the marina to get it signed, like, now? We need it for tomorrow."

Adam stood still for a beat. Then another. His pulse was louder than it should've been. He was keenly aware of the letter that was still in his back pocket. There was no way he could put it back now.

Liam was looking at him expectantly.

Adam cursed himself for not moving faster. He should've put it back. He'd meant to.

But now there was a witness.

Even worse, he'd known instantly when he felt the letter crumple into his pocket that he'd made a mistake. The letter would now be bent, creased, undeniably handled. If he put it back in its current form, she'd notice. She'd see the folds. The creases. The smudges. The evidence of fingers that weren't hers.

If she hadn't meant for him to find it, returning it would just expose that someone had found it. Someone had read it. He knew how she would react to that. And he couldn't do that.

In that moment, he decided he had no choice but to keep the letter. Not to read again. Just to keep it.

He grabbed the unsigned marina permit and turned toward the door.

"I'll take you halfway," Liam offered. "But then I need to make a delivery." He patted his messenger bag.

"Thanks Liam, but I know the way." Adam nodded, the letter still warm in his pocket, something he now carried with him that felt like the nuclear codes.

As they walked down the hall, Liam talked about something forgettable—an issue with a printer, maybe, or someone overbooking a rental space—but Adam barely heard any of it. His mind was on the letter.

He would wait. That's what he told himself. He'd wait for her to mention it. To bring it up casually, maybe, like it wasn't a big deal. Or to ask if he'd seen something strange in the folders.

Or maybe—even just maybe—to say the words out loud.

But until then, he'd play it cool. Act like nothing had changed. Even though it had. Because now he knew. And he couldn't un-know it.

As Liam turned down a side hallway, Adam nodded a goodbye and kept walking, the permit in hand and something far heavier in his pocket.

Chapter Eight

Emily's romantic track record didn't exactly inspire confidence. There was the long-distance guy she dated during her last year in New York who claimed to "love spontaneity," which apparently meant vanishing for days without warning. Then the graphic designer who ghosted her after she helped him pitch his passion project.

And of course, there was the great We-Said-I-Love-You-Too-Soon Incident, which ended with Emily crying in the rain outside a movie theatre while her then-boyfriend calmly explained that he'd "changed his mind." At least he'd been honest.

Looking back, she blamed a lot of the past several years on the idea that being loved was the ultimate goal, and that another person would save you, define you, complete you. That your real life started once someone else said you were worthy of it. The books she devoured as a kid. The rom-coms she memorized in high school. All those sun-drenched montages and heart-clutching speeches and perfectly timed rainstorms in movies. The happy endings.

She'd genuinely believed it—that love would be the most important part of her life. The best part. The thing that made all the other pieces fall into place.

But now that she was older, she knew better. Love wasn't a story arc. It wasn't a neat resolution. It was messy, unreliable, and distracting in the worst possible way.

Her last situationship had been the worst. She'd gone all in—*really* all in—a friendship she had mistakenly thought was something more. It had ended with her sitting on a train out of Brooklyn, clutching a letter she'd never sent and staring out a fogged-up window like she was in the last act of a very depressing indie film. She'd spent the ride replaying every moment that had felt real, trying to understand how it had gone so wrong so quickly.

No warning. No explanation. Just a polite shrug and a voicemail she couldn't bring herself to delete until months afterwards.

Somehow, no matter what she did or how hard she tried, her relationships always followed the same pattern: intense, consuming, romantic in the big-screen kind of way—and then, always, a slow slide into heartbreak. Someone changed their mind. Someone wasn't who she'd thought they were. Someone let her down. Always.

And she always pieced herself back together afterward. She was good at that now—gluing the cracks, filling the gaps, pretending the fractures were part of the design. But like a ceramic vase that had been broken and mended too many times, she knew she wasn't quite the same. A little more cautious. A little more brittle. A little more scared of falling all over again.

And now? She was determined to live with a new promise she'd made to herself. That this chapter—this city, this job, this life—wouldn't be defined by a man. No more rearranging her identity for someone else's convenience. No more acting like a supporting character in her own story.

This time, she would be the story.

Which was exactly why she hadn't let herself fall for Adam Kostas. Why she *couldn't* let herself fall for Adam Kostas. Why she wouldn't.

Not when everything between them was so light. Easy. Breezy. A little flirty, but mostly friendly. It felt nice. Harmless.

But Emily knew better.

She was the kind of person who rewrote her schedule for someone she cared about. Who made banana bread from scratch just because they'd mentioned liking it once. Who memorized the way someone stirred their coffee and called it love.

And Adam? Adam was the kind of person who showed up with syrup and a smirk, then made himself indispensable in a way that was dangerously comforting. But from what she knew of him, he always left when things became too close, too intense, too real.

"Adam doesn't do relationships," Daniel had once remarked over brunch. Adam had thrown a napkin at him, but hadn't disputed it.

Emily couldn't fall for that.

Not again.

Now she was pacing the hallway outside a community center filming location in Niagara County, pretending she was focused on itinerary details and camera angles, and not the fact that Adam Kostas was inside—charming the sound tech like it was his full-time job, and wearing that soft grey Henley shirt that needed to be banned immediately for public safety.

Her nervous system couldn't handle it. Her self-control definitely couldn't.

And the worst part?

He wasn't even doing anything wrong.

He was just... being him. Easy. Helpful. Unbothered. Good at doing...*things*. The kind of man who made it very hard not to start picturing things. Like Sunday morning coffee. Or long walks in the rain. How big and warm his hand would feel holding hers. Or what it would be like having him in her apartment, no Brunch Club, no buffer.

Emily clenched her fists and stopped pacing. Breathe. Focus.

This was a work day.

This was *not* the time to catch feelings.

She took a slow breath, counting backwards from five like her therapist once suggested—though it rarely worked outside of yoga or parallel parking moments—and tried to remember she was here to run a shoot, not spiral.

Then the front door creaked open behind her.

Emily turned just as Sophie Lin breezed in like she belonged on the cover of a local lifestyle magazine titled *Effortlessly Together*.

She was unmistakably camera-ready: hair pulled into a glossy low ponytail that somehow defied humidity, skin dewy in that suspiciously natural-but-definitely-product way, and a perfect sweep of berry lip gloss that caught the light just enough to be casually intimidating. Her large tote bag hung off one shoulder, oversized sunglasses hooked on one finger, and her vibe was pure *I'm booked, busy, and hydrated.*

"Hey," Emily said.

Sophie took one look at her, then followed the sound of Adam's laugh echoing from the next room—the deep, low kind of laugh that made people turn and look and wonder what it was like to be in on the joke.

Her eyebrows lifted. Just slightly. "So... Adam's here."

"Yep," Emily said. "For logistics."

"For logistics?"

"Yes."

Sophie leaned against the wall, sipping her iced coffee. "And by logistics, do you mean holding clipboards and making everyone fall in love with him?"

Emily rolled her eyes. "He's been helpful."

"I'm sure."

"Stop."

"I didn't say anything."

"You *looked* something."

Sophie grinned. "Fine. But he *is* very present lately."

"I know." Emily exhaled, pulling her ponytail tighter. "He's a good friend."

They stood in silence for a moment, the hum of fluorescent lights buzzing overhead.

"A good friend," Sophie repeated, then softer: "Do you... like him?"

Emily didn't answer at first. Because *yes* wasn't enough. Because *liking* Adam Kostas wasn't the problem. The problem was what came next—what always came next.

"I'm trying not to," she said.

Sophie blinked. "I see."

"I like how things are," Emily added, quieter now. "The group. The brunches. The rhythm. If I fall for him—and it goes sideways—I lose all of that."

Sophie nodded, thoughtful. "But what if it doesn't go sideways?"

Emily gave her a look. "Sophie."

"I'm just saying, you're already circling the drain emotionally. You might as well admit there's water in the tub."

Emily snorted. "That's the weirdest metaphor you've ever

used."

"Is it?" Sophie asked. "Because last week I described my relationship with Daniel as a 'sourdough starter—delicate but bubbling with potential.'"

"Okay, fine. *Second* weirdest."

Sophie smiled again. "Just be honest. With yourself, at least."

Emily didn't reply. She couldn't.

Because she didn't know how to say *I'm afraid I'll want too much.*

Or *I don't know how to like someone without losing myself.*

Or *I don't want to be the only one who cares more. Again.*

So instead she said, "We should get started."

Sophie gave her a long look but didn't push.

They walked into the filming space, where Adam had already coiled two extension cords like a pro, labeled three sets of batteries, and was currently explaining gaffer tape to someone who had definitely worked on more shoots than he had.

He turned when he saw them, flashing that slow, unbothered smile that made her stomach do something she pretended was indigestion.

"You're late," he said to Sophie.

"You're annoying," Sophie replied. But she was smiling.

Adam leaned against the nearest table, arms crossed, looking way too comfortable for someone surrounded by chaotic pre-shoot energy. "I'll have you know I take my unpaid logistical consulting very seriously."

"Do you also take bribes in the form of pastries?" Sophie asked.

"That depends. Are we talking croissant or muffin?"

"Blueberry muffin. Slightly warm. Bakery down the street."

"You drive a hard bargain, Lin." Adam made a thoughtful face. "But I accept."

Sophie smirked and reached into her tote bag to extract a brown paper bag. She tossed it and Adam caught it deftly in midair with a grin.

Sophie's phone chirped. "Excuse me." She turned away, leaving Emily and Adam alone.

Emily didn't say anything right away. Neither did he.

He just looked at her for a second too long—not in a way that demanded anything, just… noticing. Like she was a puzzle he wasn't done solving.

"You look focused," he said finally, opening the paper bag and peeking inside.

"Is that code for stressed?"

"No," he said. "It's code for extremely competent and also mildly intimidating. Just trying to stay out of your way and not get hit with a clipboard." He reached into the bag, extracted a small morsel of blueberry muffin top and he popped it into his mouth.

Emily cracked a smile, the tightness in her chest easing just a little. "No promises. But I'll try to aim low."

He grinned. "Not too low."

Sophie reappeared, sunglasses now perched on top of her head. "You two done with your flirty banter?"

"We don't have flirty banter," Emily said, too quickly.

"Sure," Sophie said, already walking toward the gear cases. "Let's roll, lovebirds."

Emily rolled her eyes and followed, trying very hard not to look at Adam again. Trying even harder not to notice that he was already walking beside her, like some invisible thread kept pulling them into step.

Behind them, the door shut gently. The lights dimmed. The crew buzzed around, cameras getting calibrated, mics clipped in place, and scripts double-checked out of habit, even though nothing was really scripted.

Emily took a breath and stepped onto set, heart steady, voice clear.

This was her work. Her shoot. Her idea coming to life.

And Adam? He was just here for logistics.

Probably.

Maybe.

Right?

What Emily didn't know was that the letter—now tucked into Adam's jacket pocket—was about to become the most meaningful misunderstanding of her life.

Chapter Nine

Adam stood outside the door to Emily's ground floor apartment, his hand raised, poised to knock.

He was surprised to find himself hesitating. He wasn't the type of guy who got nervous. He could land a commercial jet in whiteout conditions. He'd once given a speech at a friend's wedding with only ten minutes' notice and wearing borrowed pants held together in the back by laundry pins.

But standing outside Emily's apartment door? It was like he was a different man. Less sure of himself. Less cocky pilot, more man on the edge of something he didn't fully understand.

Maybe it was because inside the pocket of his jacket, folded into a perfect square and already reread too many times, was a letter. A letter he was fairly certain Emily had written about him.

The words were still burned into his brain.

I look at you and it feels like possibility.

Every time he thought about it, something tightened behind his ribs.

He hadn't mentioned it—not to Daniel, not to Sophie. Not to his brother. Not to anyone. He was still trying to figure out what it meant. If it meant what he thought it did. If it was real.

C'mon, he thought, shaking his head. *Pull yourself together.*

He raised his hand again to knock.

And that's when he heard her laugh. Muffled, but clear enough through the door.

"No, it's fine, Jonah. I swear. You don't have to drive up here. I've got it handled."

Adam blinked. *Jonah?*

He leaned just slightly to the side, pretending to stretch.

Emily's voice came again, with a note of fond exasperation. "Yes, I'm eating. And no, not just crackers. Why do you always assume I'm lying?"

Adam's stomach did a strange, unwelcome thing. He shouldn't be eavesdropping. But also—he kind of couldn't move.

A beat. Laughter. Soft and genuine.

Then: "Yes, I like it here. It's quiet, but not boring. The job's good. The people are nice."

Another pause. A tone shift. Her voice softening. "I miss you, too."

Adam flinched. *I miss you, too*?

Something in his chest twisted. Tightened.

He knew it wasn't any of his business, but she'd never mentioned *a Jonah* before. And now she was talking to him like he was a permanent fixture in her life. A caring one. A close one. The kind you *missed.*

He took a half-step back from the door, his thoughts scrambled. Maybe she had been seeing someone else this whole time. Maybe the letter had nothing to do with him. Maybe he'd been walking around clutching something that wasn't his to hold. Maybe the letter had been written for… this Jonah.

For a second, Adam considered leaving. But then he heard her voice again.

"Okay, okay, but please tell Mom I'm fine, and to stop worrying." A pause. A low chuckle. "I know, she's such a worry-wort."

Adam blinked. Tell *Mom*?

His brain did a double take. The tone. The teasing. The wellness check thing. Suddenly, it all clicked.

Jonah. Not a boyfriend. Not a romantic mystery. Her *brother*. She'd mentioned him once—briefly—during a post-brunch cleanup. Something about him living in Texas and being "chronically concerned."

Adam exhaled so hard he nearly laughed.

She wasn't dating someone. Or at least, not dating Jonah. He acknowledged she could be dating literally anyone else. Even so, the relief was immediate and irrational and totally pathetic, and he didn't care at all.

He was a fool.

On the other side of the door, he could hear Emily again. "Yes, okay. I said okay already! I love you, too. Bye." A pause. "No, you hang up. Okay, okay, bye."

Adam raised his hand again, and knocked—this time without hesitation.

The door opened a few seconds later, and there she was: Emily, with her phone still in hand, barefoot, ponytail askew, a pen tucked behind her ear like she'd forgotten it was there.

"Adam?"

He held up the coffee. "Peace offering. Also caffeine."

"For what?"

"Showing up uninvited." He handed her the cup. It was still warm. "I'm between flights," he explained.

Her expression softened. "You're fine. I needed the break anyway."

He followed her inside, trying not to read into anything. Just be cool. Be chill. Be normal.

Adam had been here a few times already and he always marveled at how Emily's apartment looked exactly like her: a bit disorganized, a bit cozy, and quietly clever if you paid close enough attention.

The front hallway opened into a bright, sunlit living area filled with a comfortable mix of hand-me-downs and charming thrift store finds. Her couch had a quilt tossed over one arm. Two of the throw pillows didn't match—one said ESPRESSO YOURSELF, and the other had a wine stain that looked faintly like a map of Australia.

A narrow table ran along the far wall, currently serving as a hybrid desk/kitchen counter overflow/workspace. It held a stack of campaign notes, a glass jar of pastel highlighters, two open notebooks, and a coffee mug full of mismatched pens. Her laptop was open, paused on a video timeline. The muted frame showed the canoe shack, sunlight glinting off the water behind it.

He noticed the aroma of cinnamon and slightly burnt toast—comforting, somehow. The kind of smell that said someone lived here, even if they never really stopped moving long enough to finish organizing the space.

"Sit," she said, moving a pile of clean laundry off one end of the couch. "I was just editing. Or, like, staring blankly at my screen hoping inspiration would strike."

He took his shoes off by the door, then moved into the living area and dropped into the now-cleared space.

She took the pen from behind her ear and tucked it into the spiral of a nearby notebook, then sank into the chair opposite him with a grateful sigh.

Adam looked around again, more slowly this time. There were bits of her everywhere. A dog-eared copy a rom-com novel on the coffee table. A ceramic bowl filled with keys, bobby pins, and loose change. A framed photo of her and Sophie in ridiculous sunglasses and matching pink t-shirts, mid-laugh.

His fingers tapped his knee for a few seconds. Then he said as casually as he could, "So… you sent the draft to the group chat."

She blinked. "Wait, you watched it?"

"You sent it."

"I didn't think anyone would actually click it. I just needed somewhere to dump the link while my Wi-Fi was being cursed."

He grinned. "I watched it. Three times, actually."

She stared at him like he'd just recited a sonnet. "Why?"

He shrugged. "Because it's good."

She gave a skeptical snort. "It's rough."

"It's real," he corrected. "Which is why it works."

He sat on the edge of her coffee table and pulled a printout from his jacket pocket—not the letter, *thank God*, but her campaign brief. Still, his hand brushed over the inner fold of his jacket, grazing the other paper. The *real* one. The one that had nearly scorched a hole in his conscience for days.

But it was the campaign brief he held now, slightly rumpled but professional enough.

Out of the corner of his eye, he saw her jaw drop. The fact that he'd printed it out at all made her look at him like she didn't know who he was.

He smoothed the paper on his knee before clearing his throat.

"I liked the pacing," he said, referring to his notes. "But I think you can cut the voice-over by about ten seconds. Bring the visuals in sooner. Also—maybe layer a bit more personality in. It doesn't have to sound so polished. It's better when it sounds authentic."

Emily looked at him like he was a science experiment. "Who even are you?"

"I promised to help, and so I'm doing what I can to help." He grinned.

She sat across from him, a little stunned, coffee paused near her lips. "That's... weirdly impressive."

He nodded once. Tried to keep it casual.

Because this was safer. Campaign edits. Pacing. Tone. All of it was safer than *hey, did you write a devastatingly honest love letter and leave it where I could find it, or do I just need to get a grip?*

He thought about asking. He really did.

But her face—open, tired, soft in a way she rarely let herself be—stopped him.

Also, he realized that maybe she *had* written it for someone else. Maybe she *was* seeing someone else. He had no idea. She'd never mentioned anyone, but that didn't mean there wasn't someone special in her life—someone *else* special in her life. And he had no right to press her on something that might not be his business at all.

So he didn't ask.

He gave feedback. Made her laugh. Then talked about shooting schedules and local donut shops instead. Later, they sat cross-legged on the floor eating Chinese food out of cartons, the air between them warm with quiet conversation and the occasional too-long glance.

Adam kept waiting for the moment he'd snap out of it—for the fog to clear, the pull to fade—but instead, all he could think was how easy it felt to be here. How dangerous it felt to want to stay.

And when he finally stood to leave—jacket slung over his

shoulder, heart heavier than when he arrived—he paused in the doorway.

"I'll see you next weekend?" he asked, voice light. "For the final shoot?"

She nodded, brushing a loose strand of hair behind her ear. "Yeah. Different place, same sunrise."

He smiled. "Looking forward to it."

She didn't say anything for a second. Then: "Me, too."

He gave a final wave as he left and walked slowly to his car.

The letter was still in his inner pocket.

Unfolded.

Unmentioned.

And growing heavier by the hour.

Chapter Ten

By the time they wrapped filming for the day, the sun was setting in that *Instagram-filter perfect* way that made even traffic cones look poetic.

Emily stood outside a small family-owned vineyard just outside Niagara County, arms crossed over her chest, a smile tugging at her lips as the final shot wrapped. She stretched her neck and exhaled slowly, the warm air tinged with the scent of lavender and earth.

Sophie had been there earlier in the day, bouncing between interviews and hair touch-ups with her usual camera-ready energy. But she'd left mid-afternoon—hugged everyone, claimed she was late for a train, and disappeared with a joke about how her mom in New York would "start a gentle guilt campaign" if she didn't visit soon.

That part stuck with Emily more than she expected. She hadn't been back home in months. Not since the move. Not since things had started feeling... real here. Maybe she was overdue for her own visit.

But right now, the day was golden and quiet, and Adam was leaning against a wooden post near the vineyard's entrance, sipping sparkling water from a mason jar like he'd been styled by a moody food blogger.

"You survived," she said, walking over.

"Barely," he replied. "I was attacked by flying wildlife. This job should come with hazard pay."

She grinned. "You were buzzed by *one* bee."

"One bee can end a man."

The crew was finishing up, laughter drifting over the gentle clatter of gear being packed away. It had been a good day—three locations, four interviews, one wine tasting that went off-schedule but ended with complimentary Riesling and a charcuterie board the size of a kayak.

Emily felt it in her body—sun-tired, wind-tousled, and content in a way she hadn't been in a while.

"You hungry?" Adam asked.

She nodded. "Definitely."

He nodded toward the road. "There's a place nearby. Tiny pub, patio, string lights. We passed it earlier. Looked promising."

"You remember landmarks?"

"I remember *food* landmarks."

She grinned. "Sold."

They said bye to crew, then walked the few blocks in comfortable conversation, passing stone fences and flower-filled baskets swaying gently from porch hooks. The town glowed in that golden-hour hush where even shadows looked soft.

The pub was better than she expected: mismatched chairs, candlelit tables, and a patio that smelled like rosemary and woodsmoke. A chalkboard sign near the entrance read 'Tonight's Special: Whatever We Have Left', and Emily immediately felt at home.

They ordered truffle fries, a platter of food to share, and a local IPA that went down far too easily.

Adam made her laugh harder than she had in

days—especially with his deadpan impression of the cider tour guy.

"'Fermentation… is like emotional healing.'" He mimicked the sigh, gesturing with a fry. "Slow. Messy. And not always what you expect."

Emily laughed, the combination of alcohol and completing today's shoot leaving her feeling more relaxed than she had in weeks. "Okay, but you remembered the metaphor."

"I remember weird things. It's a gift."

"Is that what makes you a good pilot?"

Adam tilted his head. "You think I'm a good pilot?"

She gave him a look. "You're still alive and gainfully employed, right?"

He smiled. "Fair point."

Then she paused. "But seriously… is it what you always wanted to do?"

Adam leaned back in his chair, tipping his beer bottle slightly between his hands. "Yeah. I think so. I was one of those kids who got obsessed with planes early. My dad took me to Pearson Airport once to watch takeoffs, and that was it."

She studied him for a moment. "What did you like about it?"

He didn't answer right away.

"It was the freedom," he said finally. "The idea that you could just… lift off. Leave everything behind and end up somewhere totally different in a few hours. No traffic, no distractions. Just sky."

Emily tilted her head, watching him. "Sounds kind of romantic."

He huffed a laugh. "Don't tell Daniel that. He'll say I'm reckless."

"You are a little reckless."

"Only with snacks and spontaneous road trips."

"And relationships?" she asked lightly, half-teasing.

He shrugged, but there was something heavier in it. "I'm trying to get better at the landing part."

Her smile faded just a bit, but she didn't push, even though something about the way he said it made her chest go a little tight. Because she thought she understood what he meant. Even if he hadn't said it. Was he warning her away?

"And you?" he asked. "Always dream of convincing strangers to rediscover small towns?"

Emily laughed softly. "Not exactly. I wanted to write. Journalism, maybe. Or travel pieces. But I wasn't good at the whole freelance hustle. I needed something steadier. Somehow, I got into event planning." She shrugged. "I liked it enough, but I knew it wasn't what I wanted to do forever." She touched the bottom of her glass and drew a finger along the condensation that gathered there. She frowned slightly, aware of Adam watching her. "This job opened up when I was still living in New York and halfway to a breakdown. And something about it just felt... right. I think marketing—storytelling—may be my calling."

Adam nodded. "You're good at it."

"Thanks," she said, suddenly shy. "It's cheesy, but I like telling stories that matter to small places. You know? Places people skip over."

"You make them feel bigger."

She looked down at her glass. "You're good at saying things that sound simple and aren't."

"I've had practice," he said. "My brother used to say I should've been a therapist. Or a con artist."

She smiled, then blinked. "Wait. You have a brother?"

He nodded, eyes warming slightly. "Just one. Evan. He's the

one who calls to check on me when I'm flying too often or not sleeping right."

"Older brother?" she guessed.

"Yeah. Three years. Married, lives in Vancouver. Has a mortgage, a backyard, and a kid who's obsessed with dinosaurs and thinks I'm the 'cool uncle with sky powers.'"

Emily laughed. "That's adorable."

"He's a good guy," Adam said, softer now. "Always has been. Type of person who'd mail me socks and underwear in college because he thought I didn't own enough. Still leaves me voice mails that are mostly just him listing vitamins I should take."

She smiled. "Sounds like he worries about you."

"He does."

"And you let him?"

"Yeah. I guess I do." Adam shrugged. "I'm used to it."

They sat in a beat of comfortable silence, the patio glowing with candlelight and the last of the sunset.

Then Adam glanced over. "And your brother… Jonah?"

Emily's eyebrows lifted. She didn't ask how Adam knew Jonah's name. Maybe she'd mentioned it before. Maybe he'd just paid more attention than she realized.

Adam leaned back in his chair. "Sounds like someone who cares about you a lot, too."

She nodded. "He does. He lives in Texas now. Has this incredibly boring tech job and a condo full of smart home devices he doesn't know how to use."

Adam chuckled. "Classic brother energy."

She smiled. "He calls at least twice a week to make sure I haven't spontaneously combusted. I think he still pictures me as the chaotic teenager who nearly set our microwave on fire trying to cook spaghetti in a metal bowl."

"Wait. Spaghetti in a microwave? Wait. Metal bowl?"

"It was college. I was ambitious."

Adam smiled. "Sounds like he's your Evan."

"Yeah," she said, her voice softer. "He is."

They finished dinner, paid for their meal, thanked the hosts, and stepped into the night. It was properly dark now, the moon overhead softly lighting their way. As they wandered back to her car, the world felt a little blurrier at the edges, but in a good way.

They stopped at the car but didn't get in.

"Today was good," Adam said.

Emily nodded. "It was."

He nudged her shoulder. "You made a donut shack feel like the emotional core of a region."

"It *is* the emotional core of a region."

He laughed. "You're not joking, are you?"

She turned toward him, one eyebrow raised. "That place has been there for fifty years. Generations of people stopped there on their way to the lake, to family reunions, to first dates and breakups and awkward summer jobs. One of the customers told me her mom met her dad there when she spilled apple cider on his shoes."

Adam blinked. "That's... surprisingly poetic for a place that sells deep-fried sugar."

"They also donate every third Saturday's profits to the food bank," she added. "And the man who runs it remembers everyone's name. Even ours."

Adam grinned. "Okay. Emotional core confirmed."

She smiled too, but softer now—because she meant it. That shack was more than its donuts. It was a landmark of tiny, forgotten stories. The kind of place people didn't notice until it was gone. The kind of place that reminded you why community mattered.

And then she felt it—that slow slide of silence. The way time seemed to stop, to soften. The distance between them not quite real.

Adam reached a hand out slowly, eyes intent on her face as if checking every nuance of her reaction. He gently tucked a strand of hair behind her ear.

She didn't pull away. Her skin tingled where he touched.

His eyes were soft, his expression serious.

She looked up at him and suddenly realized they were standing close together. Too close. She wondered what would happen next. Would he try to kiss her?

Her heart began to thud in her chest. Did she want him to?

Yes. God, yes. But wanting wasn't the problem. Wanting was the easy part, she reminded herself. It was everything that came after that was dangerous.

Because if he kissed her, everything would change. And change had consequences.

They'd built something between them: this funny, fragile rhythm with the texts and the eye contact that always lasted a beat too long. The in-between of it all. The sweet, safe space where nobody had to admit what it really was.

And she liked it there.

If they crossed that line, she wouldn't be able to pretend anymore. She'd want more. Expect more. She'd fall—completely, entirely, without brakes. Because that's who she was.

And Adam? Adam was... Adam. Thoughtful. Charming. Funny. Warm when he wanted to be. But he was also flighty. Elusive. A man who didn't stay.

She didn't want to be his next almost. His next temporary thing. His next "we had a moment" story. Not when this meant too much. Not when she liked him more than she should.

So she cleared her throat. Kicked some gravel with her shoe. Broke the moment.

She gave him a half-smile. "Thanks again for your help."

Adam's eyes flickered. He straightened, running a hand through his curly hair. He nodded. Then he reached down, opened the car door and held it open for her. She got in.

And as they drove back, windows down, music low, her thoughts drifted again to Sophie and that train to New York. Maybe she'd book a ticket home, too. Clear her head. Recalibrate.

But right now, the only thing she could think about was the almost-kiss she didn't let happen—and how close she'd come to letting everything change.

Chapter Eleven

By Monday afternoon, Emily had officially entered Avoidance Mode.

She'd answered zero texts from Adam—not that he'd sent many. Just a "Made it home" and a thumbs-up on a brunch-related pun she posted to the group chat. But still. She hadn't replied. She'd even muted notifications for the Flight Club thread. Just temporarily. Just until her heart stopped behaving like it was auditioning for a musical.

She hadn't mentioned the almost-kiss to Sophie. Or Jonah. Or anyone.

Instead, she threw herself into edits. Into work. Into highlights and B-roll and color-correcting footage until her eyes blurred.

"Okay," Liam said from the other desk, leaning back in his chair and tossing a foam stress ball into the air. "Be honest. Are you color grading that donut or planning its mysterious demise?"

Liam was the newest addition to the creative team. He'd joined them a few months ago, fresh out of college, full of caffeine and enthusiasm. Despite his tendency to not wear socks and hum obscure indie film scores while syncing footage, he'd quickly become indispensable. He had an eye for unusual camera angles, a library of free-use music no one else had heard of, and the kind of idealism that made even budget meetings slightly more bearable.

He was also the first person in the office to learn everyone's coffee order and name all the potted plants by week two. Emily had taken to calling him "Rookie" until he started casually suggesting B-roll shots that made her rethink her entire structure. Now she just called him Liam.

Today, his laptop was open to three timelines and a color wheel, but he was clearly more interested in whatever emotional spiral she was radiating across the desk.

Emily blinked. "What?"

He nodded at her screen. "That little cinnamon guy's been sitting there for ten minutes."

She looked at her monitor. Yep. She'd frozen the frame hours ago. "Just thinking about transitions."

"Sure," he said slowly. "And definitely not about your boyfriend who helped us wrangle bees and mic cables all weekend?"

"Not a boyfriend. Just a friend." She corrected automatically, then glared at him. "Aren't you busy?"

"Nope," he said, catching the stress ball one-handed. "I'm just not blind. You've been weird since Friday. And for the record? That's not your default setting. You're usually Type-A with a dash of disorganization. This is... distracted raccoon energy."

She leaned back in her chair and groaned. "I really hate how accurate that is."

Liam grinned.

They were in one of the smaller edit suites at the Niagara Tourism Board office, fluorescent lights dimmed, the air conditioning humming. The scent of microwave popcorn lingered from earlier. Emily's desk was a minefield of sticky notes, half-drunk coffee, and a planner that hadn't been updated since Thursday.

"You ever almost do something really stupid?" she asked quietly.

Liam didn't look surprised. "Like... buy a motorcycle or kiss a coworker?"

She narrowed her eyes. "I'm going to pretend you didn't say the second one."

He held up his hands. "Hey, your secrets are safe with me. But just so you know, the entire crew thought he was your boy."

Emily covered her face with both hands. "Please stop talking."

Liam chuckled. "Okay. But for what it's worth? He did a great job." He paused, then added, "And like... he wasn't even getting paid, you know?"

She peeked through her fingers. "What?"

"Adam," Liam said, sitting up straighter. "He wasn't on payroll. Not even as a contractor. I tried to submit crew lists to accounting, and they told me he wasn't on the list. That he was 'just helping out.' Voluntarily."

Emily blinked. "I know that."

"Right, but do you know *why*? He could've ghosted after day one, but he didn't. He was hauling gear and holding reflectors like it was his actual job." Liam laughed, and waggled his eyebrows. "Dude… even I know that's not something 'just a friend' does, you know?"

She shot him a glare. "You don't even know him."

"I do, kind of," Liam corrected. "We worked together all weekend. And I know *you.* And I know this campaign matters to you."

"It's only the most important project of my entire career so far," Emily agreed wryly.

Liam nodded. "So maybe you need to figure some stuff out so you can focus, you know?"

She didn't want to admit it, but he wasn't wrong

"I am focused," Emily turned back to her screen. "Just watch me focus." She clicked her mouse. "I am laser focused."

Liam let out a huff of amusement and returned to his screen, too.

Emily tried to work on transitions, on audio levels, on the part of the canoe shack interview where Sophie said "reconnect" with a little too much emphasis. But her mind kept drifting.

To the almost-kiss. To the look in Adam's eyes. To the way her heart had wanted to say yes, even when her brain was screaming no.

She couldn't fall for him. Not for someone like him. Not again. Not like that.

But avoiding him wasn't fixing it either.

Eventually, she said, "Hey, Liam?"

"Yeah?"

"If I give you the last donut from the fridge, will you finish syncing the ferry B-roll?"

"You had me at 'last donut,'" he said, already reaching for her hard drive.

Emily stood and picked up her phone. "I'm going to call my mom."

"Cool."

Emily stepped out into the hallway, still clutching her phone. She didn't even think about it—she just tapped *Mom*.

It rang once.

"Emily, sweetheart!" her mom answered, her voice warm

and obviously happy to hear from her. Emily instantly felt better. "I was just thinking about you. Are you eating? You sound hungry."

Emily laughed. "Hi, Mom. Yes, I'm eating."

In the background, she heard her dad's voice. Faint, amused. Something about peanut butter.

"He says hi," her mom added. "He's in the middle of reorganizing the pantry again. Don't ask."

Emily smiled. "Tell him I said hi, and to leave the cumin alone."

"Oh, he won't. You know he thinks cumin is the unsung hero of the pantry."

Emily leaned against the wall, sliding down until she was sitting on the carpet. "I just needed to hear a normal voice. It's been a long week."

"Oh no, everything okay? Is it work stuff? Boy stuff?" There was a pause. "Jonah said you sounded a little off when you talked to him the other day. He's been very concerned. You know how he gets."

"I'm fine," Emily said. "Just tired. It's the last week of filming for the campaign."

"Well, we're proud of you. Your brother's always bragging about you, by the way."

Emily smiled again, a little softer. "Still single and living the tech bro dream?"

Her mom laughed. "For now. He claims he's too busy dating his job."

Emily snorted. "That sounds about right."

There was a pause, then her mom's tone softened. "He worries about you, you know. Always has."

"I know," Emily said. "It's mutual."

"Will you be back to visit us some time soon, honey? We miss you."

"I miss you, too." She swallowed hard. "Is Jonah planning a trip back any time soon? Maybe we can coordinate."

"Yes, he is. Let me check the calendar," her mom said, rustling through something in the background. "Jonah's planning to come up the second weekend of next month. Apparently there's a 'League of Legends' eSport competition in Manhattan he wants to attend the week before."

Emily smiled. "That sounds like him."

"You should come too," her mom added. "Make it a full family thing. We'll make lasagna and that lemon cake you like. We haven't had everyone together in ages."

"I'd really love that," Emily said softly. "I'll book the Friday off. It will be good to see Jonah in person, too."

"He'll appreciate that. And feel free to invite a friend. Maybe Sophie. It would be great to see her again and see how she's doing." Her mom paused. "Or someone else special in your life?"

Emily made a face her mom couldn't see. "We'll see."

Her mom just hummed knowingly. "Love you, honey. Now go make something wonderful. And call again before the end of the week or you know how your dad will worry."

Emily smiled. She knew it was her mom who worried the most. "Deal."

She hung up, heart lighter than it had been all day.

When she returned to her desk, Liam had already synced the B-roll and left a sticky note that said: *Donut secured. Ferry synced. Still think he likes you.*

Emily rolled her eyes. But she smiled, too.

Then she opened the Flight Club group chat again.

Emily: *Rough cut coming together. Thanks again for helping last week.*

She hovered over send. Took a deep breath. And sent it.

Baby steps.

Avoidance Mode: deactivated.

Chapter Twelve

The airport locker room always smelled like metal, old memories, and the faint scent of jet fuel that never quite washed out.

Adam leaned back on the bench, legs stretched out in front of him, one hand resting on his flight bag, the other holding a folded piece of paper he knew he shouldn't still have.

Daniel Carter dropped onto the bench beside him, still in uniform, sipping from a bottle of neon-orange hydration fluid. "You good?"

Adam didn't answer right away. He stared at the letter.

Daniel squinted. "Is that… paper? Like, actual paper? Are you writing fan mail now?"

Adam looked down at it, then shoved it into his bag. "It's nothing."

Daniel raised an eyebrow. "Your 'nothing' has 'existential spiral' written all over it."

"It's a letter." Adam's voice dropped. "It's... personal. Vulnerable. It's not signed, but Emily wrote it."

Daniel looked interested. Waited.

Adam hesitated. Then reached back into his bag and withdrew the letter. He held it out. "Fine. Here. Read it."

Daniel took the paper. Unfolded it. Read it. Then read it

again. He blinked. "Wait, *Emily* Emily?"

Adam nodded.

"She wrote this for you?"

Adam groaned. "Yes. Maybe. I don't know." He took the paper back, smoothed the edges, and folded it carefully. "I found it. At the Niagara shoot. In the campaign files."

Daniel whistled.

Adam dropped his head into his hands. "It's definitely her handwriting. I checked."

Daniel leaned forward, elbows on knees. "Alright Sherlock, and what—now you're in love with her?"

Adam laughed dryly. "No. I mean, maybe? Hell, I don't know. Before this, she was just… Sophie's friend. Brunch coordinator extraordinaire. Type-A queen of disorganization with ridiculously good hair."

Daniel snorted. "Accurate."

Adam carefully tucked the letter back into his bag. "But this letter… I can't stop thinking about it. About her. And now everything is weird."

Daniel tilted his head. "So, what's really messing you up? The idea that the letter might be about you—or that it might not?"

"Yes," Adam said, immediately. "No. Maybe. I don't know." Then, quieter: "But mostly? That if it *is* about me... I don't deserve it."

Daniel blinked, surprised. "Whoa."

Adam shrugged. "Come on. You know me. I date people for a few months. Six months tops if I'm pretending to try. I get into it fast, get out faster. They want more, or I want out. Rinse, repeat."

Daniel nodded slowly. "There was that yoga instructor you

dated because you liked her playlist."

"And the pastry chef," Adam added. "Who turned out to be a flat-earther."

"God, I forgot about that one."

Adam smirked. "I didn't."

"And the one who tried to manifest you into quitting your job."

Adam gave him a look. "She was... weirdly persuasive."

Daniel laughed. "Dude, you have a type."

"Yeah."

Adam dropped his head into his hands. "I know. They're usually easy-going. Fun. Low-maintenance. The kind of girls who post about their shopping and 'letting the universe decide'. Spontaneous, maybe a little emotionally detached. I liked that. I thought it made things simple. But they always wanted more, or I got bored, or both."

Daniel leaned back, folding his arms. "Okay, so maybe you've been chasing the wrong kind of girl."

Adam exhaled. "But the truth is, I've been chasing girls who made it easy not to try. Who didn't ask for more than charm and clever banter. Who didn't expect anything real."

Daniel leaned back.

Adam paused, the words slow to form. Then, he rubbed the back of his neck. "Emily wasn't even on my radar like that. I mean, sure, I liked her when we first met—she was funny and beautiful and sharp as hell—but not someone I thought I could ever keep up with."

"And now?"

"Now I realize... maybe that's the point." His voice rose with animation. "She challenges me, you know? Makes me want to show up. Like, actually show up, not just charm my way through everything. She's sharp, driven, intimidatingly focused—and suddenly, bam, I'm spiraling. Wondering what it would be like to actually step up."

"Step up, huh?" Daniel smirked. "Look at you, all grown up."

Adam flipped him off half-heartedly.

"So, are you going to give her the letter back?" Daniel asked, sobering.

Adam shook his head. "I want to. But what if it wasn't meant for me? Then I've built all this feeling on a fantasy. And if it was meant for me? Then I'm definitely going to ruin it."

Daniel sighed. "You're so dramatic. Did you audition for The Bachelor while I wasn't looking?"

Adam glared. "Not helpful."

He shook his head. This wasn't him. He wasn't the guy who spiraled. He wasn't the guy who second-guessed or sat around analyzing *his feelings*. He was the calm one. The easy one. The one who cracked jokes and shrugged off complicated things with a smirk and a wink.

He wasn't supposed to be dramatic about love. But here he was—sitting in a locker room at work, agonizing over a piece of paper. God, when had he become like this?

Daniel touched Adam's shoulder. Then he stood, opened his locker, and began to pack his flight bag.

Adam watched quietly, marveling at Daniel's efficiency. He moved with practiced ease, each move economical and precise, hanging the lock in the hook, unzipping his bag and placing it open on a nearby bench.

While folding socks, Daniel spoke again. "Speaking of commitment issues, you still thinking about going for Captain?"

Adam nodded slowly. "Yeah, but what if I'm not cut out for

it? What if I'm better off being the laid-back guy who avoids the big decisions?"

Daniel looked over at him curiously, then resumed packing, grabbing a small, plastic bag with a toothbrush, toothpaste and floss from his locker and placing it in his bag. "Where's this all coming from?"

Adam hesitated, studying the floor. "My dad once took a job halfway across the country. Better pay, fancy title. My mom hated it—lost her friends, her community."

He watched as Daniel moved a pile of neatly folded clothes into his bag. Daniel was quiet, brows furrowed.

Adam continued, "He always regretted forcing that move, always second-guessed every decision after that. Maybe that's why I can't commit—career, relationships, picking a damn coffee flavor. I'm terrified of choosing wrong and being stuck regretting it forever."

Daniel stopped and stared. "Wow. And I thought this locker room talk was supposed to be about fantasy football and complaining about catering."

Adam rolled his eyes.

Daniel zipped his bag shut. "Look, Adam, you're not your dad. His mistakes aren't yours. At some point, you have to trust yourself. The Captain selection process opens soon. You've got the training, the hours, the experience."

Adam nodded. "I know."

"You love flying," Daniel continued as he shut and locked his locker. "And you're good at it. You'd make a great Captain." He paused and turned to look at Adam. "Logically, it's the next step."

Adam shrugged. "I look at some of the senior guys—tired, jaded, living out of suitcases for decades. They've got big titles and healthy pensions, sure, but also empty apartments and nobody waiting when they land. That's not the life I want."

Daniel tilted his head. "Then why do you keep saying you'll apply next season?"

"That's what I say every season," Adam admitted. Then ran a hand through his hair. "I don't know, man. I think I want it, but something keeps holding me back. Maybe it's imposter syndrome. Maybe I'm scared to get locked into a decision I may regret later. Maybe I don't trust myself enough to know what's right for me yet."

Daniel put a comforting hand on Adam's shoulder. "Sounds like maybe you're figuring out what actually matters to you. That's just life." He slung his bag over his shoulder. "Sorry, got a flight to catch."

He paused in the doorway. "By the way, maybe the point isn't what the letter meant when it was written. Maybe the point is what it means to you now."

Adam stared at his friend, letting the words sink in. "Who even are you?"

"And hey," Daniel added. "If you ever need someone to officiate the wedding, I've got my online license."

Adam tossed a balled-up paper bag at him. "Of course you do."

Daniel ducked out the door, still laughing.

Adam sat back, staring at the locker ceiling, the ghost of a smile tugging at his mouth.

Maybe he was spiraling. Maybe he was overthinking.

But maybe—just maybe—it was because for once, he'd found something worth getting a little dramatic about.

He picked up his own flight bag, tucked the letter a little deeper inside, and stood.

He had a flight to catch, too.

And maybe—if he didn't screw it up— something even better waiting for him when he got back.

Chapter Thirteen

A couple of weeks passed. Not long. Not dramatic. But just long enough for everything to settle into a quieter kind of ache.

Emily hadn't seen Adam since that night outside the pub.

She hadn't mentioned the almost-kiss. Hadn't clarified the moment. Hadn't called or texted. Just... let things cool. Let the air clear. Let herself believe that maybe if she gave it space, the wanting would shrink back into something manageable.

She threw herself into work instead.

The *Rediscover Niagara* campaign was almost ready. She and Liam had pushed through the final edits, scheduled the rollout calendar, built out the social strategy, and presented the whole campaign to her boss, Susan, with enough polish to make her feel like a proper adult.

Susan had even given a rare, non-sarcastic "Nice work," with a nod of approval. It felt like momentum.

And now? There was just one thing left to do: launch.

So Emily planned a small preview brunch—just the core team, a few partners, a little champagne, and a big screen to show the final cut. Nothing fancy. Just her apartment. Just a few plates of food and the hope that no one knocked over a mimosa this time.

She made a flyer—half joke, half legit invitation—and

texted it to the group chat.

Emily: *Casual Niagara campaign brunch. Soft launch. Waffles may be involved. Be there or be square.*

Sophie: *Can I wear my "Donut worry" sweater?*

Daniel: *Only if there's bacon.*

Adam: *I'll bring syrup. Grade A only—I have a reputation to uphold.*

Emily stared at that last text longer than she meant to.

She hadn't muted the group chat this time. But she also hadn't replied.

Until now.

Emily: *Syrup accepted. But no flirting with the pancakes this time. The waffles get jealous.*

Adam: *They flirted first.*

She smiled. Just a little.

And now it was Sunday morning, and her apartment smelled like cinnamon again.

There was a French press on the counter. Three waffle makers warming up. A stack of napkins with tiny donut icons printed in the corners. She didn't go full Pinterest—no bunting, no fairy lights—but she had set out mismatched plates and poured the juice into glass pitchers. Progress.

Liam had come early to help "taste test" the waffles.

"You know," he said, mouth full of syrup, "you're a different kind of intense today. Like, calm panic. Very zen raccoon."

"I swear to God," Emily muttered, swatting him with a tea towel.

He just grinned. "You nervous?"

"No."

He raised an eyebrow.

"Maybe."

Then the doorbell rang.

Emily wiped her hands and crossed the living room.

When she opened the door, Adam stood in the doorway. He was wearing jeans, a soft navy tee, and that half-smile that somehow looked less cocky than it used to. More quiet. More sincere.

He held up a tall glass bottle of amber liquid.

"Grade A, of course," he said.

She stepped aside to let him in, unsure whether to laugh or run.

"You came," she said instead.

"Wouldn't miss it."

They settled into the flow of arrivals—there was Lucy, her sound engineer, already halfway through a croissant and enthusiastically discussing mic placements with Gabriel, the lighting tech with a charmingly thick French accent who claimed he had been the lighting technician for Coldplay when they had come to town.

Then came Ariana, the social media coordinator from the regional office, with three phones in one hand and a tray of tiny muffins in the other. Maya, from the local arts council, popped in with a bouquet of wildflowers "because launches deserve florals," and Chris, the owner of the donut shack, arrived with two boxes of fresh donuts, and a shy sort of pride in his eyes.

Sophie and Daniel were not far behind, bearing fruit and enough energy to fill the room. Sophie wore her "Donut Worry" sweater and immediately jumped into a conversation with Chris about slogan ideas for his shop. Daniel made a beeline to the coffee machine and began making espressos and attempting to organize the mugs by color.

There were hugs, coffee, clinking plates, and a half-hearted debate about whether the *"Brunch Club"* should have a logo. Someone suggested enamel pins. Someone else suggested matching aprons. Liam was already sketching possible designs on a napkin. Sophie offered to order more *Let's Waffle About It* mugs, and started taking orders.

Emily let herself take a breath and actually watch it all unfold—her apartment full of collaborators and caffeine, maple syrup warming on the stove, and no one pretending to be anywhere else.

And somewhere in the midst of it, Adam found his usual place at the waffle station. He didn't even ask. Just stepped in like he'd always been there.

Emily let herself watch him.

He wasn't trying too hard. He wasn't putting on a show. Just pouring, flipping, quietly handing out waffles with syrup and a side of wit.

And something shifted in her. Not huge. Not loud. Just... softer.

Maybe she didn't have to be afraid of the next thing. Maybe she didn't have to figure it all out right now. Maybe brunch could just be brunch.

And friends could just be friends, right? She'd need to keep working on that one.

Emily grabbed a plate and drifted toward the kitchen for a refill, pausing halfway when she caught sight of her reflection in the microwave door. Messy ponytail, dark circles barely hidden by concealer—it had been busy the last few weeks—and a smile that wasn't forced.

A quiet moment of yes. Of I built this.

She had pitched the campaign, developed the vision and

strategy, spent the past two months working her butt off to bring that vision to life, and now she was releasing it out into the world.

But it was more than that—it was the people, the trust she'd earned, the quiet doubts she'd pushed through. It was the feeling that maybe, just maybe, she was building a life for herself on her own terms, and finally doing something that felt like it mattered. Something she was good at.

She looked away before she got emotional about her own microwave. Grabbed a cup. Rejoined the crowd.

Later, as the syrup cooled and the waffle makers were turned off, everyone began to gather around the TV screen. As people settled onto the couch and floor with their plates, Emily picked up the remote and pressed play.

The campaign video started.

And for the next five minutes, the room was quiet—except for a few laughs, a couple of oh hey, that's me, and moments of the kind of silence that meant people were really watching, really seeing it.

When it ended, there was light applause.

Then Sophie, smiling wide and just a little misty-eyed: "You did it."

Emily nodded, feeling it to her core. Weeks of scouting, filming, editing, obsessing. Of notes scribbled on napkins, lighting adjustments in unpredictable weather, and a thousand quiet moments of doubt. But it had worked. The campaign had worked.

The final video—*Rediscover Niagara*—was a warm, five-minute love letter to the region. It opened with slow shots of sunlight cutting through vineyard rows and paddle boats pushing off the dock, intercut with quiet interviews from shopkeepers, artisans, and bakers talking about why they stayed, why they built something here. Sophie's narration wove it all together: sincere, imperfect, real.

Together with accompanying stills, graphic elements, and a hashtag campaign ready to roll out across socials, local billboards, and community papers, it wasn't just good marketing. It was storytelling. Emotional. Honest. Local.

Emily beamed. Spread her arms to include everyone. "We all did it."

Everyone cheered. Someone popped a cork.

Lucy wiped her eyes and muttered something about allergies. Liam fist-bumped Maya, who had already posted a boomerang of the cheers to her Instagram story. Chris looked stunned, like he couldn't believe his storefront had made the opening shot.

Daniel and Sophie hugged Emily at the same time—Sophie proud in the loud way, Daniel in the quiet one.

Then her eyes drifted to Adam.

He didn't say anything. Just lifted his mug from his seat on the arm of her sofa, and held her gaze.

It was the smallest gesture in the room—and somehow the one that stuck the deepest. That quiet kind of pride that didn't need explanation. The kind that meant *I see you.* The kind that made her wish, for the hundredth time, that things weren't so complicated.

The conversation turned. People spread out again, picking over waffle crumbs and debating best brunch condiments. Sophie was in the corner convincing Ariana to let her try drone footage next time. Liam offered unsolicited opinions on lens flares to Brett, the crew's cameraman. Someone turned on music—something jazzy and upbeat.

Emily found herself tucked between two conversations, plate in hand, slowly scanning the room. Her room. Her people. Her work, finally out in the world.

For the first time in weeks, she let herself feel it all at once—the pride, the exhaustion, the wild blur of hope.

Maybe she hadn't figured out everything yet.

But *this*—this campaign, this moment, this crowd around her—felt like something steady.

Something worth staying for.

Chapter Fourteen

Within three days of going live, the *Rediscover Niagara* video racked up nearly 80,000 views across Instagram and Facebook, with the state of New York's repost adding another twenty thousand. Comments flooded in—locals tagging friends, visitors reminiscing about past trips, strangers asking for directions to the donut shack.

The regional analytics team reported a 14% spike in tourism site traffic and a 22% increase in direct clicks to featured businesses. On the Canadian side, the Niagara Falls Tourism office sent Emily a message that read: *"Your campaign's doing more for the falls than our drone footage ever did. Call us?"*

She saved the email.

It was a strange and heady feeling—seeing something you built go out into the world and actually work. Emily still didn't know what to do with the compliments. Or the sudden uptick in meeting invites.

But she knew how to do field visits. And with Susan's encouragement, she reached out to the Canadian side and scheduled a tour of cross-border sites that looked interesting—hidden gems, community-led businesses, and the kind of human stories she could never resist.

She'd been planning to go solo—armed with an iPad, a few

branded business cards, and the kind of caffeinated optimism she could only maintain for half a day—but then Adam had texted.

She'd mentioned her idea to visit the Canadian side of Niagara Falls in the *Flight Club* group chat, asking the two Canadians for ideas, when her phone chirped. The name Adam Kostas flashed across her screen.

She'd stared at it longer than necessary. It was their first direct message to each other. Then unlocked her phone.

Just a casual *"I'm between flights. Need a field trip buddy?"* followed by a beaver emoji.

She typed three different replies.

Settled on: *"Sure. But only if you promise not to charm anyone into giving us free samples."*

To which he'd replied: *"No promises. My dimples have their own agenda."*

So she said yes.

Which was how she ended up crossing the American-Canadian border with her passport on a breezy Wednesday afternoon, and meeting Adam on the Rainbow Bridge.

He was holding a brown paper bag and chewing something. They fell into stride beside each other as naturally as if they'd been doing it for years—matching pace without speaking, shoulders brushing lightly now and then, as if the border itself had dissolved and they were just two people walking the same path.

Adam looked easy next to her, casual in a brown jacket and jeans, sunglasses on, like this wasn't a big deal. Like meeting her on an international bridge on a weekday was the most normal thing in the world.

For a second, Emily let herself just enjoy it—the mist rising from the falls in the distance, the sunlight catching the river, the steady rhythm of footsteps side-by-side. Easy. Breezy. Dangerously natural.

"Now that we're here… what are we doing here again?" Adam asked as he guided her off the bridge and they started down the sidewalk towards the main pedestrian plaza, already buzzing with tourists and the faint smell of cotton candy.

"The American Niagara Tourism Board wants me to scope out potential partnerships with the Canadian side." Emily squinted against the sun, holding a hand up to shield her eyes as she admired the Niagara Falls from the Canadian side. They looked bigger on this side.

"So, no break for Superwoman?" Adam asked. "Don't you want to, oh I don't know, put your feet up for a few days, bask in the glorious success of your first campaign, and relax?"

Emily grinned at him. "This is how I relax."

Adam nodded, mouth full. "Thought you'd say that." He swallowed. "So, what do you need me to do?"

"Give me ideas. Tell me what's good on the Canadian side. Any hidden gems?" She elbowed him gently. "Keep me company. Keep me sane."

He grinned. "Ah yes. Emotional support provider. Got it." He reached into the paper bag and offered her a piece of a cinnamon-topped pastry. "Now try this."

She took the pastry. Popped it into her mouth. Didn't answer for a few seconds as a shock of buttery sweetness and warm cinnamon hit her tongue, rich and flaky and almost criminally good. She let out an involuntary, delighted hum.

"What *is* this?" she demanded, half-laughing.

Adam grinned. "Canadian magic. It's called a beaver tail." He opened his arms expansively. "Welcome to the good side."

Emily took a bigger bite this time, surrendering to the outrageous, sticky goodness. The pastry was still warm, crispy on the edges and soft in the middle, cinnamon sugar clinging to her fingers. It was obscene in the best way.

"Beaver tail, huh? I'm moving here," she declared, eyeing the brown bag and wondering how much was left inside.

Adam laughed, eyes crinkling at the corners. "Good. We have excellent pastries and questionable weather. Stay for both."

"We have questionable weather on my side of the border, too." Emily was still licking cinnamon sugar from her fingers, when Bev called out from the gift shop next door.

A door creaked open behind them, and a woman popped her head out of the tiny storefront next door—a cheery building with a hand-painted sign that read: 'Bailey's Bits & Gifts – Souvenirs, Sass, and Seasonal Magnets.'

"Hey now, I recognize you two," Bev called out.

"Bev!" Emily smiled broadly in surprise. "What are you doing here?"

Bev had been running a gift shop titled 'Bev's Bits & Gifts' for over thirty years and was something of a local institution on the American side of the falls. She sold handmade Niagara-themed magnets, aggressively punny dish towels, and an alarming number of bottle openers. Her shop had briefly featured in the *Rediscover Niagara* campaign.

Emily and Adam had both enjoyed working with her. Bev's judgment was quick, her gossip sharp, and her affection—for both of them—came with the kind of warm bluntness that was impossible to dodge.

"Well, well—if it isn't my favorite couple," Bev said, striding towards them. "I'm visiting my sister." She gestured vaguely behind her. "She runs Bailey's Bits & Gifts here on the

Canadian side."

Emily glanced at the shop and did a double take—it looked almost exactly like Bev's. It had the same chaotic charm—floor-to-ceiling souvenirs, slightly faded signage, and an enthusiastic disregard for minimalist retail trends.

"Seriously?"

Another woman emerged from the shop behind Bev. "Hello, I'm Bailey."

Emily shook hands automatically as her mouth dropped open. Bev and Bailey were nearly identical—same wavy grey hair, same round face, same twinkling eyes. They even held themselves in the same way, shoulders back with their hands clasped in front of them.

They laughed with delight at her and Adam's expressions.

Bailey introduced herself as Bev's twin sister—and business partner. As it turned out, her back story was as charming as the shop itself. She and Bev were American and had run the shop on the American side for years before Bailey fell in love with a Canadian and decided to open a second location here, "because love doesn't care about international shipping fees."

Emily's ears perked up immediately. A cross-border romance? Local entrepreneurs who were identical twins living on different sides of the border running the same shop on both sides of the Falls? *Featured story potential* was practically flashing in neon lights across her brain.

"We should talk," Emily said, already pulling out a business card.

Bailey beamed. "Anytime."

Meanwhile, Bev had disappeared back into the shop and was already bustling forward with something in her hands and a knowing look in her eyes.

“These are for you,” she said, handing over two colorful keychains. One was shaped like a lock, and the other like a key. “Limited edition. Couple's set. The key really fits in the lock. They fit together, see?” She beamed. “Like you two.”

Adam stilled. Just a blink. Not long. Not noticeable.

Emily smiled, automatic and bright. “Thank you, Bev. That’s... very thoughtful.”

She didn’t correct her. Not because it was true. But because she didn’t want to watch Bev’s face shift from delighted to confused. Because it felt easier not to.

“Just keep smiling like that,” Bev said with a wink. “And if I don’t get an invite to your wedding, I’m putting it in the town newsletter.”

Bev and Bailey said their goodbyes, then turned and shuffled back into the shop, already discussing how to rearrange the moose stickers.

Adam took another bite of his beaver tail. Chewed, swallowed. Then said, very casually, “So we’re a couple now?”

Emily looked at him, startled. Then rolled her eyes. “Don’t start.”

“Hey, I’m just trying to keep the public informed.”

“It was Bev. You don’t correct Bev.”

He looked at her more carefully. A longer glance. Not quite teasing anymore. “You okay with people assuming we’re together?”

“It doesn’t matter what people assume.” She took the last piece of beaver tail from the bag. Bit off the top. Sighed with pleasure as she chewed.

Adam crumpled the paper bag. Tossed it like a basketball towards the nearest garbage bin where it hit the edge and went in. Of course it did. He turned to face her, hands in his pockets now.

“Where to now?”

They resumed walking.

"You must take me to wherever you got this.” Emily pointed to her mouth as she swallowed the last bite.

Adam laughed and pointed ahead. "Come on, rookie. Let’s get you a proper Canadian baptism."

He led her up a long street, around the corner, past a haunted house and an ice cream stand, until they reached a little red-roofed kiosk with a faded, cheerful sign that simply read: ‘Taylor’s Beaver Tails.’ The smell hit her first—warm fried dough, butter, cinnamon, powdered sugar and maple—a cloud of pure temptation that made her mouth water.

Inside the open window, a young woman about their age was expertly flipping pieces of dough and laughing with a customer. She wore a red apron with a logo, her blonde hair pulled into a loose braid, and her arms moved with the easy rhythm of someone who could do this blindfolded.

Adam waved her over. "Emily, meet Taylor. She's the boss around here." Adam pointed a thumb in Emily’s direction. “American,” he explained. “She just had the last bite, so I think we’re going to need more.”

Taylor grinned, wiping her hands on her apron and leaning forward with a friendly brightness. "Hey! First beaver tail?"

"Life-changing," Emily said seriously.

Taylor laughed. "That's what we like to hear.”

“Do you… own this place?”

Emily glanced around, taking in the cozy chaos of the place—handwritten thank-you notes from tourists pinned to a bulletin board, a tiny Canadian flag stuck into the tip jar, a vintage poster of a beaver by the door. Behind Taylor, a chalkboard menu listed flavor combos in colorful handwriting—maple walnut crunch, lemon sugar, Nutella banana. A few teenagers sat on the bench outside sharing a beaver tail the size of a dinner plate, while a family hovered near the counter debating between toppings.

Taylor nodded. "My parents started this shop twenty-five years ago—one of the originals outside Ottawa. I basically grew up behind the counter. Took it over a couple years ago when they retired." She tilted her head, studying them both with an amused smile. "Couple on a food pilgrimage?"

Adam—without missing a beat—smirked. "Something like that."

Emily gave him a sharp look, but Taylor only grinned wider, like she'd just confirmed her own theory.

"Well," Taylor said, pulling a fresh pastry from the fryer, "love and cinnamon are both excellent decisions."

As Adam paid for another beaver tail, Emily quickly fished in her bag for a business card. She flipped it over, scribbled a quick note, and slid it across the counter.

"I'm actually working with the *Rediscover Niagara* campaign," she said, clearing her throat. "We're proposing to highlight local gems. If the project moves ahead, I'd love to feature you and your story—if you're interested?"

Taylor's whole face lit up. "Seriously? I'd love that! My parents would lose their minds. They think any time I get mentioned in the local paper it's a national holiday."

"We'll set up a time," Emily promised, watching in fascination as Taylor sprinkled a generous amount of cinnamon sugar over the pastry, wrapped it expertly in parchment paper, and handed it to them.

"Careful, it's hot," she said in a practiced clip. "See you tomorrow!" She was already turning toward the next customer.

As they stepped away from the kiosk, pastry in hand, Adam nudged Emily lightly with his elbow. "Second person today to assume we're a couple," he said, mock casual. "Apparently, we have excellent chemistry."

"Canadians are very optimistic," Emily said.

He chuckled, unbothered, and they started walking again—this time along the mist-sprayed promenade that curved alongside the roaring falls.

Tourists posed for selfies nearby. A little girl in a pink jacket pointed at the rainbow stretching over the river, and a couple on a tandem bike wobbled precariously past. Somewhere behind them, a street musician strummed a soft acoustic cover of "Can't Help Falling in Love."

Adam glanced at her, a quiet sort of smile tugging at his mouth. "Maybe it means we're more than just friends."

Emily's heart started to thud. She didn't know how to respond. "Riiight."

Adam continued. "It must mean we're, like, *really good* friends. We've moved beyond casual friendship."

"Yeah." Emily nodded slowly, swallowing hard. Her heart was a jumble of emotions. "Must be that."

And she tried to leave it there. She really did.

But when Adam reached over and casually brushed a sugar crumb off her cheek, she didn't stop him. Worse, she had to stop herself from leaning into his touch.

And that—more than anything—was what scared her the most. Because maybe it wasn't just how other people saw them. Maybe it was how she was starting to see them too.

Chapter Fifteen

Emily hadn't stopped moving since 7:00 a.m.

Her office at the Niagara Falls Tourism Board looked like a beautiful mess—campaign performance charts, analytics dashboards, thumbnail mockups, and three different sticky notes that said *remember to breathe*.

She had been given an empty office last week, and had promptly colonized it into a hybrid of a slightly disorganized idea lab and a cozy panic room.

She was on her third cup of tea and currently working on her fourth attempt at organizing a post-launch wrap deck that wouldn't bore the Board of Directors to death.

She wore black yoga pants and a long-sleeved shirt that read *License to Chill* in looping gold script. Her hair was pulled into a high ponytail that had started off slick but already sprouted a few rebellious wisps near her temples—like even her hair refused to stay calm for long.

The American-Canadian partnership proposal had landed—hard. In the best way. Her boss had been pleased and immediately approved the budget. Now every stakeholder wanted to speak with her, and her inbox was expanding faster than she could keep up with.

It was good.

It was exhausting.

She was mid-scroll through audience engagement metrics when Liam appeared in her doorway, holding two muffins and an expression that screamed, *prepare thyself.*

"Do you want good news or the confusing kind?" he asked.

Emily narrowed her eyes. "What's the muffin for?"

"Emotional ballast," he said, handing it over.

She accepted the muffin with suspicion. She didn't even get to bite into it before Sophie barreled into the office.

"Emily!" she beamed, flinging her arms out like she hadn't seen her in years even though they had just had brunch last weekend.

Emily blinked. "What are you doing here? Aren't you supposed to be in…" She racked her brain. "… Mexico?"

"Well, yes, but this was more important." Sophie looked around approvingly. "Nice office… it's giving girl-boss energy meets Pinterest hurricane."

Emily smiled despite herself. "Thanks."

"Anyway, I'm bringing you news of your future empire," Sophie said, flopping dramatically into one of the chairs across from her. "And also Daniel. He's in the parking lot because he got a call and had to do that whole *serious voice* thing."

Liam slipped away with a look that said *good luck.*

Sophie leaned forward. "Okay. So. Remember how Daniel flies for SkyLux?"

"I've met him, yes," Emily said dryly.

"Well, SkyLux is looking to expand its Canadian domestic network. Guess what? Niagara is one of the new routes."

Emily's brain clicked twice before catching up. "Wait. You think they want—"

"To partner. Yes. On a regional brand campaign. Fresh

destinations. Off-the-beaten path travel. They're creating a Canadian spotlight series, and Daniel pitched them using *Rediscover Niagara* as a model."

Emily sat back, muffin forgotten. "You're serious."

"Deadly," Sophie said. "They want to meet with you and your team. Like... next week."

"That's amazing!" Emily paused. "But the *Rediscover Niagara* campaign just wrapped. I haven't even filed the budget close-out yet." She clutched her hair. "And now, the American-Canadian partnership campaign has *just* been approved."

"Whoa, congrats!" Sophie looked impressed. "Maybe this is perfect timing then."

But Emily's mind was racing. The American-Canadian partnership and the SkyLux campaign were definitely project *adjacent*, but her instincts told her the vibes would be different. SkyLux would want big-budget, sleek, and high-gloss content—less grassroots charm, more airline commercial polish. The American-Canadian campaign felt homegrown and heart-first. It was grounded while the SkyLux campaign would need altitude.

Sophie's gaze turned sharp at her silence. "You're overwhelmed," she stated.

Emily shook her head. "No, no. It's great. Truly." She turned to her computer and opened a new file labeled 'SkyLux Campaign' beside the other ten folders on her desktop. "This is a fantastic opportunity for us. This can be a win-win for SkyLux and the Niagara region." Her voice gained confidence as she spoke.

"They'd want the same tone," Sophie added. "Same energy. Ideally... same creative team." She paused meaningfully. "And they know of a very specific SkyLux pilot who's already been heavily involved in the *Rediscover Niagara* campaign."

Emily raised her eyebrows at Sophie. "Meaning Adam?"

"Meaning Adam," Sophie confirmed. She beamed. "And me."

Emily felt her heart tick up. She couldn't help it—her brain had already started painting the picture. More field visits. More brainstorming sessions. More Adam.

She liked spending time with him. Liked working with him. Liked the way he listened. Liked the way he made her laugh, even when she was running on caffeine and stress. And yes, maybe she liked the way he looked at her sometimes—like she wasn't just the girl behind the campaign, but the reason it worked. He believed in her.

But was it getting dangerous? Spending more time with him? Letting those quiet moments and casual touches linger just a little longer each time?

No, Emily decided. She was a professional. She was mature. She could be normal about this.

They were friends. Good friends. And she was a fully functional adult woman who could absolutely work alongside a charming pilot without turning it into a rom-com subplot.

She straightened in her seat, mentally smoothing the edges of her thoughts.

Then Daniel walked in.

"Hey," he said, nodding. "The airline's serious about this. They want a regional story with local impact. I showed them what you did with *Rediscover Niagara*, and their marketing head said it was one of the best integrated community campaigns she's seen this year."

"Wow, thanks," Emily said, taken aback. The SkyLux

marketing team was one of the best in their industry. It was high praise.

"Adam's already looped in," Daniel added casually. "They're putting him on more of the Canadian routes to help with logistics and content liaisons. He doesn't know the details yet, but if this moves forward, he'd likely be one of your SkyLux points of contact."

"That makes sense." Emily nodded, her brain already buzzing with new ideas. "I'll book something with the team. Set up a discovery call." She paused. Took a deep breath. "I need to talk to my boss."

Sophie stood and slung her bag over her shoulder. "Daniel and I are perilously low on caffeine. We'll be back in ten. Want anything?"

"No, thanks." Emily grabbed her planner and crossed the hallway to her boss's office.

Susan Mackenzie, Director of Marketing and Communications, was the kind of leader who ran on black coffee, bullet points, and a finely tuned ability to detect excuses before they were spoken. Her office was a shrine to organized busyness: color-coded folders, sharp-tipped pens in symmetrical rows, and a desk sign that read: 'Creativity is nothing without logistics.'

Susan looked up from her laptop as Emily knocked and stepped inside. "If this is about the *Rediscover Niagara* wrap report, it's not due until Friday."

"It's not the wrap report," Emily said, shifting the planner under her arm. "It's a new opportunity."

She explained—quickly but thoroughly—about the SkyLux proposal, and reminded Susan of the American-Canadian partnership campaign that had just been approved. She kept it factual, organized, no spiraling into excitement or panic.

When she finished, Susan leaned back, her face unreadable. "And you're planning to take this all on yourself?"

Emily took a breath. "I can do it. But to do it well, I'll need support. At least a project coordinator now for the American-Canadian campaign. And if SkyLux moves forward, probably additional resources—either another contractor or more internal time from the creative consultants."

Susan tapped her pen against the desk, thinking. "You have someone in mind for the coordinator role?"

"Liam," Emily said immediately. "We work well together. He knows the *Rediscover Niagara* workflows. He's smart, reliable, and adapts well to change."

Susan nodded slowly. "All right. Draft a proposal. Timeline, resource breakdown, deliverables for both campaigns. If SkyLux gets greenlit, we'll talk expansion then. If not, Liam gets valuable experience and we get the American-Canadian project delivered on time."

Relief bloomed in Emily's chest. "Thank you."

Susan gave her a thin smile. "Don't thank me yet. You just signed up for two full-time jobs."

Emily grinned, clutching her planner tighter. "Wouldn't have it any other way."

Sophie and Daniel returned ten minutes later with matching iced coffees.

Sophie collapsed into the chair across from Emily and took a loud, slurpy sip. "Sooo... how's my favorite rising regional marketing legend?"

"Busy." Emily shot her a quick smile. "Excited about the SkyLux partnership. Worried about managing two campaigns at the same time." She paused. "But otherwise, great."

Daniel leaned against the doorframe, looking far too amused for someone who allegedly found joy in Excel pivot tables. "You sure? Because from what I hear, you're about to have Adam Kostas professionally tied to your inbox."

Emily set her mug down a little harder than necessary. "It's fine. We're friends. We can handle it."

Sophie grinned. "Mmm. Friends who take long walks across international borders and share emotionally compromising pastries?"

Emily buried her face in her hands. "Please stop talking."

Sophie laughed. "You owe us lunch, you know. We drove all the way over the border for this chaos."

Daniel nodded. "And because Sophie decided we needed to check out that retro diner you featured in the *Rediscover Niagara* B-roll. She's been obsessed since she saw the footage."

Emily laughed despite herself. "Fine. Lunch. My treat. If you survive the wait list at Laura's Diner, you've earned it."

Sophie beamed. "Victory tastes like greasy fries and questionable milkshake flavors."

Daniel shook his head fondly. "Pray for us."

Emily rolled her eyes. "Now please go away so I can start working on the SkyLux proposal. My boss needs something by next week, and I have a lot of ideas in my head that I want to get down on paper."

"We'll go to Laura's to wait for a table first." Sophie looked at her watch. "See you there in an hour?"

"Should we invite Adam?" Daniel mused aloud. "Make it a Brunch Club event? He could drive down in time."

Emily shook her head. "Don't worry. Adam's stuck on a layover today."

Daniel raised an eyebrow. "Even I didn't know that."

Emily quickly shuffled papers around her desk, avoiding eye contact. “Besides, I can barely pretend to be normal around you two right now. Adding him is just asking for a public meltdown."

Sophie snorted into her coffee. Daniel laughed outright. Emily glared at them both.

"Noted," Sophie said, winking. "No emotional land mines at lunch."

“Just friends.” Daniel nodded. “Noted.”

Emily threw a muffin crumb at them. Missed.

Sophie and Daniel left, laughing their way down the hall.

Liam appeared a second later, muffin in hand. “Soo… how did it go?”

Emily looked up and gave Liam a pointed stare. "Congratulations, you're promoted. Project Coordinator, effective immediately."

He blinked. "Wait, seriously?"

"Seriously," she said, fighting a smile. "But if you so much as breathe one word about my emotional state while you're on the clock, I will demote you back to Muffin Acquisition Specialist."

He clutched his chest dramatically. "I promise to honor the dignity of my new role."

"Good," Emily said, tossing another crumb at him. "Now go update your email signature."

He saluted. "Long live the marketing queen."

Emily leaned back in her chair once he was gone, staring at the blinking cursor on her screen.

The campaigns were huge. The timeline was tight. The pressure was real.

And Adam?

Adam was about to be woven into her work life in a way she

couldn't ignore—or outrun.

If she wanted to build something real—not just for the region, but for herself—she needed to stay clear-eyed. Stay grounded.

She could do this. She had to do this.

She could juggle two major campaigns, a cross-border partnership, and a national airline.

She could stay friends with Adam. Just friends. She could absolutely, definitely, totally keep things professional.

Emily groaned and covered her face with her hands. She wasn't sure if she was spiraling over working on two massive campaigns at once, or because her stomach did a full gymnastics routine any time someone said the word "Adam".

Probably both.

It was just... a lot.

The pressure, the responsibility, the slow and slightly terrifying realization that people actually believed in her now. She wasn't the assistant taking notes anymore. She was leading projects, shaping narratives, steering regional partnerships.

She was *in it*. And if the success of *Rediscover Niagara* had cracked something open, this next step—this new layer of corporate polish and national attention—felt like the universe daring her to admit it: maybe she'd made it. Maybe she was the kind of person who didn't just chase big things—she *caught* them.

But with Adam thrown back into the orbit of her professional life, things felt less like catching and more like juggling flaming swords in a wind tunnel.

Still, she wasn't going to drop the ball. Not this time. Not when it finally felt like she was building something that could last.

Emily peeked between her fingers and muttered to the empty office, “Okay, universe. Let’s dance.”

Chapter Sixteen

The SkyLux-Niagara partnership was officially in motion.

The regional office was buzzing with a low hum of energy, the kind that came with big projects and bigger expectations.

Somewhere near the back, Liam was adjusting a stack of coffee cups next to a sad-looking box of grocery store muffins.

Susan, their director, was running final checks on the projector setup, her sharp eyes flicking between her clipboard and the room like a general surveying the battlefield.

Emily sat at the head of the long conference table, pretending to review her agenda notes, but mostly trying to breathe past the restless flutter under her ribs.

The room was fuller than usual.

There was Susan, of course. And Liam, newly minted as her project coordinator, looking both terrified and thrilled, armed with a color-coded notepad and three pens.

From SkyLux's side, Adam was the primary content liaison—though the airline's regional marketing manager, a sharp, polished woman named Natalie Cheng, was also dialed into the meeting remotely, her face projected onto the conference room screen.

From the Canada side was a senior executive, Marcus Hale, their regional marketing lead, whom Emily had met and already knew through her work on the American-Canadian partnership. He was now also working the SkyLux project. Double-hatting, like her.

The task ahead of them was clear—and complicated.

Emily understood what they were asking for: to weave together two projects that, while complementary, hadn't been designed to fit perfectly.

The American-Canadian partnership had been built to highlight the hidden gems, the cozy corners of Niagara—the small vineyards, the family-owned bakeries, the indie craft shops tucked down winding side streets. It was storytelling at a micro-level: heartfelt, hyper-local, sincere.

SkyLux, on the other hand, wanted something bigger. Broader. Flashier. They were chasing major traffic. Bold visuals. Destination glamour. They wanted the grandeur of the falls at sunset, the sleek airport lounges, the curated luxury experiences that would convince travelers to book a SkyLux flight instead of driving across the border.

Merging the two would take finesse. It meant celebrating the heart of the region without losing the polish SkyLux expected. It meant threading a needle between intimacy and aspiration—showing that Niagara wasn't just a stop on the way to somewhere bigger. It *was* the destination.

Emily tapped her pen against her notebook, mentally filing it all away.

She could do this.

She would do this.

This meeting mattered.

This was the moment where expectations were set. Where leadership on all sides would decide whether Emily—and by extension, her whole career trajectory—was ready for bigger stages.

And, of course, Adam Kostas, ever dependable, sauntered in five minutes early. He was dressed in dark jeans, a navy button-down rolled at the sleeves, and that easy, confident half-smile he seemed to wear without thinking.

He spotted her immediately.

"Fancy meeting you here," he said, sliding into the seat next to hers like it was the most natural thing in the world.

Emily gave him a side-eyed look. “Didn’t peg you for the boardroom type when we met. And yet…”

"I have layers, Emily." He leaned back in his chair, stretching out long legs that brushed lightly against hers under the table.

Accident, she told herself. Total accident.

She shifted, clearing her throat. "Ready to dive into spreadsheets and brand pillars?"

"Living the dream," Adam said solemnly, shifting in his chair.

Their knees bumped again—this time definitely not an accident.

Across the room, Susan called for quiet, tapping the microphone with an unnecessary amount of force.

"Okay, everyone, let's get settled. Welcome to the SkyLux Niagara Campaign Kickoff!"

Murmured greetings and the rustle of papers filled the room as everyone settled in. Emily flipped to the first page of her notes, her pulse ridiculously loud in her ears. She’d spent weeks prepping for this—working past midnight on her slides, talking them through with Sophie. She was ready.

Mostly.

If she could just stop noticing the way Adam smelled like

clean laundry and sunshine. Or how his thumb was tapping a silent rhythm against the table—easy, relaxed, *distracting*.

Susan launched into the opening remarks, outlining the goals and expectations. Emily forced herself to focus, jotting key points in her notebook, nodding along.

"Content production leads," Susan said, nodding pointedly at Emily, Adam, and Marcus, "will coordinate cross-functional assets, creative approvals, and content pilots for both the Niagara tourism boards and SkyLux's regional channels."

Emily nodded crisply.

"If you need any support," Susan continued, "Liam has been formally assigned to assist with production coordination on *both* campaigns."

Liam, two seats down, waved at everyone around the table, and at Natalie on the screen. She waved back.

Emily fought a smile at his enthusiasm.

The meeting progressed. At one point, Emily spoke, her voice calm and clear as she went through her slides. She outlined her ideas, her vision for the project, deliverables, the timeline, and metrics.

Adam listened, scribbling occasional notes into a sleek, Skylux-branded moleskin. He looked maddeningly focused—brow furrowed, jaw tight, the sleeves rolled up just enough to reveal the sharp angles of his forearms. He tapped his pen once against the edge of the notebook, thoughtful. Efficient. Unbothered. And somehow, impossibly, unreasonably *hot* while doing it.

Emily blinked hard and looked back at her slides.

Across the table, Liam gave her a huge smile and a thumbs up.

Then Susan wrapped the presentation, fielding questions

first, then assigning teams for the first wave of content shoots.

"Any additional questions before we adjourn?" she asked.

Silence.

“I think we’re pretty clear,” said Marcus, closing his laptop with a click.

“I agree,” said Adam. “Great presentation.”

Susan nodded. "Good. First content meeting is this Friday. See you then."

Chairs scraped. Conversations erupted. Someone started passing leftover muffins around.

Adam lingered.

Emily stuffed her notes into a folder, hyperaware of him next to her—tall, warm, devastatingly close.

He waited until most of the room had cleared, then said, voice low and playful, "You know, if we weren’t technically colleagues right now, this would be the perfect setup for me to ask you out."

Emily froze, pen hovering mid-air. Slowly, she turned her head to look at him.

Adam’s expression was pure mischief, eyebrows raised like he was daring her to call him out.

Emily arched a brow. "Wow. Shooting your shot in a government conference room? So romantic."

He grinned, unapologetic. "Hey, I work with what I’ve got."

"Which is... fluorescent lighting, an audience of bored stakeholders, and approximately four varieties of muffin?"

"Irresistible conditions," he said solemnly.

Emily turned slowly, her lips twitching. "You know what?" she said, feigning consideration. "Maybe I should be taking notes. Clearly *some pilot* has figured out the ancient art of boardroom seduction.”

“So you *are* thinking about it.” Adam grinned. “What about just friends?”

"Oh, I’m thinking," she said, eyes sharp. "I’m thinking *if* I ever do ask you out, it’ll be somewhere with mood lighting and no risk of being interrupted by Liam offering us carbs."

Adam’s eyebrows lifted. “Wait—*if*?”

Emily gave him a dazzling, impossible-to-read smile. “Gotta keep you on your toes, Kostas.”

He blinked, then let out a short laugh. “Wow. That was... hot.”

“Then it’s a good thing we’ve established boundaries,” she said crisply. “And I’m thinking *thank god* for HR policies."

Adam smirked. "You’re no fun."

"I’m the most fun," she said primly, grabbing her laptop. "I’m also the most committed to not losing my job because some pilot thinks he’s charming."

He cocked his hear. "That’s the second time you’ve called me *some* pilot."

"All pilots," she countered airily.

He laughed, low and rough. The sound slid under her skin.

"Guess I’ll just have to prove you wrong. Professionally, of course," he added.

Emily shook her head, but she was smiling.

Around them, the last of the team trickled out, and Liam waved from the door. “You two coming?”

“In a minute,” Adam called back.

When they were alone, Emily put her laptop into her bag and finally looked at him, dropping all pretense of play. She looked at him, really looked at him.

Seeing her serious expression, he straightened.

“I want this campaign to go well,” she said quietly. “I *need* it to go well."

Adam nodded. "It will."

"And we're going to be in meetings. On site. In the editing suite. Together. A lot."

He didn't flinch. "I know."

"Which means we need boundaries."

"Agreed," he said, without hesitation. "Clear ones. Like… no flirting between 9 and 5?"

Emily exhaled a laugh, then stood, slinging her bag over her shoulder. "Let's just try not to be a disaster."

Adam tilted his head. "Professionally?"

"Professionally," she confirmed.

He stepped aside, letting her pass. "Then I'll save the charming stuff for after hours."

Emily didn't answer. But the way her smile lingered as she walked out the door said enough.

Chapter Seventeen

The SkyLux-Niagara partnership was officially in motion.

Adam, who had been a pilot flying for SkyLux for almost a decade, was suddenly grounded. With purpose. With a project. With Emily.

This time, it was official. He wasn't supporting her as a friend, but as a colleague. Instead of a friendly volunteer, it was now part of his job. He was being paid to spend time with her.

They'd wrapped *Rediscover Niagara* weeks ago, but this new campaign felt different. Bigger. Higher stakes. A national airline and two regional tourism boards with real momentum behind it.

And while the logistics team at SkyLux handled most of the back-end setup, Adam was the chosen point of contact for content. His name was on the call sheet. His name was in the Slack group. His name was sitting in Emily's inbox, probably next to a dozen others—but it was there.

They'd seen each other a few times since the launch. Group meet-ups and brunches, mostly. A few work calls. Carefully neutral banter. Polite professionalism. Emily was friendly, efficient, unfailingly kind, still playful. But different.

And so was he. He knew this project was important to her. He did *not* want to be the reason anything went sideways for her.

But pretending it didn't matter was starting to wear him down.

He liked her. That part wasn't new. He'd liked her since the moment she walked into that dinner in yoga pants and a cropped jacket, confident as hell.

And now he could see—could admit—he wanted more.

And he didn't know what to do about that.

Because the idea of messing this up—of saying something wrong, pushing too far, becoming another person who made her life harder instead of better—it made his chest ache.

What they had now? It worked. It was safe. It gave him excuses to see her and hear her voice and feel the electric buzz of standing a little too close, flirting lightly, without crossing any lines.

But some nights, he lay awake wondering how long he could keep doing this. Pretending he didn't feel everything he felt.

And yet, he was afraid that if he reached for more… he might lose her completely. He didn't think he could handle that.

So instead of speaking up, Adam did what he'd always done when it came to Emily Levine.

He stayed.

And he hoped that maybe—someday—she'd meet him halfway.

He could be patient. After all, he had the letter. It was now safely tucked into his kitchen drawer at home. He had memorized it weeks ago and no longer carried it around with him. The sentences played on a loop in his head: *I wasn't looking for this. But maybe I needed it. I think about you when you're gone.* Beautiful, intimate lines that he had convinced himself were for him.

They had to be. Right?

He was mildly perplexed that, even after all this time, she still hadn't said anything about it. Never slipped, never hinted. Not once. Which meant… nothing. She was smart. She could keep things to herself until she was ready.

All he knew for certain was that he cared about her. A lot.

So, he showed up to meetings with professionalism and a notebook. Now he smiled from across the room but kept his distance. Now he worked on being exactly what she seemed to want him to be.

Nothing more.

The first SkyLux shoot started exactly like Adam expected: too early, too bright, and with way too many laminated checklists.

He parked behind the Niagara Falls Welcome Pavilion and found the crew already half-assembled—tripods being wrestled into place, camera cases open on the grass, and Liam sprinting after a runaway lighting umbrella that was caught in an updraft.

Adam sipped from his travel mug and adjusted his sunglasses, squinting toward the chaos until he spotted her.

Emily.

Hair pulled into a haphazard ponytail. Oversized sunglasses. A lanyard full of access badges bouncing against her chest as she barked something into her phone and gestured at a junior crew member with the grace and efficiency of a drill sergeant.

God, she was hot.

He strolled toward her with a smirk. "Reporting for duty."

She barely looked up. "Do you even know what your duty is today?"

He took the laminated shot list from her hand and flipped it over to face him. "Something about 'be charming and look tall.'"

"Mostly tall," Liam added, panting as he passed by with the

lighting umbrella securely tucked under his arm.

Adam nodded solemnly. “Glad I’m finally being recognized for my true skill set.”

Truthfully, he had a decent sense of what he was doing here—not just supporting her with charm and warm banter, but he had actual deliverables. SkyLux had looped him in early. Natalie Cheng, the regional marketing manager, had briefed him over a series of emails and a video call earlier that week.

"Remember," she'd said, her voice crisp over the call, "we’re not just selling Niagara. We’re selling the experience. The SkyLux experience. Accessible luxury. Hidden gems. Travel worth flying for. This campaign should feel aspirational, but not out of touch. Think: ‘Instagrammable,’ not ‘exclusive.’ Got it?"

He got it.

He’d even scribbled the phrase *luxury but local* in his notebook and underlined it a few times. And now, watching Emily direct camera angles near a food stall selling deep-fried cheese curds, he could see exactly how those two ideas could play together.

He’d seen the stress in her shoulders during the kick-off meeting, the way her brow furrowed when the American-Canadian campaign leads suggested integrating their local storytelling into SkyLux’s flashier vision. He knew the challenge—how do you merge cozy and colossal? Family-run jam stands with first-class upgrades?

Watching her now—juggling logistics while still capturing the essence of what made Niagara feel real—he knew she could pull it off. And maybe, just maybe, he could help.

He’d pitch it to her later. Not now, when she was mid-shoot mode. But sometime soon. Because *luxury but local* didn’t just sound good—it felt right. And he had a hunch she’d agree.

Setup flew by. He moved light stands and explained waiver forms to confused tourists like a pro. Every time he looked up, Emily was there—directing the crew, checking angles, making adjustments, tightening a tripod clamp with focus and determination.

Adam realized then, wherever Emily went, he followed, because that's what he did now—drift into her orbit and pretend it wasn't the best part of his day.

They moved into position for the first shot—families in the park, couples taking selfies, someone struggling to keep a sun hat from flying away in the breeze.

Adam framed background shots for social reels and suggested B-roll angles SkyLux could use for in-flight promotions, listening closely to Emily's feedback on pacing and tone.

Emily adjusted the scene framing, walking him through what she called the "moments of pause", the in-between glances and slow pans she wanted to keep the vibe grounded.

They found a rhythm—him capturing the wider context, her zooming in on the emotion.

They worked well together. Too well. It was terrifying.

He found excuses to hover near her.

Passed her a water bottle and let his fingers linger.

Held the camera bag open just a second too long so their hands would brush.

Each time, she'd glance at him—eyes flicking up like she was trying not to look.

And failing.

God help him, so was he.

It was thrilling. It was confusing.

During a lull, she stood by the riverbank, reviewing footage on the camera.

He stepped behind her, leaned close—close enough to smell her shampoo—and murmured, "Getting my good side?"

She didn't even blink. "If you had one."

He grinned broadly. God, he liked her.

By midafternoon, they had captured nearly everything on the shot list: paddle boats, shaded trails, kids eating melting ice cream in front of the falls. The lighting was perfect. The drone hadn't crashed. The vibe? Pretty damn good.

They broke for lunch on the grass near the pavilion. Most of the crew headed toward a row of food trucks. Adam flopped down beside Emily, handing her a boxed salad with dramatic flourish.

"Nutrition," he declared. "You're welcome."

"You literally just ate a deep-fried Mars bar," she said.

"And I regret nothing."

Emily peeled open the salad lid, eyeing him with the kind of suspicion usually reserved for amateur magicians.

They ate in companionable silence, broken only by Liam shouting "lemonade crisis" near the food truck line.

After a moment, Adam stretched out his legs, leaning back on his elbows.

"Yet again, you've proven you're good at this," he said.

Emily blinked. "At…?"

"All of it. Herding humans. Keeping things fun but efficient. Making tourism shoots not feel like corporate hostage situations."

A faint blush crept up her neck. "Thanks. I really do like it."

He wanted to tell her more. That she made him want to try. That he'd never stuck with a project like this without checking out by week two. That he kept showing up mostly because she was here.

But he didn't.

Instead, he tipped his sunglasses down and said, "Tell your supervisor I deserve a bonus."

"What's your bonus now? Extra maple syrup on your pancakes?"

He couldn't help it. He leaned in, dropped his voice. "Only if you're the one pouring it."

She dropped her fork in the grass.

He chuckled, low and pleased. Teasing was second nature—but with her, it felt like dancing on a ledge. One wrong move and he'd fall right in.

"Relax, Levine," he said, softer this time. "We're just colleagues."

She muttered something that sounded suspiciously like "tragically" and reached for her lemonade like it might cool the blush rising in her cheeks.

He was still watching her when Liam jogged up, announcing break was over.

Emily stood quickly, brushing grass from her jeans. Adam offered his hand—open, steady, like a reflex. She hesitated for a breath too long before taking it.

Her fingers slid into his palm, warm and soft, but firm like she meant it.

He pulled her easily to her feet. Their eyes met. Everything inside him jolted like a live wire.

She pulled away too fast, reaching for her clipboard like it was a life raft. She cleared her throat. "Back to work."

"Back to work," he agreed.

But she was still smiling.

And so was he.

Even if it was slowly killing him.

Chapter Eighteen

Emily had no business being this jittery about brunch.

It wasn't a first date. It wasn't even a date. It was just the Brunch Club—an evolving, chaotic, highly caloric institution that she herself had accidentally co-created. Originally, it had been a one-off joke meal with Sophie, Daniel, and Adam to make use of her three waffle-makers. Now? It had become semi-regular, unofficially themed, and, today, fully booked at Laura's Diner.

She tugged at the hem of her t-shirt—which read "Mimosas made me do it" in looping pink script—and adjusted her favorite green cardigan, her hair pulled up into its usual ponytail, feeling both underdressed and too dressed up all at once.

As she stepped into the retro-tiled chaos of the diner, she was instantly hit with the scent of bacon grease and coffee.

Laura's was the kind of place where the menus were laminated and slightly sticky, the floors were checkered, and the jukebox still played using actual quarters. Booths were red vinyl, walls were crammed with framed celebrity headshots from the 1970s, and there was a rumor that the cook had once served pancakes to Madonna.

Adam was already there.

Seated in the middle booth, sipping coffee like he'd been

born for diner lighting, sleeves rolled just enough to show forearms that did things to her blood pressure.

"Hey," he said, standing halfway as she approached.

They hugged briefly, the warmth of his shoulders lingering on her cheek and hands as they parted.

"You're early," she noted, sliding into the booth across from him.

He smirked. "I like waffles. Sue me."

Before she could respond, the door jingled again and in walked Daniel, flanked by someone Emily didn't recognize—a woman with sharp cheekbones, honey-brown wavy hair, and the kind of tailored jacket that whispered corporate competence.

"Hey," Daniel greeted as they slid in. "Hope you don't mind—Liv's joining. We just wrapped a SkyLux ops meeting in Hamilton and I bribed her with pancakes."

"Hi," Liv said, offering a warm but curious smile. "I've heard great things. Especially about the 'brunch club.'"

Emily chuckled. "Accurate. Welcome to the club."

Sophie and Liam arrived minutes later, Sophie claiming the end seat and immediately launching into a recap of a chaotic morning involving her neighbor, a rogue garden hose, and a squirrel with "main character energy."

Lucy, the sound engineer from Emily's crew, joined soon after, waving shyly before sliding in beside Liam. Then Gabriel arrived and claimed the far corner of the booth.

Small talk kicked in. Menus were perused. Orders were placed. Coffee flowed.

"Mon dieu," Gabriel muttered after a moment, squinting at the drink options. "Does this place even serve real coffee?"

"Only the percolated kind made from dishwasher water," Liam quipped as he proffered his white ceramic mug to a server who filled it with a brown, watery liquid.

"I would kill for a good espresso." Gabriel sighed, eyeing the coffee pitcher suspiciously. "I'll even settle for a real cappuccino."

"I think that's just how diners work," Sophie said, grinning as she proffered her own cup to the wait staff.

He groaned. "I miss Europe."

Lucy pushed a glass cylinder of white sugar to him. "Here, use this. It helps."

As their food arrived, conversation turned to travel horror stories, regional campaign rumors, and Adam's theory that all good maple syrup brands were secretly fronted by Canadian grandmothers.

"Just look at the labels," Adam said seriously. "If there's not a handwritten font and a tiny plaid scarf on the bottle, I don't trust it."

Liv, who was seated beside him, snorted. "You're oddly passionate about this."

"Only about the things that matter," Adam said with a wink.

That earned him a laugh. Liv leaned in slightly, elbows on the table. "So you're on content for SkyLux, right? What's your role?"

"Mostly supporting logistics for now," he said. "But I've done a bit of everything. Some stills. Location scouting. Shooting b-roll when I have a second camera. Helps to know what you're asking from your team."

"You've shot before?" Liv tilted her head. "Professionally?"

Adam shrugged, clearly not expecting the follow-up. "Not full-time, no. But I've worked on some small travel features. A couple of editorials when I lived in Vancouver. I had a little side hustle with a friend—portraits, drone footage, documentary stuff."

Emily blinked. She'd had no idea. "You're a photographer?"

Adam gave her a crooked smile. "How else do you think I've been able to boss around your camera crew without getting smacked?"

"I just assumed it was sheer audacity."

"That, too."

Emily laughed, but it felt shaky. A tiny part of her twisted—pleasantly, and then not. Because Liv was nodding, genuinely impressed, and Adam was relaxed and smiling with his usual, natural charm.

Suddenly, someone jostled the table, sending the syrup bottle toppling towards Emily. She gasped and froze, hands out-stretched in horror.

Adam deftly caught the bottle in mid-air, some of the sticky liquid splashing across the back of his hand. He placed the bottle on the table carefully, then stood while the table clapped and cheered.

"What a hero!" Liam called out. Everyone whooped.

"No need, please, there's no need for that," Adam said expansively, and everyone laughed. "Now excuse me before this turns into a maple syrup crime scene." He stood, pushing his chair back, and walked quickly toward the bathroom, cupping his other hand around the dripping liquid.

When he was gone, animated conversation and eating resumed.

Emily felt a light touch on her arm. She turned to find Liv looking at her meaningfully. "Emily, right?"

"Yes, you're good with names," Emily noted, smiling.

"I try my best." Liv shrugged good-naturedly. "So… Adam. Daniel tells me you're good friends?"

Emily nodded. "Just friends," she added quickly, her voice firm.

Liv gave her an odd look. Then leaned in closer. "Well, is he single? Because he's really cute. And seems like a unicorn. You know, decent and hot?"

Emily nodded slowly. "He's officially single, yes." Out of the corner of her eye, she saw Daniel roll his eyes from across the table.

Liv sat back, satisfied. "Well then," she said. "That's good."

Then Daniel leaned forward. "But is he decent?" he asked meaningfully.

Liv looked between Emily and Daniel, confused. "Is he?"

Emily shook her head. "I'm sorry, I don't know that side of him." She turned to look at Daniel. "But Daniel might," she offered sweetly.

Daniel shrugged easily. "He's my friend," he stated simply, as if that explained everything. Then abruptly turned away to start a conversation with Gabriel about concert venues.

Liv turned back to her plate, brow furrowed. She looked up at Emily again as if she wanted to say more, but then Adam returned, the chair scraping the floor as he sat back at the table.

Liv turned to smile at him. "Back to your non-sticky self?" she teased.

"I don't think we know each other well enough for me to answer that," he joked back.

Across the table, Sophie and Liam were arguing about whether waffles or pancakes had more storytelling potential.

"Those perfectly symmetrical squares," Sophie insisted, "are like a mood board."

Across the table, Daniel, Gabriel, and Lucy were deep in conversation. Emily couldn't make out what they were talking about over the noise of the diner, only snatches of conversation like when Lucy raised her voice and said, "Oh c'mon! I didn't *mean* to join a cult—" or when Gabriel rolled his eyes and said something about "—drinking the brown water."

Beside her, Liv was now animatedly comparing lens kits with Adam.

And suddenly Emily felt like the outsider at her own table.

She pushed her fork through the edge of her hash browns, listening with half an ear as the conversation moved to drone permits in Canada.

Emily forced herself to tune back in. Forced a smile. Forced everything.

And then it happened. A look. Just one. For a split second, she caught Adam watching her.

Not just listening. Watching. Like she was the only one in the room.

It was gone as fast as it arrived. He quickly looked away and turned back to his conversation with Liv.

But it was real. And it made her heart lurch so hard she had to pretend to sip her coffee to steady herself.

Eventually, the plates were cleared, the laughter faded to post-carb contentment, the bill paid, and they began trickling out into the parking lot.

Sophie looped her arm through Emily's as they exited.

"Good brunch," Sophie said lightly. "Decent waffles. 8/10."

"Solid six for me," Daniel called back. "No whipped cream mountain."

Sophie rolled her eyes. "How many times do I have to tell you… you can't rate waffles based on toppings."

Daniel smiled and patted her on the head.

As they reached the cars, Adam caught up to her.

"Hey," he said, quieter now. "You okay?"

"Yeah," she replied too quickly. "Fine."

"Just checking," he said, studying her.

She opened her mouth to say something—maybe to ask if he was okay, too—but Liv appeared beside him, laughing about something Gabriel had said. Adam turned slightly, and the moment passed.

The group fanned out across the lot in clumps and pairs, still chatting, still caffeinated.

Gabriel climbed into his little hatchback with a martyred sigh and declared to no one in particular, "I go now to find proper espresso. May the coffee gods have mercy."

Lucy offered Liam a ride back to the office, and the two of them disappeared mid-debate about whether dogs could, in fact, be emotionally manipulative.

Daniel walked Liv to her car, the two of them still talking about SkyLux operations, while Sophie stood beside her vehicle scrolling her phone and yelling, "Don't let him gaslight you, Lucy!"

It was chaotic. Familiar. Warm.

As everyone said their goodbyes, Emily realized she had forgotten her cardigan inside.

Instead of heading to her car, she waved goodbye, then turned and went back into Laura's Diner.

Suddenly, she heard footsteps behind her. Adam caught up, falling into step beside her.

"Forgot my cardigan," she explained.

"Classic." He gestured vaguely toward the booth.

The booth had already been tidied, dishes and cutlery cleared away, and the table wiped down.

Her green cardigan hung innocently on the back of a chair.

They reached for it at the same time, their hands brushing. Neither moved away right away.

Emily flushed. Her pulse skipped, heat blooming under her collar.

She opened her mouth to say something, but before she could think of what to say, Liam appeared. “Lucy’s threatening to eat my leftovers if we don’t leave.”

Adam laughed, stepping back. “Guess that’s our cue.”

He put his hand on the small of her back as they exited into the sunlight again, side by side.

When he left her at her car and waved to her from Lucy’s car, the warmth of his touch lingered there.

Chapter Nineteen

The office was quiet. Too quiet.

Adam leaned back in his chair and stared at the loading bar crawling across Emily's laptop screen like it had all the time in the world.

Across from him, Emily sat cross-legged in her chair, chin in hand, watching a spinning rainbow wheel of doom with the intensity of someone trying not to lose her mind.

It had been five days since brunch at Laura's Diner. Since Emily forgot her cardigan and Adam nearly said something he shouldn't have.

In the days that followed, they'd texted. Light stuff. Logistics. Meetings. Nothing charged, nothing off-script. Just work.

But now they were deep into post-production, racing to meet the next SkyLux milestone. Which meant hours in the edit suite, just the two of them, elbows brushing as they scrubbed through footage and picked music beds.

It wasn't awkward—not exactly. But something had shifted. The air between them now felt like a held breath. Neither willing to exhale first.

"Render time: twenty-two minutes," Emily announced with the weary gravitas of a person who had been personally betrayed by software.

"Ah yes," Adam said, stretching his arms over his head. "Just enough time to reflect on all our life choices."

She smirked. "Or alphabetize the b-roll folders. Again."

"I'm not touching that system," he said, holding up his hands. "You have color codes, Emily. Color codes."

"Unfortunately, when you have this many files, it's necessary."

"It's terrifying."

They were tucked into the back editing room of the Niagara Falls Tourism Board, a space filled with coffee cups, tangled wires, and the low hum of machines that hadn't been turned off in three days.

Most of the team had gone home hours ago. But the two of them had stayed behind to review footage for the next SkyLux teaser—something about capturing "Niagara in motion," which translated to drone shots of waterfalls and exactly one hundred and twenty-three frames of swans refusing to fly on cue.

"Wanna play a game?" Emily asked suddenly.

Adam raised a brow. "What are we, twelve?"

She kicked his foot under the table. "Not like that. A real game. Something to pass the time."

He tilted his head. "What kind of game?"

She shrugged. "Twenty Questions? Truth or dare—minus the dare? Something stupid. Just… something."

Adam considered her. The soft lighting made her eyes look darker, like honey at dusk. Her hair was falling out of its bun, and she had a tiny smear of chocolate near her temple from the cookie she'd forgotten she was holding earlier.

"Alright," he said. "Truth or truth."

Emily grinned. "Deal. You go first."

"Okay..." He leaned forward slightly. "What's your weirdest travel habit?"

She snorted. "You would ask that, wouldn't you?" She didn't hesitate. "I alphabetize my packing list. Like... aggressively."

Adam blinked. "Alphabetize? Like A for...?"

"Adapter. Advil. Aloe vera. Then B for backup batteries. Bug spray. Bikini—obviously."

"Obviously," he echoed, trying not to picture that.

"Don't look at me like that," she said, laughing. "It calms me."

"I'm not judging. I'm just impressed. As a pilot, I've seen all sorts." He leaned back in his chair a little, smirking. "I once flew with a guy who refused to board unless his suitcase was blessed by his grandmother first. Another woman packed her pet iguana in a tote bag and didn't mention it until we were over Manitoba."

Emily laughed. "Please tell me you're making that up."

"I wish I was. I'm just saying, alphabetized packing? Not even in the top ten quirks I've seen."

"Your turn." She sipped her tea, smiling. "What's something no one knows about you?"

Adam hesitated. Then shrugged. "I once almost bought a food truck."

Emily sat up straighter. "Seriously?"

"Yep. I was twenty-two. Fresh out of school. Broke. Burnt out. I thought I'd drive up the west coast selling grilled cheese and not talking to anyone ever again."

"Why didn't you?"

He smiled faintly. "Because I'd be terrible at it. The cooking part would be okay—I can probably cook ten grilled cheese sandwiches at the same time, if I had to. But running the actual business, filing taxes, balancing the books? Spreadsheets are Daniel's thing, not mine. Plus, making chit-chat with customers would be the opposite of what I was looking for. And apparently, food safety is a whole thing."

She laughed. "I can't believe I didn't know that."

"Yeah, well. There's a lot you don't know."

Something shifted then. Not dramatically, but enough that he felt it. A quiet pause. A longer look.

He put a hand on the table. "Alright, your turn. What's the dumbest thing you've ever cried about?"

She groaned. "Easy. I once cried because I thought I lost my favorite mug—but it turned out to be in the dishwasher the whole time."

Adam grinned. "That's not dumb. That's a tragedy narrowly averted." He paused. "Describe it to me."

"The mug?" Emily blinked. "Oh, it's just a regular, white mug, but it had a saying I've found funny since I got it as a teenager. It was a gift from my brother."

"Jonah." Adam confirmed. "What did it say?"

She looked sheepish. "At the top it says, 'Here we fucking go again', with a little sun cartoon. Below the sun, it says, 'I mean, good morning'."

Adam laughed out loud. "That would be my favorite, too."

Emily pressed a hand over her mouth. "I like it so much because it's so out of my character, you know?"

"Sophie bought you waffle-themed mugs, too. To our first brunch," Adam said, suddenly remembering. "She must know this about you."

"I'm not a collector or anything." Emily shrugged with a smile. "I just like mugs with funny sayings."

"And clothes, apparently," he gestured toward her t-shirt

which today read "Stay pawsitive" with a cartoon imprint of a cat's paw.

She tipped her head to the side. "Okay, your turn again."

Adam cleared his throat and sat up straight.

Emily leaned forward. "Something that scared you that you never told anyone."

He hesitated.

"Flying," he said finally. "When I first started training. I almost quit. I didn't tell anyone. But for the first few flights, I kept waiting for everything to go wrong."

Her expression softened. "But it didn't."

"Nope." He met her gaze. "Turns out, you can be terrified and still move forward."

Their eyes held.

The room was quiet again. But not empty.

The render bar hit ninety-two percent.

Adam tapped his fingers lightly against the desk, then tilted his head toward her. "Your turn," he said. "What do you want most right now?"

Emily looked at him, startled by the question. Then she leaned back in her chair, crossing her arms loosely.

"I want this campaign to work," she said honestly. "I want people to see Niagara the way I see it. I want SkyLux to be proud they partnered with us. I want it to matter."

Adam studied her face—earnest, driven, just a little vulnerable. "It already matters," he said.

Emily smiled, and for a moment, neither of them looked away.

"Okay," she said, voice gentler now. "Last one. What do *you* want most right now?"

Adam could have lied. Could have said something safe. But

instead, he leaned back in his chair, his expression thoughtful. Emily's letter flashed to the front of his mind.

"Clarity," he said, clearing his throat. "About... a few things."

Emily's lips parted. Her gaze flicked to his, unreadable and somehow vulnerable.

"Like what?" she asked.

"Like everything," he shrugged. "Work. Love. Life." He paused. Shrugged again. "Everything."

The laptop pinged. Render complete.

For a moment, he wondered if she would press him for more, but she only nodded thoughtfully. She cleared her throat. "Back to work?" she suggested.

Relieved, he sat up in his chair. "Back to work."

As they leaned over the laptop—shoulders brushing, hearts pounding—Adam made a silent decision. He was done waiting. Done second-guessing. Once this campaign wrapped, he was going to tell her how he felt. Because maybe clarity wasn't something you found—it was something you chose. And he was ready to choose her.

Chapter Twenty

Emily wasn't proud of how hard she slammed the office supply drawer. But honestly, what choice did she have?

Adam Kostas was infuriating.

Not in the obvious, annoying way—he wasn't loud or careless or oblivious. No, he was infuriating in that slow-burn, quietly-charming, impossibly-attuned-to-you kind of way. The kind of man who made your stomach flip when he smiled, and then made you want to throttle him five minutes later when he casually upended your perfectly organized file structure with "just a quick tweak."

They had spent the last four days working on the SkyLux campaign, holed up in the editing suite, surviving on instant coffee and takeout dumplings. Somewhere between late-night render sessions and early morning footage reviews, they'd become something resembling a team. A *very* close team.

She hadn't noticed when it started—that shift from coworker to comfort. But somewhere in the late nights and inside jokes, he'd gotten under her skin.

He made her laugh when she didn't think she could. Knew when to offer help and when to back off.

When he disappeared to get coffee or ducked out for a break, she noticed the absence. She missed him. It was ridiculous, but true.

And now, he was standing three feet away, arms folded, casually watching her pace the length of the room like he hadn't just sent her meticulously labeled folders into an existential crisis.

"You renamed them again," she said, waving her hand toward the screen like it had personally insulted her. "Why would you do that?"

He didn't even flinch. "Because your file names were too long to read in the preview pane."

"They were *standardized.*"

"They were too long," he repeated gently, patiently.

Irrationally, this made her even more furious. "They were fine!"

He tilted his head. "Fine is not the hill I thought you'd die on."

"I'm not dying," she snapped, "I'm trying to keep things from unraveling."

Adam raised both eyebrows. "Because of folder names?"

"No," she said, throwing up her hands. "Because of everything. Because SkyLux needs final assets by Monday. Because I haven't slept more than five hours in three nights. Because I'm *this close* to losing my mind, and you—" she pointed at him "—you keep messing with my system, and acting like it's no big deal, and being completely unbothered."

Adam crossed the room slowly, until he stood in front of her. He gripped her shoulder.

"I'm not unbothered," he said, his voice low and even. "I'm just not panicking."

"Well, congratulations," Emily muttered, looking down.

"That makes one of us."

She tried not to notice how close he was now. Or how good he smelled. Or how the tension between them had gone from annoying to electric in about ten seconds flat.

He was touching her, his hands comfortingly warm through the thin fabric of her shirt. He didn't move back.

"You're allowed to freak out, Emily."

"I'm not freaking out."

He gave her a look. "You reorganized a binder three times this morning."

"It needed tabs!"

"You bought four different flavors of granola bars and then threw them all out."

"They were *chewy*, Adam."

He stepped closer again.

The back of her thighs hit the edge of the desk behind her.

And still, he didn't move, didn't look away.

What was he doing? She froze, heart skittering. There was something different in the way he looked at her now—not playful or teasing, but steady, thoughtful. Like he'd just made up his mind about something. Her pulse jumped. She didn't move. Didn't breathe.

"I get it," he said softly. "You care. You care so much it eats you alive. But you don't have to do it alone."

His words sank into her skin like heat. But she didn't want comfort. Not right now.

"You don't understand," she said, her voice tight. "This matters. This campaign, this partnership, this opportunity. I've worked my whole life to be taken seriously. And if I screw this up, if it falls apart—"

"It's not going to fall apart."

"You don't know that."

"I know *you*," he said.

She blinked. "You don't."

"I do." He stepped in even closer. "I know how hard you work. I know how much you care. I know that you carry the weight of every single deliverable like it's a personal promise you made to the entire population of Niagara. And I know—" his voice dipped—"that the reason you're angry right now isn't just because of file names."

Her pulse kicked up.

She was aware of everything: the space between them, the way his eyes locked onto hers, the faint curve of his mouth like he wanted to smile but was holding back.

She didn't respond.

Not with words.

And neither did he.

They stood there, locked in a silent standoff that was anything but quiet.

Then Adam mouth tightened almost imperceptibly, a flicker of resolve crossing his face.

He reached up, slowly, gently, and tucked a piece of her hair behind her ear. It was an almost familiar gesture by now. He had done it a few times over the past months. It was intimate and strangely comforting.

His fingers brushed her cheek. She wanted to nuzzle his hand, but resisted. Instead, she sucked in a breath as he leaned closer, his face hovering near hers.

"Emily," he said, barely above a whisper.

"Don't," she said, even though she didn't mean it. Her eyes flicked to his lips. They were close so. They looked soft. Tempting. Inviting.

She had imagined this. Not once. Not twice. Dozens of times.

Late at night, when her brain refused to shut off. During campaign meetings when he leaned back in his chair and grinned like he had no idea how distracting he was. Every time he tucked her hair behind her ear or looked at her like it meant something.

She'd imagined this exact moment—what his lips would feel like, how he'd taste, how it would undo her.

And now?

Now it was real. And terrifying. And very, very close.

As she watched, Adam's lips curved into a small smile. "Why not?"

"Because I don't know what this is," she said, her voice trembling. "Because I can't afford to get distracted—"

"You need a distraction." His head dipped even lower, closer. "You need to breathe. To stop holding everything together like the world depends on you." His voice dropped. "And I've been meaning to do this for a long time. Why not now?"

"Because if we're wrong—" she mumbled.

"We're not."

She looked at him. She swallowed. Her pulse was out of control. "If you kiss me right now, we can't undo it."

Adam searched her eyes. "I don't want to undo it."

He leaned even closer, his lips inches from hers. He paused. His pause was a question.

She didn't say no. She didn't look away.

What was she doing? What if this ruined everything? What if it didn't? She'd been fighting this—fighting him—for so long it had become a habit.

But the truth was, she didn't want to wonder anymore. She

needed to know. Needed to feel it, just once. Maybe just once would be enough. Maybe it would wreck her. But maybe it would make everything finally, finally make sense.

She'd imagined this so many times. And right now, with his breath brushing her skin and his eyes insistent, questioning, she realized she had the answer. She wanted him.

In a moment of reckless clarity, she lifted her lips. Closed the distance.

Their lips met—hesitant at first. A feather-light brush, almost cautious. Like both of them were afraid to want too much too soon.

Emily's breath hitched. Her hand came up to rest on his chest, anchoring herself.

Adam didn't move. Didn't deepen it. Just stayed there—his mouth on hers, waiting, still asking.

Finally, she answered. Her hands moved around to his back, drawing him closer to her. She leaned in. And then it wasn't tentative at all.

The kiss shifted—slow and deep and consuming. A release of everything they hadn't said in weeks. Everything they'd held back and buried under deadlines and friendly banter and unspoken questions.

She felt it in her chest. In her stomach. In the way her knees went weak and her pulse refused to settle.

He tasted like coffee and something distinctly him. Warm, steady, and irresistible.

His hands cupped her jaw, then slid gently down her arms to her waist as if to memorize her shape. She felt like the center of gravity. The place he had been orbiting all along.

She wasn't sure how long it lasted— seconds, minutes, maybe a lifetime, suspended in a moment that felt both new yet long overdue.

By the time they broke apart, she was breathless. And completely undone. Her hands were fisted in his shirt, and her brain had stopped functioning at full capacity.

Adam put his forehead against hers. He exhaled a quiet, breathless laugh. “I’ve wanted to do that since the first brunch.”

She stared at him, stunned. “You… what?”

“I tried to be professional. I really did.”

“Adam…”

He cupped the side of her face. “But I can’t pretend I don’t feel this anymore.”

Her heart was still pounding. “Me, too,” she admitted. But somewhere in the rational corner of her brain, the part not currently melting, she managed a whisper: “But this isn’t the right time.”

He nodded. “I know.” Despite his words, he pulled her against him and wrapped his arms around her. He was gentle. “But you were spiraling. I had to do something.” He laughed softly. His hand touched her hair.

She rested her head against his shoulder. She loved the feel of him. How solid he felt against her. How he made her feel safe. His Henley shirt really was as soft as she had imagined.

They stood like that for a moment. Quiet. Breathing the same air.

“When the project’s done,” she said softly. “We talk.”

“Deal,” he murmured.

They stepped apart slowly.

Reluctantly.

He ran a hand through his curly hair.

She took a deep breath. Held it. Released it slowly. And then she turned back to her laptop and reopened the asset folder.

Back to work. For now.

But her heart was no longer in it. Not entirely. She could still feel the phantom press of his lips against hers.

When Adam brushed her hand as he passed her another hard drive, she didn't flinch.

She smiled.

Chapter Twenty-One

At exactly 11:37 p.m. the next day, the following post appeared on Reddit in the "*Am I The Asshole*" subreddit.

Posted by u/throwRA_letterguy:

Subject: *AITA for not telling my friend about a love letter I found that might have been meant for me?*

I (30M) have a friend (29F)... let's call her "Cornelia". We are friends and have been spending more time together while working on a project over the past few months. Recently, while helping to organize some files, I found a handwritten letter. The letter reads like a declaration of love and was unsigned.

I recognize her handwriting (not a creep, since working on this project, we both leave notes everywhere). I'm 99% sure she wrote it and honestly, it's one of the most heartfelt things I've ever read.

But it wasn't addressed to anyone.

Now I'm not sure what to do, because... What if it's about me? What if it's not about me and I'm just a total narcissist? What if bringing it up makes things super weird between us?

For the record, I haven't told her I found it. I tried to put it back but crumpled it by accident and now it would be obvious someone had found the letter. I didn't know what to do, so I just... kept it. For now.

So, AITA for not telling her I found the letter? Should I bring it up, or just let it be?

BTW, I really really like her.

Adam had never posted on Reddit before—not for real. He'd lurked, sure, reading "Am I The Asshole?" And "Am I The Devil?" threads and secretly judging strangers over popcorn.

But last night, stretched across his living room sofa with his laptop perched on his thighs and his brain spinning out, he had found himself typing the whole story and hitting "post" before he could stop himself.

He knew he should talk to her. He knew it. But every time he tried to bring it up, he chickened out. So the obvious next step had been to ask the internet. Maybe a bunch of strangers could finally tip him off the fence he'd been sitting on for weeks.

He'd immediately felt a pang of embarrassment and regret, but there was no going back now. So he'd shut his laptop, put it out of his mind, and had gone to bed.

Now it was morning. Saturday, 6:48 a.m. The kitchen was still, the sky outside just starting to brighten. Adam padded barefoot across the floor, grabbed one of several branded SkyLux mugs from the cupboard, and made himself coffee.

Then he opened his laptop and, bracing himself, navigated to Reddit.

His post had exploded: 247 Comments. 1,530 Upvotes. A shiny red "Asshole" judgment.

He groaned and looked away. For a minute, he considered just pretending it had never happened. But curiosity—and guilt—got the better of him.

He scrolled through the comments, heart sinking with each one.

Techotecho88: *YTA. You literally found a vulnerable letter and hid it? Come on, man.*

Accidental_Sage: *YTA. That letter was private, and the second you realized what it was, you should've returned it. Crumpled or not. If this does turn into something romantic, it should start with honesty, not secrets.*

Mathavi-Kcap: *YTA. The letter is her private writing and you took it instead of returning it the moment you realized what it was. Give it back, say you found it among the files, and let her decide what to do next.*

SleepyyyKittyyy: *Bro put that shit back!!! If I were Cornelia and you were helping me organize papers and found it, then gently brought it up, I wouldn't be mad. If I found you had taken it, I would be furious and creeped out.*

Adam winced at that one. He saw a lone "Minor AH" and zeroed on it with hope.

Spare_Necessary_810: *Minor AH. Put it back and mention to her that you found it and let her take it from there. I think you hope it was meant for you, don't you? You could, perhaps, tell her you read it and say you envy the would-be recipient if so.*

That made him feel slightly better. But then he hit another wall of judgment:

ElleArr26: *You KEPT it??? YTA. Put it back and never*

mention that you read it. What a weird invasion of her privacy.

PleasantResult6236: *Why would you keep that? It's not yours. YTA for keeping something so personal and intimate to her and her emotions. Even if she did write it about you...IT. IS. NOT. YOURS. That's a huge betrayal of trust and boundaries*

Adam shut his laptop. For a long moment, he just stood there, letting the collective internet scorn soak in.

He knew what he had to do. He'd known it all along. He'd just been hoping for a loophole, or at least a little Reddit sympathy.

Nope.

He nodded to himself, stretched, and resolved that he was going to tell Emily about the letter. It was the right thing to do. Obviously. And he would do it. He would. One day. Some day. Soon. Definitely soon.

He drained the last of his coffee, took a deep breath, and reached for his phone.

Adam: *You up?*

Daniel: *Barely. You good?*

Adam: *Need to talk. Can I call? Might've asked Reddit for life advice.*

Daniel: *That bad, huh?*

Adam: *Worse. They all think I'm an asshole.*

Daniel: *So, standard consensus. Give me a sec.*

Adam smiled, the knot in his chest loosening just a bit. Maybe Reddit was right. But at least he didn't have to figure it out alone.

Seconds later, his phone buzzed. He hit accept.

"Hey, man," Daniel's voice was scratchy with sleep. "What's up?"

Adam leaned back against the kitchen counter. "I… might've posted on Reddit last night. About the letter. The one I found in the campaign files."

"Okay…" Daniel said.

"Yeah, and Reddit thinks I'm an asshole."

Through the phone, Adam could hear movement —muffled voices, the click of a mug on a counter.

Then: "Put me on speaker!" Sophie's voice rang out.

Adam groaned. "Sophie's there, too?"

"Obviously," she called back, not missing a beat. "Daniel told me you texted. We have a strict no-secrets-before-9-a.m. rule."

Adam slumped back against the kitchen counter. "Great."

His phone buzzed with a request to turn on the camera. He clicked "accept" and a few seconds later, Sophie and Daniel's concerned faces filled the screen. They were seated together at the kitchen table, mugs of coffee in front of them.

Adam raised his own mug in greeting.

"So, catch me up," Sophie demanded.

Adam took a deep breath. "Did you know I found a love letter written by Emily?" He asked.

"Er, no, of course not," Sophie said, a little too quickly. She shot a quick glance at Daniel, who was suddenly very focused on drinking his coffee.

Adam rolled his eyes. "So, yes, you know," he concluded.

"I haven't told anyone," Sophie said quickly, shrugging. "Not mine to tell."

"Apparently, not mine to tell either." Adam sighed. "I still haven't told Emily I have the letter, nor given it back," he continued. "And now Reddit says I'm the asshole."

Sophie winced, then shrugged. "I mean, they're not wrong."

Daniel coughed. "I'm gonna have to agree with the internet on this one."

Adam ran a hand through his hair. "So, you both think I should just… tell her?"

Sophie didn't hesitate. "Yes."

Daniel echoed, "Definitely."

Adam let out a long breath. "What if it ruins everything?"

There was a pause, then Daniel said gently, "It's better than lying by omission. At least then you'll know."

Sophie added, "Besides, you're not going to ruin everything. She likes you, Adam." She paused. "Just don't wait too long."

Adam shut his eyes. "Okay. I'll do it. Just… maybe after I've had more coffee."

"Make it strong," Sophie agreed. "You'll need it."

He ran a hand through his hair. "I'm heading to her place later today. We're working on the final edits to the SkyLux campaign."

Sophie's eyes brightened. "Oooh, can't wait to see it!"

Adam sighed. "I'll tell her there. In person."

"Good plan," Daniel said.

"Brave lad," Sophie added. "Good luck."

Adam managed a weak laugh. "Thanks."

They ended the call, and Adam set his phone gently on the counter.

The sun was fully up now, bright and insistent through the blinds, and he knew there was no more hiding from this.

He moved to the drawer by the sink, sliding it open. Inside, neatly folded beneath spare batteries and half-used notepads, was the letter. Carefully, he pulled it out, fingertips grazing the familiar edges.

Reading it again felt invasive now, especially after Reddit

had shredded him. But his eyes scanned the familiar handwriting anyway, heart thudding in his chest. Every line carried Emily's voice, her warmth, her vulnerability—things he'd come to love about her, even if he hadn't admitted it until now.

He knew Sophie and Daniel were right. He knew Reddit was right. Hell, deep down, he'd always known.

With a decisive exhale, Adam folded the letter gently and placed it carefully into a fresh envelope. Then he tucked it safely into his bag, determined.

No more delays. No more excuses. He would tell her. Today.

Adam changed into his usual running clothes, feeling an energized surge—nervous energy, anticipation, maybe both.

With his shoes laced and his heart thumping with newfound determination, he headed out the door to face the day with the kind of resolve usually reserved for take-offs —steady, certain, and ready to face whatever turbulence came his way.

Chapter Twenty-Two

Adam parked in front of Emily's building, his stomach a tightly knotted mess. He reached over to the passenger seat, double-checking his bag—laptop, USB drives, and the envelope containing the letter.

The letter. His nerves buzzed insistently beneath his skin as he climbed out of the car.

He knocked, and when Emily opened the door, his heart did an odd little flip. Her hair was gathered in a loose bun, eyes bright, face relaxed. She smiled warmly and stepped back to let him inside.

"Thanks for coming on the weekend," she said, closing the door behind him.

"Wouldn't miss it," Adam replied, his voice coming out more confident than he felt.

They settled in the living room. Emily's apartment was cozy and comfortably cluttered, but she had cleared a space for them on her living room carpet in front of the sofa. Within minutes, they were sitting cross-legged on the floor, laptops humming, cups of tea nearby. An indie playlist hummed softly in the background.

As they worked through the final revisions for the SkyLux campaign preview, Adam felt the weight of the envelope in his bag like an anchor dragging against his spine. He kept glancing at Emily, waiting for the right moment, the perfect opening. But every potential segue felt forced.

She looked so happy and relaxed. She was clearly pleased with the work they were doing, eager to finish the project, and excited to show it to the world.

He wondered how she would feel after he told her. Would she be furious? Embarrassed? Upset? Hurt? He didn't want to shatter the moment with a confession.

After nearly two hours, Emily stretched, arching her back and rubbing her neck. "I think we're just about done," she said, leaning back against the sofa. "Hungry?"

After some debate, they decided on Thai food and Emily submitted the order. While waiting for the delivery, they moved companionably around her kitchen, making fresh cups of tea, washing and cutting fruit, and grabbing plates and cutlery. When the food arrived, they pushed their laptops aside and ate together on the carpet.

"Is this pad see ew spicier than usual?" Emily asked, proffering the container to him.

Adam speared a few noodles, chewed thoughtfully, then smiled. "Maybe, but I like it."

"Mmm," Emily agreed happily, taking another bite. "Me, too."

After dinner, they tidied up and settled back in to finish the preview together.

Emily tightened the bun on her head, then pulled her laptop back into place in front of her. "We've probably got another hour or two of work left." She rubbed her hands together. "And then… We. Are. Done!"

Adam smiled at her enthusiasm.

Then he swallowed hard. His pulse quickened. His hands were damp. His throat tight. It was now or never. "Actually, before we get back into it—"

Emily looked over at him, still relaxed. "What's up?"

He reached into his bag and pulled out the envelope. "I found something a while ago. In the campaign files."

Emily sat up straighter, curiosity flickering across her face. "Okay..."

He handed it to her.

Her fingers closed around the envelope slowly, like she already suspected something. She opened it and unfolded the letter, her brow furrowing.

Recognition dawned. Then confusion. Then a flush of embarrassment that climbed in a pink wave from her throat to her cheeks. She folded the letter in half instinctively, like she needed to shield it from the room.

"You... read this?" she asked, barely above a whisper. She didn't look at him.

Adam felt every bit of air leave his lungs. "Yeah. Not on purpose. I didn't know what it was at first."

Emily blinked down at the letter, her mouth pressed in a tight line. "This wasn't meant for you. This was from years ago. I wrote it when I was in a really weird place."

It wasn't meant for you. This was from years ago. The words hit him almost like a physical blow. He wanted to reel back, but he kept himself steady. This time—this moment—was not about him.

Instead he nodded. "I know. But when I found it—I wasn't sure. It was just sitting there. No name, no date. And it was…"

"It was personal," she said quietly, still not looking at him.

He nodded again. "I'm sorry. I should've told you right

away. I just didn't know how."

Emily sat back, cradling the folded letter. "I spent hours looking for this. I saw a scanned copy in the campaign files and knew it had been backed up by mistake along with everything else. I tore through every folder."

Adam felt a stab of guilt so sharp it took effort to stay seated. "I didn't mean to keep it from you. I told myself I would give it back. I just… I got stuck in my head. I overthought everything."

"Did you think it was about you?" she asked, finally looking at him.

Adam let out a slow, broken breath. "I guess I hoped. Because I've been falling for you. And when I read it, it felt like something I never thought I'd get to hear."

Emily shook her head, looking overwhelmed. "Adam, this letter was from a different life. Before I'd ever met you. I'm not even that person anymore."

"I get that," he said, his voice soft. "But the way you write—your honesty, your heart—it made me see you differently. More clearly."

Emily stood suddenly, the letter still in her hands. She took a step back, her posture now stiff, guarded

"I don't know what you expected from this," she said, voice quieter but more brittle. "Did you think I'd be flattered? That I'd be touched you held onto something so private for weeks?"

Adam stood, too, his heart lurching. "I didn't expect anything. I just wanted to be honest. Finally."

"Well congratulations," she said, not quite meeting his eyes. "You were honest. And now I'm completely humiliated."

Her voice cracked on the last word, and Adam's stomach twisted.

"I'm so sorry. I never meant to hurt you," he said. "I swear."

Emily nodded, but it was sharp and not at all forgiving. She held out the letter toward him. "Here. You keep it."

He hesitated. "Emily—"

"Take it. I don't want it anymore." Her voice dropped. "Please, take it."

He reached out and took the letter back, confused.

"I think you should go," she said, folding her arms tightly across her chest.

"Emily, please—"

"I need you to go, Adam."

Adam swallowed hard, nodded once, and gathered his things into his bag.

"The brunch?" he asked, voice barely audible. They had planned a brunch at her place next weekend with the team to celebrate the SkyLux preview.

She didn't answer at first. Then finally, with her eyes fixed on the floor, she said, "Don't come."

The walk to the door felt like miles. She didn't follow him. She didn't close the door behind him. It just hung open for a moment as he stepped out, then clicked shut softly behind him. The sound had a sense of finality.

He stood still for a moment, stunned. The letter felt like hot coals in his palm.

The drive home was a blur. A reel of everything he should have said, should have done differently. The timing. The assumptions. The way he had let hope cloud his better judgment.

Halfway home, he pulled off the road and into a small plaza with a faded ice cream shop. He walked inside on autopilot, ordered a scoop of chocolate chip cookie dough, and sat on the hood of his car.

The ice cream tasted like cold sugar, and did nothing to soothe the misery, the self-recrimination, or the growing certainty that he'd just lost something important. That he'd massively screwed up.

He stared at the pavement as he ate, the letter resting beside him on the hood, mocking him with its worn edges and misplaced meaning.

Adam had been trying to do the right thing. He just didn't realize he'd done it far, far too late.

And now, sitting in a parking lot with melting ice cream and a dull ache in his chest, he wondered if he'd just ruined the best thing he'd never even had the chance to call his.

Chapter Twenty-Three

Emily stood frozen in the middle of her apartment long after the door clicked shut behind Adam. The apartment felt too quiet now. The music still played, a gentle acoustic rhythm that suddenly sounded tinny and far away, like it belonged in someone else's life. The letter was gone, but the air still crackled with its presence.

She ran both hands through her hair, undoing the bun and letting her hair fall around her face. Her cheeks still burned with humiliation. How could he have read that letter? Kept it? Brought it back to her like it was some kind of gift?

They had been her words. Her voice. That version of her heart, cracked open with just enough overthinking to make her want to crawl into the couch cushions and disappear.

Her phone buzzed on the coffee table. For a second, she thought it might be him.

It wasn't—just a message to the family group chat with an update from her parents on the tomatoes they had planted recently in their backyard. The message was full of emojis, and Emily smiled briefly. Her mom had recently discovered emojis and was now obsessed.

She scrolled through her contacts, thumb hovering for a moment before tapping the name. Jonah.

He picked up on the second ring. "Hey, Em."

"Hey," she said. "What are you doing?"

"Not much — finishing up some work for a client. You?"

She glanced at her laptop. "Actually… same."

"Whoa, look at us," Jonah said. "Despite our idyllic upbringing, did we both somehow turn into workaholics?" She could hear the smile in his voice.

Jonah Levine was her older brother by four years and, in many ways, her unofficial life coach and built-in emergency contact. He lived in Austin now, and had started a small company specializing in something AI-related she only pretended to understand.

He was the one who usually called her first, always "just checking in," but really to make sure she was eating something besides toast or to offer commentary on her latest life crisis.

Jonah could be dry and sarcastic, but he was fiercely loyal, the kind of big brother who once drove all night from Texas to New York just because Emily had texted him a sad face emoji after a bad breakup.

"What's going on? You never call me on Saturdays unless someone's died or you're trapped in the wine aisle."

Emily let out a strangled laugh. "Neither. But close."

"Uh-oh." Jonah's tone shifted immediately. "Talk to me. What happened?"

She curled onto the couch, pulling a blanket over her lap. "It's Adam."

"The syrup guy?"

"Yeah. Him."

"Tell me everything. Go."

So she did. From the beginning. The letter. The campaign files. The moment she realized it was missing. And then today—the food, the laughter, the quiet hope she'd felt when he looked at her like she mattered. Then the envelope. Then the sting.

Jonah didn't interrupt. He let her talk. She could picture him in his home office, his long frame slouched in that overpriced ergonomic chair, surrounded by monitors and the faint glow of half a dozen screens.

When she finished, there was a long pause.

"Okay," he said slowly, "I can see why you're upset."

"Humiliated," she whispered. "I feel completely exposed. That letter wasn't for him. It wasn't even recent. It was just a weird thing I wrote to process something old and messy—"

"Who was the letter for?" Jonah interrupted.

"What?" Emily paused, confused.

"Give me the name of the person who hurt you, Emily."

"Jonah, that's not the point." She rolled her eyes. "The point is Adam found the letter. And he read it. And he kept it."

"Hmm," Jonah said. There was a pause as he considered. "Yeah, that's rough. But let me ask you something."

"If you say 'maybe he had a reason,' I swear to God—"

"Just hear me out," he said. "You like this guy, right?"

Emily stayed quiet.

"Come on, Em. You like him."

"I do," she said finally. "I really do. Or I did. I don't know anymore."

"Then it's worth at least trying to understand what the hell was going on in his head. You said he looked nervous. Guilty. Not smug, not proud."

She bit her lip. "Yeah. He looked like he hated himself for even bringing it up."

"Exactly. So ask him why he didn't just put it back. Or tell you right away. Maybe there's a good reason. Or maybe it's just fear. You know what that's like. You lock up, you don't act, and then it's too late."

Emily shook her head, even though Jonah couldn't see her. "But it was so personal. It was mine. How do you come back from that?"

"You come back from it if you want to. If it's worth it."

Emily stared at the ceiling. "He thought it was about him."

Jonah let out a low whistle. "Yikes."

She laughed, a dry sound that caught in her throat. "Right?"

"Still," Jonah said, "if I found something like that, and I liked the person who wrote it, I might hope it was about me too. Even if logic said otherwise."

Emily didn't answer. She didn't want to give the tiny part of her that understood any space to grow.

Jonah continued, voice gentler now. "You're allowed to be angry, Em. But don't make it permanent until you're sure he meant to hurt you. Because from what you've told me? It doesn't sound like he did."

They sat in comfortable silence, the only sound the occasional shuffle as he moved.

"Thanks," Emily said eventually. "You're not totally useless."

"Put that on a mug for me."

She smiled. "We should probably get back to work."

They hung up not long after. She sat in silence for a while, letting the words settle around her. The anger was still there, but it had cooled. The sting of embarrassment hadn't faded, but it didn't feel like it would consume her now.

She ran a hand through her hair, wincing at the tangles and at herself.

Adam knew, didn't he? Of course he knew. They were adults. Grown-ups with back-stories and baggage and whole archives of relationship missteps behind them. They'd both had relationships before. He must know she'd had her heart broken before. Just as she never once assumed he hadn't loved or lost before.

And still, something about this felt different. The letter had been a version of her she hadn't shown anyone. Soft in a way that made her feel exposed. Hopeful to the point of naivety.

That girl hadn't known better.

Adam hadn't just read the letter—he'd read her. The parts of herself she'd long since packed away. She could excuse the embarrassment, laugh off the awkwardness—but she couldn't stop wondering if he now saw her as someone silly and lovesick, rather than someone who had learned what real love costs, and was still willing to try.

Because God, she was ready.

Wasn't she?

She thought about the way he touched her hand when passing her tea. The way he'd kissed her like he'd been waiting for her his whole life.

That wasn't nothing.

It couldn't be.

Eventually, she rose, stretched, and opened her laptop. The campaign wasn't going to finish itself. As she settled back into work, she couldn't help but feel something was missing beside her.

Chapter Twenty-Four

Emily had become the kind of person who owned three waffle makers and wasn't even sorry about it.

This, she decided, as she poured the first ladle of batter and adjusted the heat setting with the confidence of someone who had done this before, was character development.

She moved through the kitchen like a brunch general—syrup station prepped, fruit chopped, whipped cream chilling. Sophie had brought mimosas, Liam had brought vibes, and the rest of the group had filled her living room with all the extra waffle toppings one could want, along with the easy noise of familiarity.

She should've felt proud. The SkyLux-Niagara preview had gone out earlier that week. She'd presented it to Susan and the Niagara Canada team on Wednesday; Adam had delivered the pitch to SkyLux HQ the following day.

The feedback had been glowing.

— "Authentic, high-quality storytelling."

— "A campaign that makes Niagara a must-see destination."

— "Visually stunning. Strategically clever. A gold standard for regional tourism."

Earlier that morning, Daniel—seated now on her couch with

a mimosa in one hand and Sophie's feet in his lap—had told her he'd heard similar feedback in the office.

"They say this campaign is the best of the bunch. Hands down. We're opening three new routes, and Niagara's already the front-runner."

She should've been thrilled. And she was. Really. It was a big moment—a huge one, actually. She'd gone from a string of going-nowhere jobs in New York, hoping someone would give her a chance, to pitching, executing, and launching not one but three marketing campaigns for Niagara County.

And now she was partnering with SkyLux—a brand that routinely won awards for best-in-class marketing, ranked #1 in its industry, and set the standard for innovation and style.

This was why she'd moved away from her family in the first place: to prove she could make it on her own two feet. No boys, no distractions, no tangled mess of waiting for someone else to build her life.

She was genuinely proud of how far she had come. She was happy.

Except for Adam. He wasn't here. They wouldn't be celebrating their success together.

He'd texted that morning. Just a quick, "Hope brunch goes great." Nothing more.

She tried not to let it get to her. Really, she did. But it was hard to ignore the quiet ache at the base of her sternum. The way her eyes kept drifting to the kitchen doorway. The fact that her third waffle maker sat unplugged, almost accusingly, as if even it knew its usual operator was missing.

Sophie popped a grape into her mouth and raised an eyebrow. "Are you seriously still trying to make 'Maple-berry Morning' a thing?"

"It's thematic," Emily said, gesturing to the fruit platter with an air of wounded pride. "Red, white, and very Canadian. For my Canadian guests, of course."

"Oui, I totally agree. Everything needs less restraint and more whipped cream," Gabriel announced, swirling a spoon through the whipped bowl like it was an art installation.

Lucy giggled, hiding behind her coffee. "At least Liam didn't try to name it *Brunchapalooza* again."

Liam, who had been digging through the cabinet for hazelnut spread, popped his head out. "Hey, I stand by *Brunchapalooza.* It has branding potential."

Emily chuckled, even as she half-listened. She moved around the kitchen with muscle memory, refilling juice, flipping waffles, smiling when expected—but she felt slightly out of step with the room. Like she was trying to catch the beat of a song she used to know.

She missed him. More than she wanted to admit.

The silence in the group chat hadn't helped. The three of them—her, Sophie, and Adam—had gone from daily banter and chaotic meme wars to a trickle of "Looks good!" and "Hope you're having a good day!"

She hadn't seen Adam since the weekend before. Not since the letter. Not since the call with Jonah that had left her a little less angry, but no less confused.

She turned off one waffle maker and wiped her hands on a dishtowel. "Hey, Daniel?" she said, nodding toward the hallway. "Got a sec?"

He followed her toward the kitchen, leaving the others mid-debate over whether lemonade counted as a breakfast drink.

Emily lowered her voice. "Is Adam okay?"

Daniel leaned against the counter. "What do you mean?"

"The group chat's been… quiet. Just wondering if you've talked to him."

Daniel studied her for a beat. "We've exchanged a few texts. He's been working. Said he was tired. Didn't say much more than that."

"Oh." Emily tried to sound casual. "Right."

Daniel's gaze sharpened slightly. "Is something going on?"

"No. Maybe. I don't know." She rubbed the back of her neck. "Something happened between us and… I'm confused," she finished lamely.

"Is that why he's not here today?" Daniel asked quietly.

Emily nodded, then shrugged. "I'm not sure what to do next."

Daniel shifted. "This sounds like a Sophie conversation."

Emily shook her head. "No, no. I already know what she'll say." She paused. "You're his friend, so… just wanted to make sure he was okay."

Daniel studied her for a long moment. Finally, he said, "I don't know exactly what happened between you, but I'm not blind. He looks at you like you're the last flight home and he's already missed too many."

Emily raised an eyebrow. "You sound pretty sure."

He gave her a look. "Let's just say... sometimes we don't handle feelings well. Doesn't mean they're not there."

She gave a weak smile. "You're very confident for someone who doesn't know what happened."

"I know him. That counts for something." He reached out and squeezed her shoulder.

Emily nodded. "Thanks."

They rejoined the others a few minutes later, and she let the conversation wash over her like a tide—warm, comforting, a little noisy. She nibbled on the edge of a waffle. Dipped it in some maple syrup, then some whipped cream. It was perfectly crispy, the cream rich, and the syrup sweet on her tongue.

Gabriel was recounting an attempt to teach a finger painting workshop to a group of toddlers. "And then a child just started to lick the easel. Like it was a popsicle. I said nothing. I turned away."

Sophie had collapsed in a fit of laughter. "You turned away? That was your strategy?"

He tsked. "I am not trained in child psychology. Or hygiene emergencies."

Lucy raised her coffee in mock salute. "To the Brunch Club. Where we all have a very specific set of skills, and Gabriel should never ever be in charge of actual children."

They laughed. They toasted. They ate.

Emily watched them all with soft eyes and a quiet heart.

She didn't bring up Adam again. Didn't let herself check her phone.

But when she packed up the waffle irons later and found a note he'd left in the utensil drawer two weeks ago—a folded napkin scrawled with *"Bet this waffle maker still likes me better"*—she closed the drawer slowly and pressed her hand to her chest.

He hadn't stopped mattering.

Not to her. Maybe they just needed time.

They'd finished the work. The project was out in the world now, orbiting between inboxes and conference rooms. Maybe things would settle.

And if it didn't?

Well. She'd survived worse.

Still, part of her hoped it wasn't over. Not yet.

Chapter Twenty-Five

Adam was scrubbing the same spot on the kitchen counter for the third time before the knock came. Not a text. Not a call. An actual knock on his door, followed by Daniel Carter standing in his doorway like a man on a mission, sleeves pushed up, resolve practically radiating from him.

"Hi," Adam said flatly, opening the door.

"You ducked brunch," Daniel replied, stepping inside without being invited. "That's basically a misdemeanor in our group."

Adam sighed. "Nice to see you too."

Daniel lifted a brown paper bag and gave it a small shake. "Peace offering. Sophie's leftover brownies. Still warm-ish. I may have eaten one in the car."

Adam raised an eyebrow. "You bribing me with food?"

"I'm bribing you with brownies," Daniel corrected. "Let's not pretend we're above that."

Adam gave a half-smile despite himself. "Fair."

Daniel dropped the bag on the counter, shrugged off his jacket, and plopped onto the couch like he'd been personally invited.

"So." Daniel raised an eyebrow. "You avoiding all of us, or just Emily?"

Adam rubbed the back of his neck. “That subtle, huh?”

“She made enough waffles for a small village. And hardly ate any.” Daniel spread his hands. “So yeah. Subtle as a foghorn.”

Adam ran a hand through his hair, debated what to say. Then he shrugged. “She asked me not to go.”

Daniel tilted his head. “Want to talk about it?”

“No.”

Daniel waited.

He didn’t push. Just leaned back against the couch, kicked off his shoes, put his phone and keys on the coffee table, and grabbed the remote. He turned on the TV, kept the volume low, and started flipping aimlessly through channels—news, sports, a cooking show with someone flambéing aggressively.

He settled on a nature documentary narrated by someone British and soothing. “Look,” he said casually, gesturing to the screen. “Beavers. Did you know they mate for life?”

Adam didn’t respond.

Daniel stretched one arm along the back of the couch. “By the way,” he said casually. “Emily’s maple-berry concept? Underrated.”

Still nothing from Adam.

Daniel reached for his phone. “I swear to God, if you don’t start talking soon, I’m texting Sophie and telling her to come over because you say you’ll only talk to her.”

Adam groaned. “God, please don’t do that.” He let out a breath. “Fine.”

He crossed the room, then stopped halfway and turned around. “Do you remember that letter I told you about?”

“Hold on.” Daniel held up a hand. He picked up the remote. Muted the TV. Turned his attention back to Adam. “I’m guessing it didn't go so well when you gave it back to her?"

Adam nodded. He sat in an armchair across from his friend and ran an agitated hand through his hair. "She kicked me out. Told me not to come to brunch today." He paused. "She didn't understand why I'd kept it instead of giving it back right away."

"Why did you keep it?" Daniel asked. There was no judgment in his tone—just curiosity.

Adam exhaled. "After I found it and understood what it was, I went to put it back, but then Liam showed up. I didn't want him to see the letter so I shoved it in my back pocket… and crumpled it."

Daniel nodded slowly, understanding dawning.

"If I had put it back, she would have known someone had found and read it. She would have been mortified. If I had told her *I* found it, she still would have been mortified. I didn't know what to do. I thought I was protecting her." He trailed off miserably.

Daniel was quiet for a moment. Then: "You need to explain that to her."

Adam looked up. "It wouldn't matter."

"Why not?"

Adam swallowed hard. "Because it wasn't for me. The letter. It was never about me."

Daniel sat up straighter. "Okay," he said carefully. "So, it wasn't for you. That doesn't mean—"

"It means everything I thought was happening between us was based on something that wasn't real," Adam cut in. "That letter—that was the reason I started seeing her differently. Not because of some lightning bolt. Because of a goddamn hand-written letter that wasn't even for me."

Daniel raised an eyebrow. "You seriously think you made up

your feelings for her?"

Adam didn't answer right away. His voice, when it came, was quieter. "I don't know. It's like—I let myself believe something because it felt good. I thought I was falling for her. But now I can't stop wondering if it was just… wishful thinking. Projection. Like I borrowed someone else's story and convinced myself it was ours."

Daniel sat forward. "You didn't fall for her because of a letter. You fell for her because she's Emily. And you know it."

Adam shook his head. "Yeah, well. The timing sucked. The project was everything. She trusted me with her work, her vision—and I twisted the time we spent together into something else. Something personal."

"It was personal," Daniel said. "To both of you."

Adam didn't respond.

Daniel sighed. "Look, I'm not telling you to go throw rocks at her window. But I know Emily. And I know you. And whatever happened, she's confused. She misses you."

Adam looked up at that. Something in his chest shifted—unsteady, hopeful, raw. "Did she… say something to you?"

"She asked about you," Daniel said. "Pulled me into the kitchen at brunch yesterday and asked if you were okay."

That got him.

"She's not okay either," Daniel added. "So maybe stop brooding here alone and go do something about it." He paused. "And maybe don't wait too long to do it."

Adam nodded, quiet again.

Daniel reached down and began to put his shoes back on. "I should probably go or Sophie really will come to find me soon." He grabbed his keys and his phone, then looked at Adam.

"You're not a mind reader. Neither is she. If you want her to know the truth—tell her. Don't just sit here waiting for the story to write itself."

Adam offered a tired smile. "Thanks for the pep talk, Coach."

Daniel grinned. "Anytime." He grabbed the paper bag off the counter and handed it to Adam. "We don't do big emotions often, but when we do? Brownies are involved."

Adam chuckled. "Tell Sophie I said thanks." He took out a brownie. No napkin, no plate. Just bit into it like a guy with zero shame.

Daniel rolled his eyes, then moved toward the door, pausing with one hand on the handle. "By the way, did you know Liv asked about you?"

"Liv?" Adam was confused for a second. "Oh, SkyLux Liv?"

Daniel nodded. "She asked Emily at brunch a couple weeks ago if you were single."

Adam's mouth dropped open. Then he groaned. "You're kidding."

Daniel's mouth quirked up on one side. "Nope."

"What did she say?"

"Emily? She said yes, officially, you're single."

Adam closed his eyes and covered his face with a hand. Then paused. "In those exact words?"

"Yup." Daniel clapped Adam on the shoulder. "Just thought you should know." He opened the front door and stepped out. "Take care of yourself, man. And give Emily a chance to understand what's going on in that overcomplicated pilot brain of yours."

"I'll try," Adam said.

Daniel tilted his head. "Sooner rather than later. Before the next Brunch Club, okay?"

Then he was gone, the door clicking shut behind him with a quiet finality.

Adam stood for a moment, staring at the empty space where Daniel had been.

He picked up the half-eaten brownie and took another bite. It was a little squished, slightly warm, definitely too sweet—and still, somehow, exactly what he needed.

He walked into the kitchen and leaned against the counter, letting the silence settle around him like a blanket.

So. She had asked about him. She was worried about him. Maybe she missed him, just a little.

And he missed her.

But everything still felt tangled. Too many things left unsaid.

Maybe it was time to start saying them.

Chapter Twenty-Six

Emily wasn't nervous. Not really.

Sure, she was currently double-knotting her sneakers with the intensity of someone preparing for a hostage negotiation, but that didn't mean she was nervous or flustered or harboring the emotional equivalent of a shaken soda can. She was just thorough. Prepared. Strategically ready-for-anything.

It wasn't her fault SkyLux had decided that the final phase of the Niagara campaign needed "additional atmospheric footage from scenic roadside locations."

Which was how she found herself standing in her apartment lobby at 8:05 a.m. with a packed overnight bag, a checklist, and a travel mug full of tea she would absolutely forget to drink until it was cold.

And then the car pulled up. It was a silver Jeep Wrangler, dusted with September leaves and radiating that unmistakable promise of road trip adventure. The kind of car that said, "I'm adventure-ready and rugged." Of course, Adam drove something a little bold, a little outdoorsy, and secretly kind of sexy.

When he stepped out of the car—solid, familiar, and achingly Adam—her pulse skipped.

He wore dark jeans, a plain black tee, and sunglasses he probably didn't need that early in the morning—but of course he still managed to look like a brochure for a rugged Ralph Lauren fall campaign.

"Morning," he said. His voice was warm, yet flickered with uncertainty and something unreadable.

"Hey." She gave him a small, tentative smile that didn't quite land.

"You ready?"

"Sure," she said, locking the door behind her. "Let's hit the road."

The awkward energy followed them into the car like an uninvited third wheel.

They drove in silence for the first fifteen minutes, the only sounds the hum of the tires and the occasional GPS instruction.

Emily stared out the window and tried to focus on anything other than the fact that they hadn't seen each other or spoken in almost ten days. Even the Flight Club group texts had trickled away to almost nothing.

She tapped her fingers against her knee, uncertain what to say, how to feel. Tried to think of something casual. Breezy. Unloaded.

"So," Adam said finally, "did you see the SkyLux engagement numbers? Apparently the teaser got reposted by that Toronto travel influencer. The one with the tiny dogs?"

Emily smiled faintly. "Yes, Susan sent me the analytics."

"Cool. Yeah." He nodded. "Cool."

Another stretch of silence passed. A field of cows blurred by.

She sipped her tea.

"You didn't have to come," he said quietly. "The crew and I would have managed."

"I know," she said. She gave a small smile. "I wanted to.

Thanks for picking me up on the way."

"Of course." Adam nodded, tapping the steering wheel.

Outside, the clouds were starting to break—patches of sun casting stripes across the two-lane road. Inside the car, the temperature felt all wrong. Too hot. Too cold. Too uncertain.

Emily swallowed. "About last week—"

"Emily, I—" Adam began at the same time.

They both stopped. Shared a quick smile, the tension between them softening.

Adam exhaled. "If you're up for it, I'd like to clear the air," he said quietly.

Emily glanced sideways. "Yeah. We should."

He gave a quick nod, eyes still on the road. "But we're ten minutes out, and I don't want to have to cut our conversation short."

"Agreed." She forced a half-smile. "Let's keep it professional for now. We'll talk tonight."

"Tonight," he echoed.

And just like that, the moment slipped away—neatly packaged, tucked into the glovebox of things they still hadn't said.

But something shifted between them. As they pulled into the gravel lot, the silence in the car felt easier—like some of the pressure had finally let up. By the time they stepped out into the bright morning, Emily's shoulders had dropped a fraction, and Adam's voice was lighter as he greeted the crew.

Everyone fell into familiar rhythms. Lucy fussed over audio levels, Gabriel joked about nearly starring in local news with last year's seagull incident, and Brett teased them all while prepping the drone.

As Adam helped unpack the gear, pulling a heavy black case

from the back of the van, he called out, "Remind me why we're here again?"

Gabriel said dryly, "To film leaves. So many leaves."

Lucy added, "And maybe capture the poetic beauty of Canadian geese, if they don't attack us first."

Emily laughed. "We're here because SkyLux wants scenic fall footage. And we're going to make it look so damn good they'll forget they ever asked."

Adam raised an eyebrow. "Challenge accepted."

Their small crew had done enough projects together by now that words were almost optional. They moved in sync. Comfortable. Efficient.

Emily and Adam slid back into autopilot—checking lighting angles, scouting where the early fall leaves would look best on camera. She found the perfect shot between a lake and a giant weeping willow tree. He directed the drone shots like a pro. She threw leaves in the air at the perfect moment. They passed each other light reflectors with the kind of unspoken rhythm that made it easy to forget how much they weren't saying.

But it crept in. Between the camera clicks. The too-long glances. The way he handed her a pastry at exactly the right moment without asking if she was hungry.

When the last sequence was finally shot and the golden hour light faded, they packed up in a quiet kind of peace.

Lucy, Gabriel, and Brett left in their company van, still laughing about how Gabriel had once mistaken a prop goose for real wildlife and tried to position a mic boom over it.

Adam and Emily, meanwhile, had agreed to take the longer route home. The plan was for the crew to head back to their office and offload the heavy equipment, while Adam and Emily would drive partway back that evening, and capture some last minute drone footage over Niagara River at dusk. It was already late, so they'd grab a quick dinner and spend the night at a small roadside inn before finishing the trip in the morning—giving them time to debrief about the shoot and recharge before work picked up again. It was practical. Efficient. Logistically sound.

Dinner was a formality. Burgers at a roadside diner that boasted "The Best Milkshakes in Buffalo". She ordered vanilla. He ordered chocolate.

Then they sat across from each other in a diner booth far too small for emotional distance.

For a while, they talked about everything *but* what mattered—reviewing the day's shoot, comparing favorite moments, discussing the latest Marvel movies. Adam declared the fries "passable but not transcendent," and Emily countered that the milkshakes deserved their own press release.

The conversation meandered, laughter softening the edges of the tension between them. Emily leaned back in the booth, feeling a little more herself for the first time all week.

But as the plates cleared and the chatter faded, the silence thickened.

Halfway through his milkshake, Adam broke the spell. "So… about the letter."

Emily froze, her straw halfway to her mouth. She set the glass down carefully, like it might detonate. All that earlier ease evaporated in an instant, nerves snapping taut. The words hung between them, their weight impossible to escape.

"Okay, I'm listening." She folded her hands on the table and waited.

Adam took a deep breath. "I found the letter stuck between two contracts in the folder. I opened it and—I don't know. I started to read it." He stirred his milkshake with the straw.

"When I realized what it was, I couldn't stop."

"Why couldn't you stop?"

"Honestly?" His mouth twisted into a wry smile. "I think, at that moment, I thought—I hoped—that you had written it for me."

"It wasn't," she said softly. "It wasn't for you."

He nodded. Cleared his throat. "I know that now," he said, voice rough. "At the time, I thought… I thought maybe it was. And it messed with my head."

Emily looked down at the rim of her milkshake glass, tracing it with a fingertip. "Why didn't you just put it back?"

"I meant to." He leaned forward, elbows on the table. "But Liam walked in while I was holding it. That's when I stuffed it in my pocket so he wouldn't see it, and… I crumpled it." He shrugged. "Then I felt weird. Like… if I put it back all crumpled like that, you would know someone had read it."

Her brows drew together, not angry—just confused. "Why didn't you just tell me?"

"Honestly? Because I didn't want to embarrass you. That was my first thought." He hesitated, then added, "You're a private person, Emily. You don't just hand out pieces of yourself. That letter felt like… something deeply personal. Like a part of you I wasn't meant to see. And once I had, I didn't know how to give it back without making it worse."

He dropped his gaze, looking miserable. "And because, somewhere in my stupid brain, I thought maybe… maybe it was about me. That you were just too afraid to say it." He blew out a breath. "And that made it even worse."

Emily let out a soft breath, more ache than frustration. "I wrote it for someone I thought I loved. Back when I was trying to unlearn all the ways I made myself smaller to fit someone else's life."

Adam looked at her, something deep and quiet moving behind his eyes. "I think I was trying to do the opposite. I saw something vulnerable in that letter. Something honest. And I projected all of it onto you—onto us."

Emily hesitated. "But the feelings you had… were they all because of the letter?"

"No." He was quick this time. Sure. "It cracked something open in me. But that's not why I started falling for you. That came later. Every time you made me laugh. Every time you stood up for your work. Every weird waffle pun and your chaotic file-naming system and the way you believe in your campaigns so fiercely it's contagious."

Emily blinked, her breath catching slightly.

Adam cleared his throat. "But I understand if it's too late. If I've broken your trust."

She didn't answer right away. Instead, she reached for a fry, broke it in two, and stared at the jagged edge like it might help her find the words.

Finally, she said, "It wasn't the letter, Adam. It was the silence afterward. That you kept it. That you didn't trust me with the truth."

"I know," he whispered. "I'm sorry."

She looked up, her gaze steady, the emotion raw in her eyes. "You have no idea how humiliating it is—knowing someone read that. It wasn't just a letter, Adam. It was basically my heart, unfiltered, circa a very questionable year."

Adam winced in sympathy, then managed a weak laugh. "Trust me, I know humiliating. I spent waaay too much time thinking a love letter was written for me when it wasn't." He rubbed the back of his neck, smiling ruefully. "That's a pretty special kind of ego-bruising."

Emily snorted despite herself, pressing her hands to her cheeks. "Okay, you win. I think you're ahead on the humiliation scoreboard."

He smiled, sheepish. "Not a competition I ever wanted to win, but… here we are."

For a moment, the tension eased—a flash of shared mortification softening the ache. They both let out a breath, laughter dissolving the last sharp edges of tension.

"So…" Emily sighed. "What happens next?"

He reached across the table, and his finger gently traced her knuckle. "Maybe we figure that out together."

And that, for now, was enough. No declarations. No pressure. Just the faint hope that maybe, just maybe, they were starting to find their rhythm again.

They drove to the small roadside inn SkyLux had booked. Two rooms, across the hall from each other—a merciful detail.

Emily unlocked her door. "Thanks for today." She lingered in the doorway. "And for driving."

"You're welcome." Adam looked tired. And thoughtful. Like he wanted to say more.

They exchanged a quiet smile. It seemed neither wanted to end the night just yet.

Adam pointed down the short hallway, to a glass door that led to a small balcony over the motel restaurant. Through the door, Emily could see it was empty of people and gently lit by string lights.

"You want to sit for a bit?" he asked. The air was warm, the night quiet. He looked at his watch. "Meet you out there in fifteen minutes?"

"Sure, I just need a few minutes to freshen up," Emily

agreed immediately. It felt like exactly what they both needed.

"Of course." Adam opened his own door and flashed a quick smile. "See you soon."

Emily nodded. "See you soon."

Chapter Twenty-Seven

The motel balcony overlooked nothing special. Just a strip of highway, a gas station with flickering fluorescent lights, and the faint neon glow of a diner sign promising ten different flavors of pie.

When Emily stepped outside with a hoodie zipped up over her pajamas and her hair piled into a messy bun, she found Adam already out there, seated on a wooden bench by the railing, hands folded around a disposable coffee cup like it held something warmer than it probably did.

She padded across the balcony and sat beside him. For a minute, they didn't speak.

He glanced at her cup. "Tea again?"

She nodded. "Black currant. Which sounds fancier than it tastes. Yours?"

"Machine coffee," he said, making a face. "With three creams and four sugars to make it palatable."

Emily huffed a laugh, then leaned her elbows on the railing. The night was cool, not cold, and she pulled her sleeves over her hands.

"It's nice out here," she said quietly.

"Yeah," Adam replied. "It is."

The wind picked up slightly, rustling the trees in the

distance. Somewhere behind the motel, a truck started its engine and rolled out of the lot.

Emily watched the lights fade, then said, "I'm worried about the campaign."

Adam turned to her, surprised. "Really? I thought you were thrilled with how it turned out."

"I am. Kind of." She traced the rim of her cup with one finger. "It's beautiful. Polished. Strategic. But... it's also really slick. Maybe too slick. It doesn't show the small stuff. The weird little local places I fell in love with when I first got this job."

Adam considered that. "You mean like Bev's gift shop?"

"Exactly. And that couple who hand-paint their own fudge boxes on the Canadian side." She shook her head. "I pitched SkyLux on rediscovery, not reinvention. And somehow, I feel like we leaned a little too hard into the brand-side polish."

He didn't answer right away. Then: "We could still fix that."

She turned to him.

"Let me get something from my room." He stood and left her.

She stared after him, heart suddenly racing. Was she pushing too far? Adam was, after all, the SkyLux campaign liaison. But before she could spiral further, he was back, holding a notebook.

He sat beside her.

"Look what I wrote weeks ago when we started shooting." His voice was quieter than usual, but threaded with something brighter—not quite excitement, but hope. Like maybe, finally, they were on the same page again.

He opened the notebook to a page in the middle, then pointed to a sentence he had written and underlined. In his large familiar scrawl, he had written, 'Luxury but local'.

"You wrote that?" Emily stared at him. "Weeks ago?"

rest lightly on her other shoulder.

And that, for now, was enough.

Emily looked down at her tea. The lid had gone loose, and a faint trickle ran down the side of the cup. She wiped it with her sleeve. "I missed you."

He raised an eyebrow. "Yeah?"

"Yeah," she said, her voice low. "It felt weird not talking to you. Not sharing the wins. The stupid jokes. Everything."

Adam leaned back in his chair and stared up at the stars—barely visible through the motel's orange glow. "You know, I kept thinking about that damn cardigan."

Emily blinked. "What?"

"Your green cardigan. The one you left at the diner. The one you wear all the time. I kept seeing it and thinking it looked like something a person would wear when they wanted to feel safe."

Her mouth parted slightly. "Maybe that's exactly why I wear it."

"I figured." He glanced sideways at her. "You always look like yourself in it."

She smiled. "It's not even that comfortable. It's part wool. It's itchy."

"It's not about the comfort."

"No," she agreed. "It's about the feeling."

They were quiet again.

Finally, Adam said, "I think you're right about the campaign. The extension's in play. SkyLux hasn't finalized the rollout. If we move fast, we could have something ready in two weeks. Something that actually feels like Niagara."

Emily nodded. She tucked loose strands of hair behind her ears. "If approved, I want to start with Bev and Bailey. And maybe feature Taylor and her beaver tail business. She told me she's thinking about opening a food truck."

"Great. Let's book them all." He tapped the notebook. "Let's work on a proposal tomorrow and I'll submit it to Natalie for approval."

She gave him a sideways look. "You're really all in?"

"Did you see what I wrote?" he asked, lifting the notebook. "Of course, I'm in. On the campaign. On the story. On whatever this turns out to be."

She felt something in her chest settle—like everything was falling back in its place.

"Okay," she said. "Then let's make this good."

"We will."

They sat there for a while longer talking about their ideas for the extension and which of Lucy's endless playlists should be banned from the production van.

Eventually, Adam stood and stretched. "Alright. Early start. I should let you sleep."

Emily stood too, clutching her cup. "Right. Six a.m."

They left the balcony together. He paused at his door. "Hey, Emily?"

"Yeah?"

He smiled, soft and tired. "Good night."

She nodded. "Good night."

Then she slipped back into her room, shut the door gently behind her, and leaned against it for a long time.

The stillness wrapped around her. The hum of the motel's old neon sign buzzed faintly through the walls. Across the hall, she heard Adam's door click shut.

Emily didn't move. Not yet.

She inhaled—and caught the faintest trace of his cologne. Woodsy, clean, with something sharp and citrusy underneath. It must've brushed off when he leaned close earlier. When he tucked her hair behind her ear. When they had nearly…

She closed her eyes.

It was just a scent. Just a breath. But it lingered like a ghost.

Maybe they weren't back to where they started.

Maybe they were just somewhere new.

And maybe—if they were careful—they'd get it right this time.

Chapter Twenty-Eight

The morning was crisp in that very specific Canadian way—cool air warmed by sunbeams that filtered through early-fall trees just beginning to flirt with gold.

Adam pulled into the small lot next to the food truck and stepped out onto the gravel with a sense of purpose. He hadn't realized how much he'd missed this—being outside, working the camera, feeling like part of something that actually mattered.

If he never saw the inside of an editing room again, it might still be too soon.

"Crew's already unloading," Emily said as she joined him. Her hoodie was half-zipped over a t-shirt with the Niagara Tourism Board logo, her hair in a loose braid that swung as she walked. She glanced over at the checklist in his hand. "Taylor's inside prepping. Said to grab her whenever we're ready."

Adam followed her gaze to the bright teal food truck, freshly detailed and gleaming in the morning light. *TAY'S TAILS* was stenciled across the side in a playful script, flanked by a cartoon beaver wearing aviator sunglasses.

"She's really upgraded," he said, impressed.

Emily smiled. "The truck's new. After inheriting the main shop from her parents, she always knew she wanted to take it mobile. Said it felt like the next evolution."

Adam watched a crew member stringing up soft lighting beside the truck's awning, another setting up a boom mic nearby. "That's our cue."

Emily nodded, calling out instructions with a quiet authority that made people listen. Adam moved beside her, directing camera placements and approving the framing of the first few shots. They worked like clockwork now—finishing each other's sentences without meaning to, adjusting for each other's instincts.

The SkyLux extension had gone through—barely—but it meant they had a few extra days to create something that felt real. Human. Local. They were on the Canadian side today, collecting footage that would round out the cross-border storytelling and give Niagara the charm the first reel had missed.

Taylor stepped out of the truck, apron already dusted with sugar, and greeted them with a grin. "So," she said, brushing her hands on her hips. "How do I look? Like someone who makes the best beaver tails this side of the border?"

"You look like someone who could sell happiness," Emily said.

Taylor laughed. "Good. I need to. I'm testing out a new cinnamon-maple glaze today. If it doesn't work, I'll have to bribe the customers with coffee refills."

"I'm an excellent taste tester," Emily offered with a grin.

"Deal." Taylor beamed.

The camera crew finished setting up as Taylor walked through a few takes, sharing her story on camera—how her parents had opened the original restaurant thirty years ago, how she grew up in it, how she used to do homework behind the counter while her parents served customers and discussed marketing and flavor ideas.

Now, with the truck, she had freedom and flexibility—and a mission to bring those same classic Canadian treats to more corners of the world.

"She's a natural," one of the sound guys muttered.

Adam nodded. "She really is."

They spent the rest of the morning capturing everything—wide shots of the truck parked against the early foliage, close-ups of hands pressing dough, slow-motion sugar shakes, and Taylor's unmistakable laugh as she offered Emily a taste test.

The cinnamon-maple glaze passed with flying colors.

By noon, they were breaking down the shot list and repacking cables when Emily turned to him.

"Bailey's expecting us at the gift shop by two."

"Bev coming?"

Emily smiled. "She'll be there."

The gift shop hadn't changed much since the last visit—still crammed with souvenirs, still chaotic, still one badly placed wind chime away from full sensory overload.

Bev and Bailey were both there to warmly welcome them when they walked in. Both sisters were extra chatty and shared with Emily that they were wearing matching lipstick shades for the shoot.

The crew rolled in behind them, already spreading out, testing light against the stained-glass panels and racks of maple-themed dish towels.

And this time, Sophie was there, too.

Building on the success of the *Rediscover Niagara* campaign she'd led for the American side of the border, the Canadian side had insisted she be brought in as part of the expanded "local heroes" reel. Sophie's reels had been high-performing, emotionally rich, and exactly the kind of content that swayed execs in conference rooms and committee calls.

Her presence lent the project cohesion. And credibility.

Emily had handed over interview duties for the afternoon shoot—at least in part—to Sophie, who now stood beside Bev and Bailey in a cozy corner of the gift shop, holding a mic like she'd been born to do it. She wore a loose blouse and pants, and loopy, layered gold jewelry that managed to look tangled yet charming at the same time.

"So," Sophie said, her voice warm, "what made you decide to bring the shop across the border?"

Bailey beamed. "Love, mostly. I met my husband during a holiday weekend. He convinced me to move here—said Canada had better snacks."

Bev smiled fondly at her sister. "And yet she still asks me to smuggle snacks from Trader Joe's every time I come up for a visit."

Sophie laughed, nodding. "And what makes this version of the shop different?"

Bailey leaned in, all twinkle and sass. "More maple. More snow globes. Fewer customs forms."

Everyone laughed.

Adam watched it all from behind the camera—Bev's genuine smile, Bailey's hand resting gently on her sister's shoulder, Sophie tossing in just the right amount of mischief to keep things light. Emily stood just out of frame, arms crossed over her chest, her expression soft with pride.

It was exactly the kind of magic they'd hoped to capture when they first pitched the extension. Heartfelt. Human. The sort of story that turned a simple campaign into something people would actually remember.

They wrapped just after four and loaded the gear into the van, the afternoon sun casting a warm sheen over everything.

Sophie slung a large tote over her shoulder and began to give out cheerful goodbye hugs. “Daniel’s family dinner,” she announced, like it was both an obligation and an Olympic event. “Velvet chairs. Bread that costs more than a mortgage. Wish me luck.”

Before she left, she sidled up beside Adam, lightly bumping his shoulder. “So,” she said, voice teasing, “you and Emily still doing your little dance of ‘will they, won’t they,’ or has someone finally learned how to tango?”

Adam rolled his eyes, feigning annoyance. “We’re professional collaborators, Soph. Strictly business.”

Sophie raised a knowing eyebrow. “Uh-huh.”

“We’re all mature adults here.”

Sophie laughed, patting his arm gently. “Sure. Just don’t wait until the wrap party to figure it out.”

“Who said anything about waiting?” he muttered, unable to hide the smile now.

She grinned triumphantly. “That’s what I thought.”

Then she vanished with a wink and a swirl of perfume, leaving Adam shaking his head, amused despite himself.

Adam found Emily standing in the shade beside the crew van, arms crossed, looking tired but proud.

“This was the right call,” Emily said. “These stories—they’re the heart of the campaign.”

Adam nodded. “Agreed.”

For a second, she didn’t say anything else.

Then she added, a little softer, “Thank you. For pushing this through. For showing up—for all of it.”

He glanced over at her. “Of course.”

With everything packed, they hugged Bev and Bailey goodbye, and climbed into their cars. As they drove away, Adam glanced back one more time, watching the twin sisters wave from the porch.

They weren't polished. They weren't curated. But they were authentic and unforgettable.

This was what they'd been chasing all along.

Not glossy transitions or perfect lighting—though those still mattered. But something warmer. Quieter. More real.

This was Niagara the way people actually knew it. Handwritten signs. Homemade fudge boxes that didn't match. Twin sisters with laugh lines and stories that spanned both sides of a border and decades of love.

Adam had admired slick airline ads and glossy resort reels across four continents. But this wasn't content. This was community. Bev's butter tarts and Bailey's warm laugh—these he'd remember.

He exhaled, the kind of breath you only release when something finally *feels* right—not polished, but real.

And the way Emily looked—hair wind-tousled, cheeks flushed, eyes shining from the inside out—he knew she saw it too.

The real story had always been waiting here. It just needed the right people to tell it.

Chapter Twenty-Nine

Emily opened the door in sweatpants, a pineapple-print hoodie, and the unmistakable posture of someone who had just removed a bra and was not planning to put one back on tonight.

Sophie walked in holding a greasy paper bag like it was an Olympic torch. "I brought burgers. And fries. And those tiny packets of mustard you like even though they taste like socks."

"You know me so well," Emily said, stepping aside and motioning toward the couch. "Make yourself at home. I'm already dead inside."

Sophie kicked off her boots and beelined for the living room like she'd lived there in a past life. "You need mood lighting," she said, flicking on a low lamp. "And probably emotional support pastries. But the burgers will do for now."

They settled in. The food went on the coffee table. The mugs filled with tea. Slippers were located. Blankets were claimed.

It was a whole ritual. They started with the fries. Always.

"I swear," Emily said, mouth half-full, "if SkyLux doesn't approve that extended reel, I'm going to print out the beaver tail footage frame-by-frame and build a visual thesis titled *Why You're Wrong*."

Sophie smirked. "Honestly? I'd read it. Especially if you add a maple-cinnamon glaze section and a footnote about butter tarts."

"I already have the butter tart data set. Bev fed me three."

"She feeds everyone three. It's how she traps you emotionally."

They ate in companionable silence for a while, the kind of quiet that only best friends could pull off—one that didn't demand filling, just sharing filled by the sounds of chewing and "Mmm, that's good" and "I need more ketchup, please".

Eventually, the wrappers were crumpled, the tea was lukewarm, and only two fries remained.

Sophie eyed them. "This is the part where we fight."

Emily nudged one toward her. "I concede."

They sat back, bellies full, socks mismatched, and brains softened by sodium and carbohydrates.

"So," Sophie said, sipping her tea with mock sophistication. "Talk to me about Adam."

Emily groaned and threw a napkin at her. "I knew it."

"Come on. It's me. We've done everything from closet crying to eyebrow bleaching together." Sophie threw the napkin back at Emily. "I even went on an insane fake honeymoon with a man I didn't know—because you signed me up for it."

Emily raised her eyebrows. "You're now married to that man. You're welcome."

"Good point. But that's beside the point." Sophie stood and moved around the coffee table, her voice fading slightly as she disappeared into the kitchen. "The point is, you're not allowed to keep your feelings now."

She reappeared with the kettle and refilled their cups with hot water.

Emily tucked her feet up under her and nodded her thanks. "It's not that I'm hiding them," she protested, raising her voice slightly as Sophie disappeared back into the kitchen to return the kettle. She shrugged. "I'm just…" Her voice dropped. "I guess I'm not ready to call them feelings yet."

Sophie reappeared and just gave her The Look. The one she'd used in high school when Emily claimed she was "totally over" that boy from the yearbook committee.

Emily sighed. "I mean, it was weird, right? We kissed. Sort of. Then didn't. Then worked together like nothing happened. Then almost kissed again. And now we're—what? Filming beaver tails in slow motion and pretending we don't both remember every second of every almost-moment?"

"Okay, first of all," Sophie said, plopping back into her seat, "you don't 'sort of' kiss someone unless you're twelve and there's a fence between you. You leaned in. He leaned in. You didn't almost kiss. You *actually* kissed. You made out."

"But then we stopped. Said it didn't count." Emily frowned. "For now."

"And how'd that make you feel?"

Emily picked at the corner of a napkin. "Like I was both relieved and rejected. Like… I get it. I respect it. And also hate it. Does that make sense?" She sighed heavily, tipping her head back against the couch. "I think mostly, I'm scared to ruin it. Whatever 'it' is."

Sophie tapped her mug thoughtfully. "You're both overthinking. You know that, right?"

"Obviously," Emily admitted with a reluctant smile. "But what if we're better as friends? What if crossing that line means losing everything we've built? I don't know if that's worth the risk."

Sophie gave her a gentle, knowing look. "Emily, you can spin a hundred 'what ifs' if you want to, but the question that matters is simpler: Do you want him in your life as more than a friend?"

Emily hesitated, chewing her lip. "I think I do."

"Then eventually, you'll have to stop tiptoeing around each other," Sophie said gently. "Because tiptoeing is cute for a while, but eventually, someone loses a toe."

"Someone loses a toe?" Emily repeated.

Sophie smirked. "Might have got my analogies mixed up, but you know what I mean."

"Yes, I know." Emily huffed a smile. "And you're right. As usual."

Sophie smirked. "It's my cross to bear."

There was a long pause.

Then Sophie cleared her throat. "Also… I wanted to tell you something Daniel mentioned about work."

Emily looked up.

"Apparently Natalie Cheng—SkyLux Natalie, not nail salon Natalie—was seriously impressed with you. With the whole campaign, but you specifically. From concept to execution."

Emily blinked. "Wait, what?"

"Yep. She told Daniel you've got a sharp eye for a story, and that your instincts are exactly what SkyLux's marketing needs more of."

Emily sat up straighter. "Are you serious?"

Sophie nodded. "And I think you might be hearing from her. Soon."

For a moment, Emily just stared at her. "That's… amazing."

"It's huge," Sophie said. "And so deserved." She paused, voice dropping as she reached for Emily's hand. "Seriously, Em. You built something beautiful. You pulled all those pieces together—SkyLux glamor, the Niagara spirit, pastries, and people—and made it make sense. You made it matter."

A rush of pride washed over Emily—unexpected, overwhelming. Coming from Sophie, who lived and breathed campaigns for a living, who'd worked with the best and worst of them, it meant more than she could say. This wasn't just friendly encouragement; it was real.

Emily blinked. "I might cry."

"Go on, then. I won't stop you. I'll even hold your tea."

They both laughed. The moment passed, but the warmth lingered.

Sophie picked up her mug and warmed her hands around it. "Imagine you get a slick marketing job at SkyLux—like a proper job with a title and everything?" She sighed dreamily. "You could move to Toronto."

"Like you?" Emily side-eyed her friend.

"Beaver tails. Ketchup chips. Real maple syrup. Do I really need to keep going?"

"Oh my god," Emily leaned forward. "We could be neighbors again!"

Sophie widened her eyes. "Yes! Brunch Club every weekend!" She pumped her fist in the air. Spilled some tea. "Oops."

They laughed again, even as they both grabbed napkins to clean up the spill. Then they settled back into their seats, blankets back on their laps.

After a while, Emily said, "Do you think I messed things up with Adam?"

Sophie shook her head. "No. I think you both got scared. And now you're dancing around it like two introverts at a wedding."

Emily let out a breath. "I don't know what to do."

"You don't have to know right now. Just don't shut the door if he knocks."

Emily looked at her. "That was almost poetic."

"I'm full of surprises. Also fries." Sophie shrugged. "Let's talk about something less emotionally risky—like whether cinnamon-maple glaze should be a limited edition candle."

The last fry was ceremonially split. And for the rest of the night, they talked about everything else—family, the future, whether wearing too much perfume was passive aggressive or just aggressive, and why was it always just one sock that went missing.

By the time Sophie finally left—wrapped in a borrowed hoodie and still ranting about the politics of brunch reservations—Emily felt something she hadn't felt in weeks.

Not clarity. Not certainty. But ease. Like she'd finally come up for air.

The apartment was quiet again, but it didn't feel empty.

She curled into the couch, pulled the blanket back over her lap, picked up a book, and exhaled.

For the first time in a long time, she was okay with not knowing what came next.

Chapter Thirty

Pearson Airport was humming with its usual chaos—families clustering near gates, solo travelers clutching overpriced coffee, pilots moving like purposeful ghosts through security lanes and terminal corridors.

Adam moved among them in uniform, a black roller bag trailing behind him and the familiar weight of his ID badge pressing against his chest.

It had been a long day—back-to-back regional flights, a quick stop in Ottawa, and now he'd finally landed his last leg back in Toronto. But for the first time in weeks, he felt clear. Like something inside him had shifted back into place.

Maybe it was the flying.

Maybe it was getting out of his own head.

Or maybe, he thought, as he passed the food court and waved at a familiar gate agent, it was simply being back where he belonged. In motion. In the air. Doing the job he'd trained for—not holding reflectors and analyzing camera angles.

He rounded the corner near Gate C34, heading for the crew lounge, when he heard a voice behind him.

"Well, well. Look who finally got his act together."

He turned.

Carol Baker was exactly as he remembered—glossy hair,

perfect makeup, and a blazer sharp enough to cut glass. She looked like someone who never once missed a closing pitch.

He smiled. "Carol. Wow."

She looked him up and down with an appreciative smirk. "Still in uniform, I see."

He shrugged easily. "It's work."

She raised an eyebrow. "Last I heard, you were flirting with marketing. Something about 'ground-level storytelling' and 'brand resonance.'"

"Your gossip is up-to-date." Adam smiled. "But it's temporary. A detour."

She laughed. "You? In marketing? I said to my sister, 'There's no way Adam Kostas trades cockpit views for Canva templates.'"

He chuckled despite himself. "You're not wrong."

Carol tilted her head. "So, what happened?"

Adam hesitated, then shrugged. "I realized I was chasing something that looked good on paper but didn't feel right. I missed flying. Missed the rhythm of it. The focus. The peace."

She crossed her arms. "Huh. Didn't think you were the self-reflection type."

He nodded, unbothered. "Neither did I."

She gave him a pointed look. "That wasn't your vibe when you dumped me two years ago."

"Sorry about that."

She waved a dismissive hand. "That's all water under the bridge now, isn't it?" Her eyes narrowed, sharp with curiosity. "So, is there a new girl in the picture?"

He gave a short, easy laugh, automatically reverting back to the person Carol expected him to be. "Isn't there always?"

Carol's smile turned knowing. "Well, I hope she likes room

service, inconsistent schedules, and being ghosted."

Adam didn't flinch. "She likes stories. And cinnamon. And places with names most people overlook on a map."

Carol blinked. "Huh. She sounds real."

He met her gaze. "She is."

There was a beat. Then Carol smiled, just a little. "Good for you."

He nodded. "Good luck with your pitch."

"I'll crush it," she said, already walking away. "Don't screw it up, Adam," she said over her shoulder. "We both know you're better at take-offs than landings."

Adam watched her go, then turned and headed for the lounge.

He didn't linger at the airport longer than he needed.

An hour later, he was back at his apartment—a tidy space on the eleventh floor just outside downtown Toronto. The kind of place that still had the faint scent of fresh paint from a recent reno, with exactly two mugs in the cabinet and a half-dead succulent on the windowsill that he kept forgetting to water. Its perseverance inspired him. It was still technically alive, like his social life. Barely.

He dropped his keys in the ceramic dish by the door, kicked off his shoes, and shrugged out of his uniform jacket, draping it over the back of the kitchen chair. The place smelled like clean laundry and something faintly metallic—like rain off the balcony railing. The apartment was quiet, just the soft hum of the fridge and the faint city noise outside—car tires over wet pavement, a streetcar bell somewhere in the distance.

He made coffee out of habit, standing barefoot on the cool tile of his kitchen, staring at the little blinking orange light on the kettle like it might offer him answers.

And that's when he saw it.

A flash of unexpected color out of the corner of his eye, something the color between sage and seafoam.

It was Emily's cardigan draped over the edge of his couch like it had been waiting for him to notice. He didn't even remember her leaving it there—maybe during one of the editing marathons, or the planning sessions when they'd taken over his living room with storyboards and empty tea mugs.

He walked over. Picked it up. Held it in his hands. He brought it to his chest for a moment, then sat down with it still in his lap.

It was soft, slightly pilled at the cuffs, and one pocket was stretched from overstuffing. The kind of cardigan you wore when you needed comfort, not compliments.

He liked that she'd brought it here. That she'd been comfortable enough to forget it.

He fought the urge to put his face into it. That would be too weird, right?

He gave in and brought the sweater to his face. It smelled faintly like lavender and something warmer. Like cinnamon. Like her.

As he sat there, thoughts racing, he realized something that had been inching toward him for weeks but now landed with full force.

He really liked her. Emily.

Not a passing crush. Not just admiration. Not just idle curiosity about what being with her might feel like. No, this was deeper. Quieter. But undeniable.

Carol had been fun. Clever. Beautiful. They'd gone to cool restaurants and had long conversations and shared playlists. He'd liked her, sure. But he'd never missed her like this. Never thought about her the way he thought about Emily—unprompted, constantly, in small moments and big ones. He'd never wanted to know what Carol was thinking all the time, or felt the gravitational pull to be near her even when they weren't speaking. He'd never felt like that about any woman before.

But with Emily?

With Emily, he'd always found himself in her orbit—because he wanted to be there. Not to impress her. Not to win her. Just to… be near her. To hear her laugh. To watch her eyes light up when she talked about the economic importance of pastry-based tourism. He knew the cadence of her sighs, the tilt of her head when she was considering an idea, the exact way her brow furrowed when she was choosing between font colors.

It wasn't obsession. It was something gentler. More natural. Like breathing.

He didn't need to analyze it anymore. He didn't want to. He just knew. He wanted her in his life. Not just in brainstorms and brunches, not just in field shoots and friendship. In real ways. Consistent ways.

He'd been an idiot. He'd spent so much time obsessing over that damn letter. Trying to read between the lines, to figure out what it meant or didn't mean.

But none of it mattered. The letter didn't matter. What mattered was what he knew now.

He'd been trying so hard not to fall. But the truth was, he already had.

Emily made him want to be better—not different, not someone else, but more present. More intentional.

She didn't need him to build her a campaign. She'd done that herself. What they needed wasn't another campaign. It was honesty.

He grabbed his phone and opened his notes app.

Typed one line: *Ask her out. A real date. Just… ask.*

He closed his eyes for a second. Then opened them again.

The campaign officially launched tomorrow.

He'd wait a day.

But then he was going to find her. And this time, there wouldn't be any hesitation.

Chapter Thirty-One

Emily hadn't expected a party.

She'd returned to the office expecting a fresh cup of tea in the break room and some leftover paperwork. What she got instead was the sound of applause and the smell of fresh waffles.

"Surprise!" Liam called from behind the oversized 'SKYLUX NIAGARA LAUNCH PARTY!' sign taped—slightly crookedly—to the glass wall of the meeting room.

Emily blinked. "Wait… what is this?"

"Brunch," Liam said proudly, gesturing like a magician. "Pop-up. Celebratory. Congratulatory." He leaned in and whispered. "Just go with it."

Inside, the long meeting table had been transformed into a feast. There were boxes of mini quiches, trays of cut fruit, a pyramid of pastries, and a waffle tower that leaned to the left like a breakfast-themed Leaning Tower of Pisa. Various dips, spreads, and bottles of ketchup and syrup were placed at strategic locations across the table.

Someone had even brought in mimosas—non-alcoholic, of course, but with fancy glassware and everything.

Susan appeared at her side, holding a cup of tea and looking deeply pleased with herself. "We wanted to mark the occasion properly. The campaign's officially live on both sides of the border, and the feedback from our Canadian partners is already coming in."

Emily blinked. "Already?"

Susan nodded. "Very positive. They loved the 'local heroes' reel. Said it felt authentic and proud and—this was my favorite—'delightfully unpolished in a polished way.'"

Emily laughed. "That feels… accurate."

"I thought so." Susan sipped her tea. "SkyLux also tagged the videos in their newsletter this morning. Their marketing lead left a comment under the Canadian rollout: 'Real stories, real voices. This is what cross-border collaboration should look like.'"

Emily's eyebrows shot up. "Natalie wrote that?"

Susan nodded. "The very one."

Emily felt something like pride bloom in her chest. The good kind. The kind that wasn't tinged with stress or self-doubt or imposter syndrome. Just… pride.

"Go on," Susan said. "Celebrate. That's an order."

The next hour was a blur of hugs, waffle servings, blurry group photos, and clinking drink flutes. Liam tried to build a second waffle tower. It collapsed by the third layer. Someone ate it anyway.

In the background, someone had put on a playlist that looped back to Taylor Swift three times, and someone else passed around the whipped cream.

Emily found herself sitting in the corner with her plate balanced on her lap, watching it all with a dazed smile.

This team—this tiny office on the edge of a regional tourism board—had pulled off something she was actually proud of. Not just because it worked. Not just because it had good lighting and tidy transitions.

But because it mattered. Because it had heart.

She'd told real stories. Made space for real people. And for once, she hadn't second-guessed every decision along the way.

It wasn't perfect. But it was hers.

She looked around. It was theirs.

Eventually, people began to drift out. Meetings to attend, calls to return, files to upload.

As cleaners arrived in the room to tidy up, Emily refilled her cup with hot water, said a few more "congrats!" and "thanks!" before wandering back to her office.

Liam passed by and offered her the last mini quiche and a wink before disappearing with a tray of used coffee mugs.

And then she was alone again, holding a warm cup of tea and a cold quiche, sitting in a comfortable, familiar office chair, and looking at her laptop.

She put everything down on the desk and took a moment to exhale.

And then, just because, she opened her email.

Nothing urgent. A few congratulations. A few internal updates. One from a project manager at SkyLux thanking her for her "grace under pressure and the uncanny ability to find charm in fudge boxes and food trucks."

She smiled at that. The project manager sounded like her kind of people.

Emily then opened the campaign folder and scanned through the files one more time. They were all where they should be: local footage, travel receipts, updated captions, signed releases. Later, she would write the wrap-up report and finalize the budget, chasing down any last receipts.

She was just about to shut down her laptop when her phone buzzed.

Adam: C*ampaign looks incredible. Just finished the SkyLux launch party in Toronto. Champagne, name tags, execs pretending they helped. You'd have loved it.*

Emily smiled. She pressed "reply" and her thumbs moved across her screen.

Emily: *Just finished here, too. Impromptu surprise launch party in the office. Liam organized a brunch.*

Adam's reply came ten seconds later.

Adam: *He really does believe you're the Brunch Queen.*

Then came the second text.

Adam: *See you soon?*

She stared at the screen, and for the first time in a long time, she felt a kind of quiet certainty. Her reply came easily.

Emily: *It's a date.*

Chapter Thirty-Two

Emily arrived home around six, kicked off her shoes, reheated a box of leftovers someone had insisted she take, and ate her dinner standing over the sink.

The launch day glow was still clinging to her in small ways, but mostly, she just felt tired. The good kind. The kind that comes after finishing something worth finishing.

She'd just settled onto the couch with a mug of tea and zero intention of being productive when the knock came.

Soft. Hesitant. But definitely not the wind.

She padded to the door in socks and a sweater that didn't match her pajama bottoms, hair piled in a messy bun that looked more chaotic than curated. She peeked through the peephole—and froze.

It was Adam.

She opened the door. "Hey."

"Hey," he said, looking more uncertain than she'd ever seen him. He ran a hand through his hair, the curls springing up briefly before flopping back into place. "I know it's late. But is it too late? I can come back tomorrow." He held up a bag. "I brought popcorn."

Emily blinked. "You didn't have to—"

"I know," he said quickly. "And I'll go if you're too tired."

Her heart had started thumping so hard, Emily thought she would never be tired again. She stepped back. Gestured. "I'm not tired. Come in."

He did. Shrugged off his coat. Set the bag on the counter. "I wasn't sure what mood you'd be in, so I brought sea salt and kettle corn. And raw kernels, too. I can actually make fresh popcorn on a stove."

"Of course, you can." Emily crossed her arms, amusement softening her features. "This feels like a flex."

"It is." He started unpacking supplies like it was a mission. "You got a pot with a lid?"

"Middle cabinet. Left side. I demand proof of popcorn wizardry."

Ten minutes later, her kitchen smelled like toasted sugar and butter, and Adam was narrating the popping process like a cooking show host.

They ended up on the couch, popcorn in a bowl between them, a movie flickering on the TV—but they weren't watching it. Not really.

Eventually, they turned the volume down. They talked. Laughed. Ate half the popcorn without realizing. And slowly, their arms brushed. Their legs nudged. Their hands touched. Neither moved away.

Eventually, Emily leaned against him. Put her head on his shoulder. "You came all this way."

"I did." He lifted his arm and put it around her shoulders, drawing her closer to him.

"For no reason," she added. "The campaign's finished."

He nodded. "No more footage to review. No more late nights debating font choices or subtitle lengths."

She rested her head on his shoulder, letting herself feel

it—really feel it—for the first time. The quiet rightness of being here. With him. He smelled like clean cotton and something warm, like sunshine after rain. He was solid next to her, steady in a way she hadn't realized she craved until now.

She looked up at him. "Why?"

He looked at her then, eyes steady. "Because I couldn't wait. Because I kept thinking about how we left things." His eyes warmed. "And because I missed you."

She swallowed. "I missed you, too."

"And…" he trailed off.

"And?" She prompted softly.

He smiled. "Well, we promised to wait until after the campaign."

Emily nodded.

"And it is now after the campaign," he stated matter-of-factly. He cleared his throat. "Actually, I wanted to ask you on a date, like a proper date. I even made a note about it on my phone. But I feel like we've already been on twenty dates."

She smiled at that. It felt true.

He reached up and tucked a strand of hair behind her ear. "And I thought… I just want to be here. With you. If that's what you want."

She looked up at him. Tilted her head up. "It is."

He leaned in, slow and sure.

This kiss was different.

No hesitation. No caveats. No pretending it didn't count.

It was warm and certain and deep—like they were both finally exhaling at the same time. Her hand curled into his shirt. His fingers traced her cheek, her jaw, her waist.

He pulled back just a little, eyes unfocused. "Can I stay?"

She nodded. "Please."

Adam didn't move immediately. He waited, watching her, like he was giving her a chance to change her mind. When she didn't, his hand slid slowly, warm fingers spreading and gently cupping the back of her neck. Then he lowered his head again to kiss her with more urgency this time.

They moved together slowly. The popcorn bowl was gently nudged aside. The lights stayed low. There was no need for ceremony, no rush. Just a kind of quiet unfolding—each button undone, each breath drawn, each glance held for longer than was strictly necessary.

Half-dressed, she led him down the short hall, still holding his hand. Her bedroom door was already open. A small, cozy space—books stacked haphazardly on the nightstand, a candle burned down to its wick, a jacket half-draped over the armchair.

He looked around briefly before turning back to her.

"I've never been in here," he said softly.

She smiled. "You're here now."

Her bed was unmade. And for once, she didn't care. Neither did he.

They kissed again, deeper this time. His hands slipped beneath her shirt. Hers found the hem of his tee and tugged gently.

Her sweater joined his jacket on the chair, followed by her bra. His belt dropped to the floor beside the bed. Her fingers brushed the waistband of his jeans as his lips trailed a path down her neck. The lamplight caught on the curve of her shoulder, the flutter of her lashes, the soft arch of her back as she welcomed him in.

There were no whispered promises. No grand declarations. Just touch. Just breath. Just the steady rhythm of skin on skin, of old tension dissolving into something tender and real.

He moved like he already knew her—how to take his time, how to read the small gasps she made, how to pause when her hands pressed against his chest just to feel the beat of his heart. She traced the scar near his collarbone with her fingertip. He kissed the freckle below her ribs.

She tugged him closer. He settled above her. Around her. Within her. Every part of him felt like a question, and every part of her answered.

There was a moment, halfway through, where they both stilled—foreheads pressed together, breaths tangled, like they couldn't believe it was finally happening. Like they were afraid to blink in case the moment disappeared.

But it didn't. It deepened.

And when it was over—when they were lying there, bare and breathless—he reached for her hand beneath the covers and laced his fingers through hers.

She didn't let go.

And for the first time in a long time, neither of them dreamed of being anywhere else.

Chapter Thirty-Three

Emily woke slowly, as if her body knew not to rush this.

There was sunlight filtering through the slats in the blinds—soft and golden, the kind that made everything feel like a Sunday morning. For a moment, she didn't move. Just stayed there, eyes still closed, wrapped in warmth.

And then she remembered.

Adam.

Her arm stretched instinctively, brushing over smooth sheets—and warm skin.

He was still there.

His breathing was steady, slow. She blinked open one eye and turned her head to find him on his side, facing her, one hand tucked beneath the pillow, the other resting loosely on her waist.

She smiled.

Last night hadn't been a dream. He had come over. With popcorn. With quiet declarations and soft questions and that look in his eyes that made her heart stutter. And then… well, everything else.

She closed her eyes again, not to fall asleep, but to keep the moment a little longer. To hold onto it.

Eventually, Adam stirred. His hand tightened briefly around her waist, as if he were anchoring himself, too.

"Mmm." His voice was rough with sleep. "Morning."

"Morning," she whispered back.

His hair was a mess. His face was soft, unguarded. He opened one eye. Then reached out to touch her hair.

"You always look like this in the morning?" Adam murmured. "Because it's kind of criminal."

She grinned. "Sweaty, tangled, and probably with pillow lines on my cheek?"

"Exactly. Dangerous." He brushed her hair back. "Beautiful."

She looked at him. His voice had turned husky with the last word.

His fingers continued down from her hair, gently tracing the side of her neck. Then his hand flattened over her shoulders, a warm presence, before sliding slowly down her arms.

Emily shivered slightly under his touch. He shuffled closer until their noses were almost touching. Her hand slipped under the blanket to press against the hard planes of his back, her fingers flexing against the smooth skin.

She lifted her face to his and they kissed. He was soft, gentle, careful, questioning. When her hand found his waist to pull him closer, he groaned and deepened the kiss.

They didn't rush. There was no reason to. The second time was different. Less urgency, more reverence. His hands and mouth moved like he was learning her all over again, like he wanted to memorize the way she arched into his touch, the sound of her breath.

Emily responded just as fully—open, present, a little stunned at how easily this had happened and how right it still felt. There were no lights, no rehearsals, no cameras—just them.

When they collapsed again, warm and tangled in the

aftermath, neither spoke for a long while.

"I think I drooled on your pillow last night," Adam eventually mumbled into her hair.

Emily laughed. "It's fine. I think I elbowed you in the ribs at some point."

"It was an affectionate elbow. With lots of charm."

"I don't think anyone's ever called my elbow charming before."

His arms tightened around her. "All of you is charming."

They stayed like that for a while, exchanging soft jokes and slower kisses, until their stomachs finally staged a rebellion.

Adam was the first to move, brushing his lips over her temple. "Now I really want coffee."

Emily smiled. "I'll allow it."

They stumbled into the kitchen dressed in underwear and oversized shirts. Adam found coffee beans and turned on the coffee machine. Emily pulled out eggs and toast. They moved around each other like they'd been doing this for years.

Soon, the apartment smelled like coffee and breakfast. Adam sliced an avocado. Emily scrambled eggs. They bumped hips, stole sips from each other's cups, and kissed over the cutting board.

They finally sat at the small kitchen table—two plates, two mugs, bare feet brushing underneath.

"This is weird," Emily said after a beat.

Adam paused. "Weird how?"

"Weird wonderful," she said. "I mean, this *is* like our twenty-first date."

Adam grinned as he buttered his toast. "It's my favorite one so far."

Emily rolled her eyes, but she smiled. "Me, too." She put

avocado slices on her toast and passed him the pepper. "I still can't quite believe you drove over an hour and across a country to be here last night."

"To be with you? I'd do it ten times over." He refilled her coffee cup and added exactly one sugar cube, just as she liked it.

"Yes, but you didn't know what would happen," she pointed out. "Like, what if I'd said no, I'm tired, go home?"

He set his mug down. "Then I would have gone home." His words were simple, matter-of-fact. "Would've sucked, but yeah—simple as that."

"I also can't quite believe we're actually here." She frowned slightly. "Like this. Now. In this moment. Having breakfast together after…" She trailed off.

"I know." He put his hand on top of hers. Blew out a long breath. "I get it. It's surreal."

She nodded. "Surreal is a good word."

"Hey."

Emily looked at him.

She could hear the shift in his voice before she saw it on his face. His eyes locked on hers, all of the usual sparkle—the mischief, the easy banter—gone. Not in a bad way. Just… quiet. Serious. Enough to make her heartbeat skip.

He looked at her like he was weighing something. Like he was choosing his next words carefully, and that they mattered.

She put down her coffee. Waited.

He cleared his throat. "We don't have to define this right now. We don't have to make it anything you're not ready for. I just want you to know—I'm here. I'm not going anywhere." He squeezed her hand. "And I can be patient."

She shook her head, cutting him off. "I don't really… do casual."

His brow lifted slightly.

She rushed on. "It's not a rule. It's just… how I'm built. When I care, I care hard. When I fall, I fall all the way. I don't know how to love in pieces." She met his gaze. "Does that scare you?"

Adam didn't answer right away. He looked at her—really looked at her.

He saw the uncertainty in her eyes.

He set down his fork and reached for her hand.

"It used to," he said, wanting to be honest. "That kind of intensity used to make me run. But not with you."

Emily held her breath.

"I've been in relationships where I showed up halfway. Where I kept a door open just in case. But with you…" He exhaled. "It's different. I'm not holding anything back."

She swallowed. "Really?"

"I don't know how to explain it. It's not even a decision. It just… is."

Emily blinked hard, nodding.

He rubbed his thumb across the back of her hand. "I don't want easy. I want real. All of it."

A smile spread across her face, slow and sure. "Good."

He lifted her hand to his lips. "All in?"

"All in."

Later, they curled up on the couch, the remains of breakfast growing cold on the table behind them.

Emily tucked her feet beneath her, draping the blanket over both their legs. Adam slouched deeper into the cushions, his arm draped comfortably around her shoulders.

He traced small circles on the back of her hand. "You know," he said, voice low, "if this is what Sunday mornings look like now, I'm definitely renewing my subscription."

Emily smirked. "Oh, you think you're getting the premium package?"

He grinned, squeezing her hand. "At least the deluxe trial."

Emily smiled, snuggling closer. "It's almost perfect," she sighed. "Except I still can't find my green sweater. I swear it vanished into the void."

Adam's eyes lit up with mischief. "You're missing your famous cardigan? That's practically a crime."

"Don't mock my emotional support sweater," she grumbled, but her tone was teasing. "It's the perfect couch cocoon."

He chuckled, brushing his lips across her hair. "Don't move." Then he slipped out from under the blanket and crossed the room to his bag by the door.

Emily propped herself up on her elbow, brow raised. "What are you up to?"

He unzipped the bag and held something up—soft, green, familiar. "I meant to give this back to you last night," he said sheepishly. "Found it on my couch last week. I thought it'd be another good reason to see you again. In case I needed one."

She sat up fully now. "My sweater."

Adam crossed the room and handed it to her. "I didn't mean to keep it hostage. But… I kind of liked having it around."

She took it from him, smiling as her fingers brushed the fabric. "You brought it back," she said. "Thank you."

"I did," he murmured. "But only because I'm hoping you won't need it anymore."

She tilted her head. "Why's that?"

"Because next time, I'll be the one keeping you warm." He patted his chest.

Emily grinned. "I never knew you were so cheesy."

“I defy definition,” Adam said, rejoining her on the sofa.

He reached out and pulled her to him again. She wrapped the sweater loosely around them, then relaxed against him. She pressed her cheek against his chest, the steady beat of his heart beneath it, his arms wrapped around her.

“I could stay like this forever,” she murmured.

Adam smiled, his lips brushing her hair. “Then don’t go anywhere.”

She didn’t answer. She didn’t have to.

Chapter Thirty-Four

The drive to Emily's childhood home in upstate New York took just under four hours, including one bathroom stop, two snack breaks, and exactly one roadside debate over whether kettle chips or french fries were the superior road trip snack.

By the time they pulled into the long gravel driveway flanked by overgrown hydrangeas and a tire swing, Emily felt that odd, familiar tug in her chest.

"Wow," Adam said, stepping out of the car and stretching. "This place screams *home* in a way that makes me feel like I should be wearing a varsity jacket and experiencing emotional growth."

Emily snorted. "Once you meet my mom, that'll happen within the first ten minutes."

The front door opened before they even made it to the porch.

Jonah emerged, all six feet of him in a hoodie that probably cost more than Emily's rent, waving dramatically and holding a reusable coffee cup like it was a prop in a tech startup commercial. "The prodigal child returns!"

"Technically, I've never been prodigal," Emily said, pulling her overnight bag from the trunk.

"You've definitely been dramatic."

Adam leaned toward her. "Is this the one with the smart

toilet?"

"Unfortunately," Emily muttered.

"Still can't figure out how to turn off the motion sensor," Jonah said, hugging her tightly and then turning to Adam. "You must be The Pilot."

Adam shook his hand. "You must be The Brother."

"Correct. I come with sarcasm and wi-fi troubleshooting skills. Also, I've already explained to Mom how to use the new smart oven I bought her so she can make her famous lasagna tonight. You're welcome."

Inside, the house smelled like lemon cleaner, fresh basil, and Emily's entire childhood. Her mom appeared in the kitchen doorway, a dish towel slung over one shoulder.

"There's my girl!" she beamed, pulling Emily into a hug. Then she turned to Adam with the kind of appraising warmth that only mothers could wield. "And you must be Adam. I've heard so much about you."

Adam blinked. "You have?"

"She talks," her mom said with a wink, nodding at Emily. "And we listen. Come in, both of you. Dinner is almost ready. Jonah's already taste-tested the garlic bread. Repeatedly."

"I was confirming crispness," Jonah called from the couch. "I'm providing a service."

They settled in quickly—drinks poured, awkward introductions rapidly replaced by casual teasing. Adam fit in faster than Emily expected. Her dad even nodded in approval after a brief conversation about aviation fuel efficiency in commercial route planning.

High praise, considering the man once gave her prom date a 30-minute lecture on mortgage rates.

Dinner was loud and messy in the best way. Plates passed

back and forth. Jonah made dramatic declarations about his fridge trying to kill him, citing "at least three suspicious beeps" and an accidental grocery order of twelve avocados. Their dad asked Adam detailed questions about flying planes in bad weather conditions. Adam took it all in stride. Their mom insisted everyone try her famous lemon cake.

After dinner, they moved to the living room. Jonah gave them a tour of his latest smart home frustrations ("I swear my television is *listening* to me") while Emily curled up in her favorite old armchair and pulled their cat, Puff, onto her lap.

At one point, Adam glanced over and caught her smiling.

"What?" he asked quietly.

She shook her head, hands scratching gently across Puff's fur. "You're just… really good at this."

"Good at what?"

"Being here. Being… you."

He bumped her shoulder gently. "I like your people."

"They like you, too."

He looked down at Puff who looked supremely bored. "Not sure about your cat, though."

"Puff just looks like that. He actually likes most people," she declared. She picked him up and plopped him onto Adam's lap where Puff circled once, twice, then lay down. When Adam tentatively touched his back, Puff immediately began purring.

Emily grinned. "See? You've now been officially welcomed by every member of this family."

She didn't say it aloud, but part of her had been nervous about this visit. Nervous that Adam, used to sleek lounges and travel schedules, would feel out of place here in a house where the dishwasher had to be jiggled just right and the hallway rug had been the same since 1999.

But he didn't seem out of place at all. He seemed at home.

Later, while Jonah set up an overly complicated trivia app on the family TV ("It connects to my phone, which connects the TV, and it should know who is speaking by voice recognition"), Emily slipped away to grab something warm to wear from upstairs. Adam followed.

They ended up in her old bedroom.

It looked almost exactly the same. Posters on the walls. Fairy lights above the window. A bookshelf crammed with YA paperbacks and old journals. The bedspread slightly faded but still covered in pineapples.

He grinned. "You weren't kidding about the pineapple phase."

"Listen," she said, hands on her hips. "It has a *strong aesthetic*. I stand by it."

He moved closer, fingers brushing a charm bracelet on her dresser. "What was she like? Teenage Emily?"

Emily shrugged. "A little intense. A lot awkward. Loved planning themed parties. Overthought *everything*."

"So... basically the same, just with less hair mousse?"

She narrowed her eyes. "I will kick you."

Emily rummaged in her bag and pulled out her green cardigan. "I can't believe I almost lost this," she muttered as she put it on.

"Maybe nothing's ever really lost." Adam smiled. "It's just waiting to be found."

She turned to him slowly. "Did you just fortune-cookie me?"

He grinned. "Maybe."

She rolled her eyes but didn't stop smiling. "You're lucky you're cute."

"You say that like it's new information."

As they switched off the light and turned to head back downstairs, Adam touched Emily's arm. She paused and turned to look at him.

He gently took her arm and drew her towards him. "Just wanted to say thanks for bringing me."

She softened. "Thanks for coming."

He kissed her forehead gently. "You're incredible, you know that?"

She leaned her head against his shoulder. "I'm in pineapple pajamas."

"Still incredible."

That night, they stayed up way too late—playing trivia, helping her dad fix a loose kitchen drawer, sitting on the porch with mugs of tea. Jonah told a deeply embarrassing story about Emily trying to learn guitar in middle school. Emily countered with a story about Jonah's first failed attempt at flirting with a flight attendant using video game references.

By midnight, Emily's cheeks hurt from smiling.

And when they finally crawled into bed—together this time, in her childhood bedroom room with a slightly squeaky mattress—she fell asleep with his hand in hers and the quiet hum of crickets outside the window.

This wasn't a fancy resort.

It wasn't a campaign shoot.

It wasn't even remotely perfect.

But it was hers.

And now, maybe—just maybe—it was his, too.

Chapter Thirty-Five

Emily woke up to the smell of pancakes and the sound of someone—probably Jonah—arguing with the coffee machine.

"You are not out of filters," he barked at it. "I checked. I *restocked*."

She grinned into her pillow, then rolled over to find Adam already pulling on a hoodie. His hair was a little wild.

"Up for a field trip?" he asked.

"Only if it ends in carbs."

"Deal."

Fifteen minutes later, after Jonah declared the coffee machine a "menace to society" and threatened to post a review online about it, and their mom handed them each a granola bar "just in case", while their dad waited patiently with his shoes on by the front door, the five of them finally piled into Emily's car.

Puff was not allowed to go with them, much to his own vocal displeasure at the screen door.

Destination? A retro photography museum Jonah had found online with exactly three Google reviews—all of them five stars and a comment which claimed the place was "haunted and smelled like darkroom chemicals."

It sounded perfect.

The building itself was a converted fire hall, red brick with ivy crawling up one side and a crooked sign out front: 'The Click: A Vintage Camera Experience.' The inside smelled like history and probably expired film. It was also, inexplicably, blasting Fleetwood Mac over the recessed speakers.

Emily was immediately delighted.

Jonah looked confused.

Their parents wandered toward a display of Polaroids while Adam drifted to a glass case filled with 35mm cameras and began muttering names like they were old friends.

Emily sidled up beside him. "You good?"

He looked at her like she'd just offered him a first-class upgrade and a puppy. "This is heaven. This is photography *nerd heaven*."

"You're really into cameras?"

He nodded, eyes sparkling. "My grandfather was a photographer. Had a darkroom in the basement. Used to let me help develop prints when I was a kid. He's the one who gave me my first camera."

Emily blinked. "That's the most wholesome thing I've ever heard."

He pointed to a battered Nikon. "That's the one I learned on."

The museum guide—a guy with a beard, suspenders, and an expression that said he took shutter speed seriously—overheard them and perked up. "You shoot film?"

"Used to," Adam said. "Haven't in years, but I still remember the feel of winding the spool. The sound it made when you got it right."

Emily had never seen him like this. Not in airports. Not on set. There was something quieter about it. Focused. Joyful.

"Right on, man," said the guy, giving a thumbs up, before

returning to the front desk to help other visitors.

"Why didn't you stick to photography professionally?" Emily asked as they moved to the next case.

He smiled softly. "As you know, I tried it briefly. But flying won. At least, flying pays the bills."

She took his hand. "I'm glad it did."

They spent another hour there, Emily taking photos of Adam posing with ancient flashbulbs and Adam giving a photography history lesson to her father and Jonah. Her mom bought a tote bag that said *F-Stop the World* and made her dad take a picture of her in front of a Rolleiflex.

By the time they emerged into the sunshine, Adam moved with an ease she hadn't seen before.

"Okay," Emily said, stretching. "One museum, zero ghost sightings. What's next?"

Her mom pulled out a dog-eared brochure from her purse. "There's a hiking trail not far from here. Ends at a waterfall."

Jonah narrowed his eyes. "How steep is this trail?"

"Moderate," their dad said cheerfully. "Which means your mother will call it relaxing and you'll call it cardio."

"Hey, I lift," Jonah protested.

"Technically not cardio," Emily said.

"I yoga."

"Still not cardio."

Twenty minutes later, they were following a winding path through a shady forest that smelled like moss and adventure. Emily held Adam's hand.

Jonah complained for the first twenty minutes. Then again when he stepped in a puddle. Then not at all, because the view stole the breath right out of all of them.

The waterfall wasn't huge, but it was perfect—tucked into a

rocky alcove, surrounded by wildflowers, the sound of the water like a steady, soothing soundtrack.

Emily sat on a sun-warmed rock, Adam beside her, their shoulders touching.

"This," she said quietly, "was a good idea."

"A hundred percent," he said, tilting his face up to the sun.

They didn't say much after that. Just sat there, breathing in the moment, the faint spray of the water cool on their faces.

Later, Jonah suggested an ice cream stop.

"I'll go if they have pistachio," he declared.

"They do," Emily said without checking.

"Liar."

"It's called manifesting."

They ended up at a roadside creamery with a neon sign that read 'Lickety Split,' and picnic tables painted in pastels.

Emily got mint chocolate chip. Adam got maple walnut. Jonah tried something called "Birthday Explosion" and deeply regretted it. Their parents split a banana split.

"I can't believe this table is still here," Emily said, wiggling on the bench. "We used to come here after every parent-teacher conference." She looked at her brother. "Jonah once stole the napkin dispenser and blamed a raccoon."

Jonah didn't even look up from his cone. "Raccoon had it coming."

Emily laughed so hard she nearly choked on her mint chip.

Afterward, they drove home with the windows down. Jonah fell asleep in the backseat with his head against the door. Emily's mom hummed along to an old Eagles song on the radio. Her dad pointed out landmarks like they were old friends.

And Adam… Adam just held her hand on the center console. Quiet. Easy.

At the house, they all took turns calling dibs on the one good shower.

Later, after a quick shower and her nighttime routine, Emily passed Adam a clean towel and gestured to the still-steamy bathroom.

Adam touched her arm. “Uh, is there a hairdryer?” he asked.

Emily smirked. “Seriously?”

He touched his own hair. “It doesn’t look this good by itself.”

She laughed. “It’s under the sink.”

Then she padded downstairs to say good night. Her parents had to work the next day, and Emily and Adam planned to leave in the morning.

“My girl,” her mom said, embracing her warmly. “I had such a good day today. Thank you for coming to visit. You know we always love it when you do.”

Emily hugged her dad next. “It’s been nice to meet Adam,” he said as he patted her shoulders. “He seems like a good guy.”

They said their good nights.

On her way to the stairs, she poked her head into Jonah’s room. He was already propped up with his laptop, headphones on, and a half-eaten bag of chips beside him.

She knocked lightly on the doorframe. “Night, nerd,” she called.

He slid one headphone off and looked over at her, expression soft. “Hey. You good?”

She nodded. “Yeah. Today was… really nice. This whole trip was nice.”

He gestured for her to come closer. When she did, Jonah pulled her into a quick, sideways hug—careful not to spill the chips. He lowered his voice. “Seriously, Em. You’re doing good.

Don't let your brain tell you otherwise."

She rolled her eyes, but her smile was grateful. "Thanks, Dr. Jonah."

He grinned. "Night. Wake me if you need backup for a midnight snack raid."

She brought a glass of water to her room, put it on her night stand, and collapsed onto her childhood bed in pineapple pajamas and a smile she couldn't shake.

A few minutes later, Adam knocked softly on the doorframe. "You asleep?"

She sat up. "Not yet."

He came in, freshly scrubbed from the bathroom, his hair warm from the hairdryer, and shut the door behind him. He flicked off the overhead lights. She shifted over and he crawled into bed beside her. He opened his arms and she slid between them, resting her head on his shoulder.

Neither of them said anything for a minute.

Then she whispered, "Today was really good."

He nodded. "Yeah. It was." His hand played idly with a strand of her hair.

She nuzzled against him. "Even the haunted camera museum?"

He kissed her hair. "Especially the haunted camera museum."

The lights stayed off. The house creaked around them, old and familiar.

"Hey, Emily?" Adam murmured after a while.

"Yeah?"

"I think I want to take a photography class again. Something small. Local. Just for me."

She smiled into the dark. "I think that sounds perfect."

They fell asleep wrapped in old quilts, new beginnings, and the quiet certainty that this—whatever this was—mattered.

Chapter Thirty-Six

Adam had never been the kind of guy who got sentimental over calendar reminders, but the recurring Brunch Club event—every other Sunday at 11:00 a.m., location: Sophie and Daniel's—was something he actually looked forward to now.

Even if it meant waking up early after a red-eye.

Because Emily would be there.

And that had somehow become his new baseline for a good day.

They were eight months in now—officially, very thoroughly together. They alternated weekends between her place in Niagara and his in Toronto, navigating travel schedules and work commitments with surprising ease. Every time he left her, it felt like it wasn't enough. Every time he saw her again, he wondered how he ever thought anything else had made him happy before.

He kept waiting for the old fear to kick in. That anxious itch in his chest that usually showed up whenever things got too serious. When someone left a toothbrush at his place or asked about his five-year plan. That pull to run.

But with Emily? It hadn't come. Not even once.

Instead, he felt like he'd found the version of himself he didn't know he was missing.

The version who set reminders because he liked the feeling

of being expected.

The version who actually read the side of the cake mix box to get it "just right."

Who made space in his carry-on for her favorite tea.

Who didn't flinch at long conversations about the future because—for once—it felt like something he wanted to run toward, not from.

He liked who he was around her. Not a performance. Not a compromise. Just more... himself. More grounded.

Someone who laughed more easily.

Someone who lingered longer.

Someone who'd learned that home wasn't always a place. Sometimes it was a person, sitting cross-legged on the couch in cozy socks, asking if he wanted more syrup on his waffles.

Now they were pulling up to Sophie and Daniel's building with a box of pastries in hand and a playlist titled *Brunch Vibes* playing softly through the car speakers.

"Are we late?" Emily asked, checking her phone.

"Only fashionably," Adam replied. "Besides, we brought sugar. That buys forgiveness."

They took the elevator up to the condo—a beautiful three-bedroom Daniel and Sophie had moved into a few months earlier after Daniel's promotion. He'd transitioned to a strategic operations role at SkyLux, which meant fewer flights and more meetings. Sophie had promptly turned the third bedroom into an "inspiration space," which was mostly bookshelves, mood boards, lamps, and one very dramatic armchair.

The Brunch Club had started as a joke—waffles and mimosa experiments and too many group texts—but it had become something real. Every other Sunday, the same group gathered: Sophie, Daniel, Liam, Gabriel, Lucy, and others, along with the occasional rotating guest appearance from a friend-of-a-friend or rogue sibling.

When the elevator doors opened, they could already hear laughter from the hallway. Adam reached for Emily's hand.

She looked up at him and smiled.

The door opened before they knocked.

"You're late," Sophie said, stepping aside with a grin. "But you brought carbs, so you're forgiven."

Adam looked at Emily. "See?" He handed over the pastry box. "It's from that place near the Don Valley that uses actual maple sap. Emily made me double back to get it."

Sophie accepted the box, nodding solemnly. "Pastry standards are important."

Inside, the table was already set—mismatched plates, cloth napkins folded by Liam into various shapes, and a carafe of something sparkling and orange sitting center stage. Daniel stood behind the kitchen island, flipping pancakes with casual efficiency.

The two men man-hugged with clasped fists between them in greeting. Then Adam immediately went to the two waffle makers already set-up on the counter by the fridge. The waffle-makers were now on permanent loan from Emily. One had stayed behind in Niagara.

Liam popped up from the couch, waving a mug. "Ademly has arrived!"

Adam winced. "We are not calling ourselves that."

"You don't get to decide your ship name," Sophie said, already plating pastries. "The people have spoken."

Adam flashed back to the first time they had walked into a Brunch Club event holding hands. Eight months ago. That first weekend after everything shifted.

They hadn't planned to be obvious. But they were late then, too, and when Sophie opened the door, Emily's fingers were still laced with his.

No one said anything for half a second—just a beat of silence—and then Daniel raised both eyebrows and grinned. Sophie let out a theatrical gasp. Liam cheered like it was a playoff game.

"Finally!" someone shouted—probably Lucy.

"Mais, c'est cool!" That had definitely been Gabriel.

Emily had blushed, and Adam had kissed the top of her head and said, "Er, surprise?"

After that, everyone just got on with it, and nothing had really changed. It was as if everyone had already known and accepted that Adam and Emily belonged together. It had just been a matter of time.

More importantly, Brunch Club became a regular event. It was now their thing. Their little constant in the ever-shifting logistics of airline schedules and tourism campaigns.

And honestly? Adam loved it.

He loved how Sophie always made something with whipped cream, how Daniel always cooked the bacon extra crispy, how Liam brought obscure jam combinations, and how Emily always looked like she belonged here—laughing with her whole body, eyes crinkled, hair wrangled into a soft knot at the nape of her neck or an unruly bun on the top of her head.

He used to flinch at the word 'routine.' Now, he found himself looking forward to it.

They settled in. Plates were passed. The maple pastries were devoured within five minutes.

"So," Daniel said, topping off Adam's coffee. "How's the Toronto commute treating you?"

Adam shrugged. "Could be worse. I use the drive to decompress. Or listen to podcasts about plane crashes to keep things spicy."

Emily elbowed him. "Don't do that."

Liam gestured with his fork. "You two still alternating weekends?"

"Mostly," Emily said. "Depends on his flight schedule and whether I have back-to-back meetings."

"She's got the entire Niagara region wrapped around her finger now," Adam added. "They just gave her a tourism award last month."

"Stop," Emily said, half-laughing, half-hiding behind her coffee. "It was for the whole campaign team. Not just me."

"You were the team lead," he said, nudging her gently. "They should've given you a crown."

Sophie gasped. "Should we get you a crown? For next brunch?"

"Yes," Liam agreed immediately. "For the brunch queen."

Daniel leaned back in his chair. "You two make this long-distance-ish thing look easy."

"At least we're not Toronto-New York," Adam said, referring to the time when Daniel and Sophie had each been living in their respective cities.

"It's not always easy," Emily said honestly. "But it works."

"It really does," Adam said. "I keep waiting for the other shoe to drop. But it hasn't. I just… I miss her when she's not around. And that used to freak me out, but now it just feels like how it should be."

The table went quiet for a second.

Sophie smiled. "That's how you know it's real."

"And disgusting," Liam added. "But mostly real."

They all laughed, and then the conversation shifted—someone asking about a new client, Sophie ranting about a bizarre hotel review she'd read, Lucy trying to convince everyone to do a themed brunch next time. ("I'm thinking international breakfast foods. Let's rotate continents. Who's got Asia?")

Adam leaned back in his chair, a coffee mug in his hand.

Emily was laughing again, tossing a strawberry into Liam's mug, her nose scrunching like it always did when she was genuinely delighted. Sophie had flour on her cheek. Daniel was mock-arguing with Liam about whether dim sum counted as brunch. The sun was streaming in through the big corner windows of the condo, painting the hardwood floor in long golden strips.

And Adam realized—this wasn't just a good day. It was a good life.

Later, while Daniel packed up leftovers and Liam tried to create a new hip hop-only brunch themed Spotify playlist, Adam stepped out onto the small balcony. The city buzzed below. The air was crisp and smelled faintly of bread and traffic and spring.

Emily joined him a moment later, sliding her arms around his waist from behind.

"Hey," she said softly.

"Hey." He turned, wrapping his arms around her.

"You good?"

He nodded. "Better than good." Then he hesitated. "Can I say something that might sound cheesy?"

She leaned her chin on his shoulder. "Absolutely."

"I think this is the first time I've ever been in a relationship and not felt like I'm losing myself."

Emily tilted her head. "What do you feel instead?"

"Like I'm finding it."

She didn't say anything right away—just held him tighter. Then whispered, "Me, too."

He turned around, enfolded her in his arms, and rested his chin on the top of her head. The city kept buzzing. Someone honked below. Inside, someone turned up the volume on the music again.

But out here, on the balcony, it was just them.

Eight months in. And still, somehow, it felt like the beginning.

Somewhere in the distance, a church bell rang. A dog barked. Emily's thumb traced a small circle at the base of his spine. He let himself breathe it all in.

Chapter Thirty-Seven

Emily was in the middle of fighting with her office label maker when her phone rang.

The label maker—ancient, temperamental, and possibly possessed—had just spat out a half-printed sticker that read "CAMPAIG" before jamming. Emily, who had gone precisely four hours and seventeen minutes without caffeine was entering a state known clinically as 'murder-adjacent.'

She glanced at the screen.

Natalie Cheng. SkyLux.

Her stomach did a small, curious backflip. She answered, trying to sound less like someone who'd just threatened a label maker with scissors.

"Hello?"

"Emily! Natalie Cheng here," said the cheerful voice on the other end. "Am I catching you at a bad time?"

Emily looked at the half-mauled sticker. "No, not at all. Perfect timing."

"I'll get straight to it—we've had a position open up in our Toronto office. Marketing lead, regional strategy with a digital emphasis. And your name came up."

Emily blinked. "My name… came up?"

"I've followed the campaign," Natalie said. "Niagara's

results were exceptional. Your ability to blend strategy with story-telling is exactly what we're looking for."

Emily's brain went momentarily blank. Somewhere behind her, the label maker gave a smug little *click.*

"I… wow. Thank you. That's a lot to take in."

"Totally understandable. This isn't a formal offer yet—just a conversation. We can chat details when you're ready. But I wanted to reach out personally. I think you'd be a great fit." Natalie paused. "Will you think about it? It would require you to move to Canada, but we've got a great immigration specialist on the HR team here who could manage that for you."

Emily managed to string together a coherent thank-you and promises to follow up by the end of the week. Then she hung up.

She stared at her phone, and said aloud: "Puff, I think I'm having an identity crisis."

Puff, who had taken up residence on the only sunlit corner of her desk, opened one eye. Then went back to sleep.

Her parents had dropped Puff at her place last week. They were now on a month-long cruise across the Atlantic, and likely eating fresh pasta somewhere in Italy now. Meanwhile, Emily had grown accustomed to Puff's diva-like habits—including chirping at sunrise, demanding filtered water, and routinely sitting on her laptop.

"Thanks for the help," she muttered, then stood and paced her office like a sitcom character trying not to yell *plot twist!*

SkyLux. In Toronto. With Adam.

She plopped back into her chair and stared at the wall where she'd pinned a printed photo of the beaver tail truck from last year's campaign.

Could she leave Niagara?

Her mind did a rapid-fire scroll:

— Susan's morning tea lectures about municipal grant writing
— Liam's chaotic sock collection and near-religious reverence for b-roll
— The smell of the falls and the river after rain
— The little cafe that knew her order by heart
— Her desk, her mug, her people

Ugh.

And yet, on the other hand:
— Adam, every day, no commute
— Progressing her career by being part of a larger team with national reach—this was everything she'd been working for
— Learning new things instead of fixing the office printer's paper tray for the fiftieth time
— More Brunch Club with Daniel's fancy espresso machine

She buried her face in her hands. "Why can't this be one of those sitcom jobs where people just magically move and no one notices?"

Puff yawned. Stretched. Slept again.

Her phone buzzed. A text from Adam.

Adam: *How's your day?*

She stared at it. Thought about how he kissed her forehead every time he left, how he still remembered her coffee order even though she changed it every season.

Emily: *Just got a call from SkyLux.*

Pause.

Adam: *Job offer?*

Emily: *Sort of. Nothing formal.*

Adam: *Based in Toronto?*

Emily: *Yes.*

A beat.

Adam: *Want to talk about it tonight? I can come by after my flight.*

She smiled, then bit her lip.

Emily: *Yeah. That'd be nice.*

Adam: *Tell Puff I'm on my way.*

Puff, who now greeted Adam at the door like a long-lost spouse returning from war, had grown disturbingly attached. Emily had once caught him pawing at Adam's sweatshirt and refusing to move after Adam left for a work trip.

She put her phone down and tried to go back to work. She lasted four minutes.

Then she gave up entirely and wandered into Liam's editing suite, where he was aggressively color-correcting footage of a couple walking through a grove of trees.

He turned briefly. Saw her expression. "Do we need to have a pastry-supported crisis session?" he asked. "Because I'm all out. Sorry, just had the last croissant."

"I might be moving to Toronto," she blurted.

He almost knocked over his iced tea. "Wait, what?"

"SkyLux called. Natalie. They're hiring."

Liam blinked. "And…?"

"And I don't know. It's a great opportunity. It's the next step, career-wise. It's a big deal. But it's… not here."

He looked at her for a long moment. "Okay, selfishly? I'd miss you like crazy. Who else will yell at me about font choices? Or talk me down from drinking my sixth coffee?"

"Exactly."

"But," he added, more gently, "maybe that's how we know it's the right move. If it's hard to leave, it means you mattered here. You made your mark."

Emily blinked. "Stop being wise. It's upsetting."

Liam shrugged. "You can take the girl out of Niagara…"

"Still not comforting."

"You'll figure it out," he said with a confidence she didn't feel. "You always do."

Back at her desk, she found herself holding her second favorite coffee mug—a chipped ceramic one that said *World's Okayest Strategist.* It had been a joke gift from her colleagues. She'd grown deeply attached and now used it every day when at work.

"I can't take all this with me," she whispered to herself. "Or can I?"

Puff meowed like he was done with the drama.

She rolled her eyes. "Okay, fine. Let's go home." She went to get Puff's travel bag.

By the time she got home, she was a walking spiral of indecision. She paced. She stress-cleaned. She tried to do yoga and nearly fell over.

When Adam showed up, carrying Indian food and a warm smile, she threw herself into his arms before Puff could. Puff meowed loudly, looking personally offended.

"I'm glad you're here," she mumbled into his chest.

He just held her.

Later, over takeout containers of butter chicken, garlic naan, and melting mango ice cream, Emily explained the phone call with Natalie.

Adam focused on eating but she knew he was quietly listening. When she finished, he just looked at her, waiting.

Finally, she asked: "Would it be weird if I took the job because it's in the same city as you?"

He set his spoon down. "No. It would be weird if that was the *only* reason. But it's not, is it?"

She shook her head. "No. It really isn't."

"Then it's not weird. It's life. People make choices for the people they love. That's not weakness. That's the point."

She exhaled. "It would mean starting over. Again."

"I wouldn't say it's starting over." He picked up his spoon again. "Can I ask you something?"

Emily nodded.

"Why the hesitation?" he said gently. "I thought this was what you wanted—something bigger. A new challenge. You've worked your ass off for this. So… what's holding you back?"

Emily toyed with her napkin. "I don't know. Maybe I'm just scared to want it now that it's real. Like, what if I get there and it's not what I thought? Or worse, what if I get there and *I'm* not who I thought?"

Adam reached for her hand. "You'll be exactly who you are now. Just with better office snacks."

She smiled, but it faded a little. "Okay, then let me ask you something."

"Shoot."

"Why didn't you apply for Captain?"

That caught him off guard. He leaned back slightly. "Wow. Okay."

"You've been qualified for months. You say it's the next step, but you haven't even filled out the paperwork. Why?"

Adam didn't answer right away. "I guess… I wanted to be sure I wasn't chasing it just because it was next. I wanted to know it was something I still wanted—not just a title or a milestone to tick off."

She pointed her napkin at him. "Exactly."

He chuckled. "Wait, does this mean we're hesitating for the same reasons?"

She tilted her head. "Well, I also really like where I am right now. The work is interesting and my colleagues are great."

Adam nodded slowly. "And for me, you and this project—Niagara, SkyLux, all of it—it reminded me there are other ways to lead. Other ways to matter."

They both shrugged at the same time, then shared a smile.

"Sometimes the next step's still the right one, even if you take it slowly," Adam said thoughtfully. "It's not hesitation—it's respect for the weight of the choice."

Emily stared at him. "Have you been talking to my mom?"

Adam laughed. "No, but I'd like to. I still dream about her lasagna."

They ended the night on the couch, her feet on his lap, a movie on the screen, lights dimmed, their future still blurry—but a little less scary.

Puff jumped up on the sofa, stared them both down with the judgment of a thousand ancestors, then—without warning—nudged Emily's foot off Adam's lap and plopped himself down in the warm spot with a self-satisfied *mrrrp*.

Emily looked at him, betrayed.

Adam grinned. "He's clearly chosen his favorite."

"Rude," she muttered, reaching for her wine glass.

Her other hand found Adam's large, warm one. And she didn't let go.

Chapter Thirty-Eight

Emily accepted the job—not just in theory, but in emails, in signed documents, in a celebratory group text that ended in twelve emojis and a waffle GIF. It was happening. She was moving to Toronto. She'd said yes to a new city, a new title, a new chapter.

And yet, standing in a chic Toronto boutique where all the clothes hung on minimalist wooden hangers and the price tags whispered threats about her financial future, it still didn't feel quite real.

"This one says 'I take meetings with confidence and quietly own too many reusable coffee mugs,'" Sophie announced, holding up a navy pantsuit with a subtle pinstripe.

Adam, seated in the corner of the fitting room area with an iced coffee and the vacant stare of a man who'd spent far too much time in women's clothing shops, looked up. "That looks great," he agreed for the forty-seventh time.

Emily disappeared into the fitting room while Sophie flopped dramatically into the seat beside him.

"She's stalling," Sophie said.

"I know," Adam replied. "She tried on the same sweater twice and pretended it was different colors."

Emily's voice floated from behind the curtain. "I can hear

you."

"We know," they said in unison.

She emerged a minute later, tugging at the sleeves of the new blazer. It looked fantastic. Professional but not boring. Structured but still her.

Sophie raised her eyebrows. "That's the one."

Adam nodded. "Definitely."

Emily glanced at herself in the mirror. "This doesn't mean I'm suddenly a blazer person."

"It does," Sophie said. "But in a cute, 'blazer over vintage tees' kind of way."

Emily smiled, just a little. "Okay. Fine. Put it in the yes pile."

They moved through the racks with purpose—Emily picking out versatile staples, Sophie tossing in the occasional wildcard, and Adam offering commentary only when asked. His answer was always a nod and, "That looks great."

By the time they reached the checkout, Sophie asked, "So, you're really signing the lease tomorrow?"

Emily hesitated. "That's the plan."

Adam handed over one of the shopping bags. "It's a great place. Decent view. No weird smells. You even get a bathtub, not just a standing shower."

"But..." Sophie prompted, looking between them like a tennis match was about to start.

"But," Emily said slowly, "we've also been talking about maybe... not doing that."

Sophie blinked. "As in, moving in with this one?" She jerked her thumb at Adam, who just sipped his coffee.

"I already offered," he said, his voice even. "My place is closer to SkyLux. We'd probably end up sleeping there most nights anyway."

Emily nodded. "He's right. But…"

"But," Sophie repeated.

"I don't know. It feels like a big step," Emily admitted. "Like I'm merging into his life instead of building my own."

Adam leaned on the counter beside her. "It wouldn't be like that. You're not moving into my schedule. It's our life. We'd make it work however you need."

"That's a very reasonable response," Sophie said approvingly. "Now excuse me. This is turning into a private moment and I need to look at overpriced accessories I don't need."

As she wandered off toward a display of gold hoop earrings, Emily looked at Adam.

"I don't want to crowd your space."

"You wouldn't," he said gently. "You already live in my space, Em. You just haven't moved your stuff in yet."

She bit her lip. "And if it doesn't work?"

Adam didn't flinch. "Then you get your own place. No drama. No weirdness. I'll even help you move out and assemble your furniture—with only minimal swearing."

Emily stared at him, something warm and nervous catching in her throat. "That's more awkward."

"Maybe," he said. "But for me, it's worth the risk."

She didn't say anything right away. Instead, she glanced around the boutique—at the concrete floors, the dried eucalyptus bundles, the display table stacked with motivational desk calendars. Everything sleek and styled and slightly intimidating.

Finally, she exhaled. "Fine. I'll sign the lease. But only month-to-month."

Adam pulled her into his arms. "Okay. But only if you agree

not to buy any new furniture for the first few weeks."

She opened her mouth to protest. Then closed it again. "Deal."

They left the store with three bags, one questionable leopard print scarf Sophie insisted was "power-lunch material," and a quiet sense that things were changing—but in the right direction.

They walked to a nearby café, where Daniel was already waiting at a back patio table with two espresso cups and a plate of croissants so aggressively flaky they had taken over a third of the table.

"About time," he said, pushing his sunglasses up. "I was starting to feel abandoned."

"You're in linen," Adam said, eyeing his pale button-up shirt. "Why are you always in linen?"

"Because I'm emotionally stable and have access to a steamer," Daniel replied smoothly. "Also, it's spring."

Emily flopped into the chair across from him. "We've been shopping. Sophie bullied me into structured pants."

Daniel looked at Adam. "And you survived?"

"Barely," Adam said, grabbing a croissant.

Daniel nodded. "Respect." They fist bumped.

Sophie rolled her eyes but she was smiling.

Everyone settled in, ordering coffees and hanging shopping bags on chairs. They chatted for a few minutes—small talk, Toronto weather gripes, Emily's official employment status—before Daniel turned to Adam.

"So, are you going for it?"

Adam blinked. "What?"

"The Captain upgrade. The simulator's open. They're scheduling tests in May."

Emily looked at him. "You didn't tell me that."

"I just found out this week," Adam said. "It's not guaranteed. It's a process."

Daniel sipped his espresso. "But it's the next step."

Adam nodded slowly. "Yeah. It is."

Emily felt her heart shift—just a little. "Do you want it?"

Adam looked at her, eyes steady. "Yeah. I do. I've been flying long enough. I'm ready."

Daniel smirked. "I'll even write you a reference letter. I'll leave out the part where you once forgot your headset in the lounge."

"One time," Adam muttered.

Emily smiled. "You'd be amazing. Captain Kostas has a nice ring to it."

"Better than 'World's Okayest Strategist,'" Daniel said.

"Hey," Emily warned, "that mug is iconic."

Daniel picked up a mini shopping bag beside Sophie. He raised his eyebrows. "I thought it was Emily who was shopping and you were only along as emotional support?"

Sophie leaned over and kissed him on the cheek. "Let's just say there was a limited-edition lipstick involved and I blacked out."

A server arrived and everyone ordered coffee or tea and pastries.

Sophie turned to Emily and squeezed her hand. "Now tell me, did you cry at your goodbye brunch?"

Emily groaned. "Ugh. Yes. Like a loser. Liam made a custom mimosa flight and named them after inside jokes from past campaigns. Susan brought a PowerPoint presentation of 'Lessons Emily Taught Us,' which included 'Always carry sun block' and 'Never trust a drone on a windy day.'"

Adam laughed. "Please tell me you filmed it."

"No," Emily said, "but someone definitely did. I saw phones. There will be footage."

"Were there waffles?" Daniel asked.

"Of course. They were shaped like North America," she said. "Susan called them 'edible patriotism.'"

Sophie clutched her heart. "I really loved working with the Niagara team. They were awesome."

Emily picked at her croissant, the flaky edges crumbling between her fingers. An ache in her chest made her blink faster than she wanted.

"I already miss them," she said softly. "It's weird. I know this job is the right move. But it still feels like I left a part of myself there."

Adam reached across the table and gently squeezed her other hand.

Daniel nodded. "You're allowed to grieve a little, even when you're moving forward."

"And to impulse-buy a new espresso machine to cope," Sophie added.

Emily raised an eyebrow. "Is that your coping mechanism?"

"No, mine is buying a water carbonator," Sophie replied.

Daniel shot her an affectionate glance before adding, "Plus matching Himalayan salt lamps, custom throw pillows, a weighted blanket, and a sous vide machine."

They all laughed, and the conversation drifted into future plans and new routines. Adam mentioned wanting to tweak his flight schedule to accommodate simulator time, and Daniel promised to help quiz him on emergency procedures. Sophie offered to test Adam's nerves by pretending to be a difficult passenger mid-study session.

"If you can handle me demanding hot towels and inquiring

about your flight credentials, you can handle anything," she declared.

Adam smirked. "Honestly? I'd pass just to get out of that conversation."

They ordered another round of coffees and shared the last pain au chocolat like it was a peace offering. The sun filtered through the patio canopy, warm and golden and filled with the kind of light that made you believe in good things happening.

Later, walking back toward the subway, Adam caught her hand.

"You sure about the apartment?"

Emily nodded. "I think so. It's a buffer. A space that's mine. But yours is still… home."

"Okay." He kissed the top of her head. "You can have both."

She squeezed his hand. Her voice was quiet but certain. "I think I finally believe that."

They kept walking—two people, one city, and the comfort of knowing they were no longer figuring things out alone.

Chapter Thirty-Nine

Emily's alarm buzzed at 6:45 a.m. She blinked once, twice, and groaned as she realized—yet again—she was not in her apartment. Technically, she still had one. Realistically, she hadn't slept there in weeks.

Beside her, Adam stirred. "Work?" His voice was low and sleepy.

"Second week," she said softly, already swinging her legs over the edge of the bed. "Can't be late."

He made a dramatic sound of protest and buried his face in the pillow. "I was having a dream about a brunch-themed escape room," he mumbled. "I was *so close* to unlocking the maple safe."

She smiled faintly as she padded across the room to grab the cardigan draped over the back of a chair—it hung in Adam's apartment like it belonged there. Like she did, too.

Puff was stretched out dramatically across Adam's armchair. He blinked at her once, then went back to sleep, clearly unbothered by her schedule.

He had been meant to go back to her parents after their cruise. That had been the deal. A temporary stay while they indulged in too much pasta and European port cities across the Atlantic.

But when her parents had tried to collect him, Puff had let out a yowl so loud and despairing that her mother paused mid-sentence and said, "I think he's made his feelings known."

Her dad, halfway through booking flights to Greece, had looked at the cat, then at her, and simply said, "Better for all of us, really." Apparently, their retirement would be full of travel and adventure—and blissfully litter-box-free.

So Puff stayed. He now ruled the condo with silent authority, greeting Adam like a returning hero, ignoring Emily unless his cat litter needed cleaning, and sitting on her laptop to assert his authority. He had a cat bed. He never used it.

Emily smiled at the ridiculousness of it all and headed out the door, a reusable coffee cup in hand.

At SkyLux, her second week was off to a running start. Natalie Cheng had looped her into campaign meetings and brand brainstorms before she even finished her welcome muffin. There was an energy here—a mix of corporate polish and wild creativity—that felt weirdly familiar.

She navigated her morning meetings without sweating through her blazer and even made a few coworkers laugh during a presentation about seasonal flight promotions. At one point, she caught herself using phrases like "target engagement metrics" and "return on investment" without cringing. She wasn't sure when that had started happening, but it didn't feel fake. It felt earned.

During lunch, she found herself alone in the break room with a quinoa bowl and a seat by the window. The view was impossibly cinematic—Toronto in soft focus, the CN Tower watching over her like a benevolent older sibling.

She pulled out her phone and texted Adam.

Emily: *I may have accidentally agreed to present at the*

Wednesday all-staff.

Adam: *Proud of you. Also mildly concerned. Do you need a PowerPoint intervention?*

Emily: *I'll be fine. Probably.*

A pause.

Emily: *Where are you?*

Adam: *I would give you a hug if I could, but I'm in Kansas between flights now. Back tonight. Pick you up?*

She smiled.

Emily: *Can't wait.*

That night, Adam picked her up from the SkyLux building entrance. He'd landed at Pearson Airport an hour earlier. The sun was starting to set, casting everything in honeyed light, and Emily felt the soft exhale of satisfaction that came from a long, productive day at the office—doing work that felt important, with colleagues who made her feel part of the team, and had already invited her to her first team trivia night.

"I think I'm going to give notice on the apartment," she said as they pulled into the underground parking lot of Adam's apartment building.

Adam kept one hand on the wheel and glanced at her with a smile. "Yeah?"

"I haven't been there in weeks. I water the one plant, pick up more clothes to leave at your place, and then come right back here. It feels dumb to keep it. And expensive."

"It doesn't sound dumb," he said. "It sounds like it was the right thing for you to do, and now it's not."

She looked at him. "You okay with that? Like, officially?"

"With officially living with you?" he said. "I've been campaigning for that for months now."

She rolled her eyes, but her heart was doing that warm

flutter thing it did when he said exactly what she didn't realize she needed to hear.

They walked around the corner to pick up Thai food from their favorite corner spot and then curled up on the couch together. Puff made himself comfortable on Adam's lap and fell asleep in a smug little roll of fur.

Adam leaned into Emily's side, absently running his fingers through Puff's fur. "I keep waiting for this to feel like too much," he murmured.

Emily didn't answer right away. She turned to face him. "And does it?"

He shook his head slowly. "No. It just feels like mine. Like… ours."

She smiled. "Because it is."

The next morning, while Adam was still asleep and Puff was busy knocking a pen off the kitchen counter just for fun, Emily walked over to her old apartment.

It felt strange, stepping inside after so many nights away. The air was still. Familiar, but not comforting. It reminded her of her old apartment in New York. She had felt the same way there.

Her mail was stacked neatly by the door, and the plant on her windowsill looked surprisingly alive. She was impressed by its will to survive. It had the same tenacity as Adam's plant. Maybe they belonged together.

She moved through the space like a guest, pulling open drawers and gathering what she needed. A few sweaters. A backup charger. A notebook she liked.

And the mugs. Her beloved, ridiculous mugs.

She wrapped each one carefully:

— "Here We Fucking Go Again—I Mean, Good Morning," the

sarcastic sunshine mug from Jonah, a relic from her college years.

— "Let's Waffle About It," a gift from Sophie after the first brunch meeting.
— "Let's Waffle About It," again, but with glitter lettering—Daniel's version.
— "World's Okayest Strategist," chipped but still perfect in every way.
— A My Little Pony mug that said "SUPER ULTRA EXTREME AWESOMENESS" on one side with Rainbow Dash on the flip side.
— Her Niagara Tourism Board travel thermos, which still smelled faintly like Liam's overbrewed tea.

Among others.

After wrapping each one, she placed them gently into a tote, then glanced around the kitchen one last time. It didn't feel like goodbye. Just the quiet closing of a chapter that had already finished telling its story.

Back at Adam's, she put her plant beside Adam's plant on the window sill. Then she moved to the kitchen to unpack her mugs, lining them up one-by-one in the cabinet next to his sleek, black espresso mugs and the SkyLux-branded travel cups.

She stood back, looked at the chaotic line of mismatched handles, and sarcastic slogans, and smiled. It was a visual map of past, present, and future.

Puff jumped onto the counter and knocked over the glittery waffle mug.

Emily caught it mid-air and held it up triumphantly. "Nice try."

Adam wandered in a minute later, yawning and shirtless.

Her pulse picked up like it always did.

He scratched behind his neck and looked around. "What's happening in here?"

"Claiming territory," she said, pointing to the cabinet.

He peered at the mugs, then turned to her with a slow grin. "You know what this means?"

She blinked. "That I'm a sentimental hoarder?"

"That, too," he said. "But also… you live here now."

He came to stand behind her and wrapped his arms around her. She leaned against his chest, pressing into his solid warmth. "Guess I do."

And just like that, it was official—not because of paperwork or declarations, but because her mugs had found their place. So had she.

Chapter Forty

Emily woke up to the smell of coffee and something suspiciously lemony wafting through the apartment. For half a second, she forgot what day it was. Then she opened her eyes, blinked at the ceiling, and remembered.

Brunch. At Adam's—and now also her—apartment. With everyone.

It would be the first brunch they'd hosted here, as brunches were usually held at Sophie and Daniel's place. Their place was bigger, but Adam and Emily had rearranged the furniture and borrowed a few extra chairs from the neighbors to ensure everyone who came would be comfortable.

Emily stretched and rolled over. The bed was empty. Adam was already up. That wasn't a surprise. He'd been acting suspiciously energetic all week. Whispering with Sophie. Texting Daniel at odd hours. Rearranging their pantry with a level of focus usually reserved for flight checklists.

She knew something was up. She wasn't a complete idiot.

Still, she had no idea when—or how—it would happen. And she wasn't about to ruin the surprise. She kind of wanted to be surprised. Kind of wanted to see if he could pull it off.

Puff was snoring in the armchair like a tiny freight train. She padded into the kitchen in bare feet and an oversized T-shirt that read “Coffee is My Love Language”.

Adam turned when he saw her. He was wearing an apron.

“Morning,” he said, too casually.

She tilted her head. “How long have you been up?”

“A while.”

“Uh huh.” She walked past him, stole a strawberry from the counter, and kissed his cheek. “I need to brush my teeth.”

By the time she got dressed and helped finish setting up for the coming brunch, they’d transformed the apartment. There were flowers. Real napkins. A brunch-themed playlist playing softly in the background. A chalkboard sign read ‘Welcome to the Brunch Club.’

Daniel and Sophie arrived first. Sophie looked at her with the kind of gleam in her eye that made Emily instantly suspicious. They hugged and both Daniel and Sophie immediately made themselves at home.

Then came Liam with his latest girlfriend (possibly named Lexi?), followed by Gabriel, Lucy, Brett, Ariana, Maya, and to Emily’s surprise, Jonah, who arrived carrying two large grocery bags and declared, “I didn’t know what to bring, so I brought options.”

As soon as her brother walked in, Emily knew something was *definitely* up.

“Wow, Jonah,” she exclaimed in surprise. She gave him a tight hug. “What are you doing here?”

“Nice to see you, too.” Jonah grinned easily. “It’s not that far, is it? Only a three hour flight. I came to watch the Texas Rangers annihilate the Toronto Blue Jays.” He shrugged a little too casually. “Thought I’d stop by and say hi while I’m here.”

“You came all this way to watch a baseball game?” Emily demanded, narrowing her eyes.

"Jonah, hey!" Adam boomed, a little too loudly, appearing at their side. They did the man hug thing. "So good to see you. Thanks for coming all this way. Wanna help me make some waffles?"

Jonah looked relieved. As they moved toward the kitchen, Emily heard her brother say, "Why do you have three waffle makers?"

In the next few minutes, brunch was buzzing—clinking cutlery, overlapping conversations, a waffle maker working in the background. Everything was loud and familiar. Her favorite kind of chaos.

Emily was in mid-conversation with Sophie debating whether the Brunch Club needed official uniforms—Sophie wanted embroidered robes; Emily insisted on matching aprons with slogans like "Whisk Takers"—when something behind Emily seemed to catch Sophie's attention.

"Sorry, Em," Sophie said, brightening. "I'll be right back."

"Sure."

Emily watched curiously as Sophie moved to the middle of the living room and raised her mimosa glass. She cleared her throat.

"Attention, everyone! Attention, please." She turned to survey the room and seemed satisfied everyone had stopped talking. "Before we all pass out from maple syrup overload, I'd like to say a few words."

Emily frowned. Sophie was doing her ceremonial toast voice. That was rarely good.

"Actually," Sophie continued with a grin, "I'm passing the mic to someone else today. Adam?"

Emily blinked.

Adam came to stand beside Emily, clearing his throat. His

hand brushed hers and stayed there.

Emily blinked again. She'd never heard him give a speech before. And yet here he was. Ready to speak in front of their friends. Holding something behind his back.

"I didn't prepare anything," he started. "Which is probably a mistake. But I've learned that sometimes the best things in life happen when you don't have a plan. Just good intentions."

When Adam turned to look at her, Emily froze. Her stomach flipped. He took her right hand in his left one and squeezed. His right hand remained behind his back.

"You moved into my apartment one mug at a time," Adam said, eyes never leaving hers. "And now my cabinet is chaos."

There was laughter, a soft collective inhale.

"I didn't realize that love could be like that. Quiet. Persistent. Slightly ceramic."

More laughter.

"But I want it. All of it."

He dropped to one knee.

Emily's breath caught. The whole world narrowed to just him.

"Emily Levine—will you marry me?"

She stared at him. At the small velvet box in his hand. At the ring—simple, elegant, exactly right.

Emily's hands flew to her mouth. "Oh my god," she whispered. Then louder, "Yes. Yes!"

The room erupted—cheers, clapping, someone popped a champagne cork that hit the ceiling. Puff, startled by the commotion, bolted out of the room with a loud *mrrrow*.

Adam stood, slid the ring onto her finger, and pulled her into his arms.

"You did it," she whispered.

"You said yes."

She pulled back just enough to look at him. "Of course I did. I was just waiting to see when you'd crack."

He grinned. "How long have you known?"

"You and Sophie were texting one-on-one," she explained.

Adam raised her left hand and looked at the ring. "Do you like it?"

"I love it." Emily moved her hand around, the ring catching the sunlight from the window. "It's exactly the style I've always dreamed of."

He nodded. "You can thank Sophie for that."

"It fits perfectly," she added, her voice catching.

"Bar of soap," he said cryptically, with a shrug.

Sophie crowded in with a squeal and hugged them tightly. Daniel clapped Adam on the back. Then everyone else came around. There were hearty congratulations, oohs and ahhs about the ring, tight hugs, high-fives, and one spontaneous chant of "Brunch Wedding! Brunch Wedding!" led by Liam and joined by half the room before anyone could stop them.

The rest of the morning blurred into warm laughter and happy chaos. More waffles. More hugs. Jonah made an elaborate toast involving video game metaphors. Gabriel cried again. Sophie confiscated Emily's phone to post the first photo of the ring.

It wasn't perfect. There were crumbs everywhere, someone spilled juice on the rug, and Puff refused to come out from under the couch. But it was close.

Later, as people were leaving, there were endless hugs at the door—some tearful, some giddy. Everyone wanted a closer look at the ring, to offer one more round of congratulations, to snap a few more photos.

Sophie insisted on at least three different selfies with Emily's hand front and center.

Daniel hugged her twice, then once more for good luck.

Jonah demanded a formal handshake from Adam, then clapped him on the back and said, "Welcome to the family, bro—don't mess it up."

He then enveloped Emily in a bear hug that lifted her off her feet.

When the door finally clicked shut behind the last guest, Emily closed the door and leaned back against it, letting out a long, shaky breath.

She looked down at the ring on her finger—still a little stunned. She wiggled her hand so the diamond caught the afternoon light streaming in through the window.

Around her were the remnants of another successful Brunch Club: half-empty glasses, leftover pastries, crumpled napkins, and the faint scent of maple syrup.

Adam was already stacking plates, humming tunelessly as he moved around the dining table. When he saw her standing by the door, happy tears in her eyes, he set the plates down and crossed the room to her.

He took her hand in his, turning it gently, admiring his own handiwork with a mock-serious nod. "You know, I had help. But I still get all the credit, right?"

She laughed. "Let's say… ninety percent."

He brushed a kiss across her knuckles, lingering for a second. "I'll take it."

Then he opened his arms and Emily eagerly leaned into his solid frame, wrapping her arms around him. They fit together like a lock and key. She sighed happily and snuggled closer. Adam's arms tightened around her.

She had no idea what kind of wedding they would plan. She suspected it would involve waffles. And Sophie's Pinterest boards. It would probably be over brunch.

But that didn't matter. They were already building the life she hadn't dared to imagine—one that, this time, wasn't a campaign or a story or a well-timed post.

It was real.

It was hers.

It was theirs.

Epilogue

Six months later

Adam was rifling through his dresser drawer, looking for a spare passport photo when his fingers brushed against something soft, papery.

It was the letter. Still folded. Tucked between a stack of foreign currency and an old, forgotten SkyLux lanyard.

He pulled it out slowly, turning it over in his hands. The paper was slightly creased, a little worn around the edges. He hadn't seen it in months—not since moving the last of Emily's boxes into the closet and rearranging his drawer system to accommodate her alarming number of punny t-shirts and cozy socks.

Back then, the letter had felt like a question mark—something unresolved between them. The day she handed it back, it had scorched his palms, heavy with guilt and regret.

Now, it felt like a footnote.

He sat on the edge of the bed, holding it in his palms for a long moment. Then, with a small smile, he folded it back neatly and tucked it into the back of the drawer.

"I don't need this anymore," he said softly.

From the kitchen, Emily called out, "Did you find it?"

He grabbed the passport photo and tucked it into his back pocket. "Yes, got it," he replied, standing and leaving the room.

He headed for the kitchen, swept her into his arms, and kissed her shoulder with a grin. "And now I've found something even better," he growled.

Her squeal of surprise and delight was the sound he'd never stop chasing.

After all the wondering, all the almosts, this was better than anything he'd ever imagined—and he wouldn't trade a minute of it.

Did you fall for the slow burn, the banter, and perfectly timed forehead kisses?

If this story made you smile, swoon, or stay up way too late reading *just one more chapter*—I'd be so grateful if you left a review. Reviews help indie authors like me reach new readers and keep the stories coming. You can leave a review on Amazon, Goodreads, or wherever you grabbed this book. Seriously—it means the world.

Want to know what I'm writing next in the series? Come hang out with me on Substack at tracywrightbooks.substack.com or follow me on TikTok, Instagram, or Facebook: @tracywrightbooks.

Thank you for spending time with my characters. I hope they made you laugh, feel, and maybe believe in love just a little bit more.

Until the next chapter,
—**Tracy**
www,tracywrightbooks.com

Manufactured by Amazon.ca
Bolton, ON

50089845R00155